SALSA AND SECRETS

Also by Joanne Pence

The Cook and Inspector Mysteries

DEATH ON A SILVER PLATTER - A QUICHE BEFORE DYING -
THE MARINARA MURDERS - CLOSE ENCOUNTERS OF THE
DEADLY KIND - DEATH BY DEVIL'S FOOD - BLIND DATE'S
BITTER END - THE TAVERNA AFFAIR - THE MUSIC BOX
MYSTERY - TRUFFLES TO DIE FOR - COOKING SPIRITS - ADD A
PINCH OF MURDER - SALSA & SECRETS

The Rebecca Mayfield Mysteries

ONE O'CLOCK HUSTLE - TWO O'CLOCK HEIST

THREE O'CLOCK SÉANCE - FOUR O'CLOCK SIZZLE

FIVE O'CLOCK TWIST - SIX O'CLOCK SILENCE

SEVEN O'CLOCK TARGET - EIGHT O'CLOCK SPLIT

NINE O'CLOCK RETREAT - THE 13th SANTA (Novella)

Ancient Secrets Series (author J.M. Pence)

ANCIENT ECHOES - ANCIENT SHADOWS

ANCIENT ILLUSIONS - ANCIENT DECEPTIONS

ANCIENT PASSAGES

The Donnelly Cabin Inn Novels

IF I LOVED YOU - THIS CAN'T BE LOVE - SENTIMENTAL
JOURNEY - A CERTAIN SMILE - TIME AFTER TIME

Others

SEEMS LIKE OLD TIMES - DANGEROUS JOURNEY

DANCE WITH A GUNFIGHTER - THE DRAGON'S LADY

THE GHOST OF SQUIRE HOUSE

SALSA AND SECRETS

THE COOK AND INSPECTOR MYSTERIES
BOOK 12

JOANNE PENCE

QUAIL HILL PUBLISHING

Quail Hill Publishing

Eagle, ID 83616

Visit our website at www.quailhillpublishing.net

First edition Quail Hill Publishing ebook: April 2017

Second edition Quail Hill Publishing ebook: September 2025

First edition Quail Hill Publishing Paperback: April 2017

Second edition Quail Hill Publishing Paperback: September 2025

SALSA AND SECRETS

1

————

Merritt's Café had been a fixture in Jackpot, Arizona, for over twenty-four years. LaVerne Merritt, self-described "chief cook and bottle-washer," ran the place with a pride that bordered on territorial. What she loved most, though, was being with her customers. Heaven forbid she miss out on a good story because she was standing over a hot stove.

From her station at the counter, LaVerne had the best vantage point in Jackpot. The café sat smack in the middle of Main Street—all five dusty blocks of it. From behind the counter or while refilling mugs, she had eyes on every passerby. Not that there were many at this time of year. The tourists had vanished with the summer heat. Now, just about the only folks who came through town were lost.

She was topping off Junior Whitney's coffee when she spotted an unfamiliar vehicle. She would have poured the cup to overflowing if he hadn't cried out.

Pot in hand, LaVerne edged toward the apple-and-grape café curtains and squinted out the window. Her small, angular face twisted into a scowl. She adjusted her thick bifocals, her drooping eyelid giving her the look of being perpetually unimpressed. Her brittle, over-processed blond hair stood straight up, crackling like miniature lightning bolts.

The car wasn't a pickup, which was strange for these parts. But it also wasn't an American sedan or a respectable SUV like a Ford Explorer. The vehicle crawling down Main Street looked... foreign. Literally. The glare off the windshield made it impossible to see the occupants. It slowed nearly to a stop.

She pressed her nose to the glass, leaving a small foggy imprint. Her frown deepened.

Could be a reporter. Or some fancy-pants investigator from the FBI or some other Fed agency—who knew? Ever since word got out about Hal Edwards' death, she'd been expecting the buzzards to circle. Investigators. Reporters. Curious onlookers. Jackpot had just enough mystery to whet their appetites.

The car parked, nose-in, in front of her diner, close enough she could see the hood ornament.

A Mercedes? A Mercedes SUV here in Jackpot?

"Lost Californians," she muttered with a shake of the head, but kept watching.

A tall man stepped out of the driver's side. Thirties, good-looking, dark brown hair, aviator sunglasses. Jeans and a green plaid shirt—trying to blend in, but the Mercedes gave him away.

He moved to the passenger side and opened the door.

A pair of high-heeled yellow sandals appeared first—no straps, just a slip-on style that screamed impractical. He offered his hand, and out stepped a petite woman in a yellow-and-white dress, her wavy dark brown hair catching gold glints in the sun. Lavender-tinted wraparound sunglasses covered her eyes. She looked like a movie star who must have taken a wrong turn somewhere around Palm Springs.

LaVerne's lips curled. She watched the woman fluff her hair, adjust her dress, and totter toward the sidewalk. Then her heel snagged between the wooden slats. Perfect!

LaVerne let out a snort of laughter. Definitely lost Californians. They wouldn't last a day here.

She scurried back behind the counter, wiping her nose print off the glass with her sleeve.

Angie Amalfi gripped the arm of her fiancé, Homicide Inspector Paavo Smith, as she tugged her Prada heel from between the boards.

"I didn't think towns still had wooden sidewalks," she said, sliding her foot back into the shoe. "I thought that was only in ghost towns set up for tourists."

"This is the real thing," Paavo said, holding her steady.

"It reminds me of Disney's Frontierland when I was a kid."

He gave her a look but said nothing.

Late afternoon sunlight bathed Jackpot in a golden haze. The town's main street was lined with an automotive shop, gun store, hardware, and feed supplies. A gas station and Circle K anchored one end, a Halmart store the other. Angie blinked at the sign. Halmart, not Walmart.

A few sad-looking motels flashed neon VACANCY signs. Behind them, narrow side streets stretched toward small clusters of modest homes.

A week earlier, the man who had raised Paavo after his father's death and mother's disappearance, Aulis Kokkonen, received a phone call from one of his oldest friends. Doctor Loomis Griggs, who had studied medicine in San Francisco where he met Aulis, and now lived just outside Jackpot.

When Paavo was young, Doc—as everyone called him—had invited Aulis and Paavo to spend time with him on his ranch.

They were some of Paavo's most memorable summers. Of course, when he grew older—around age sixteen—he considered himself much too "cool" to go on a vacation to a small town and ranch with his guardian. And as Aulis grew older and Doc busier, their visits also stopped.

But when Doc phoned Aulis, he said troubling things had happened in the town after the death of a former patient of his, a man in his seventies, named Hal Edwards.

Aulis had sensed some real worry beneath Doc's jovial and garrulous conversation, and Doc wasn't one to fret unnecessarily. Seeing Aulis's concern, Paavo decided to phone Doc Griggs. Just hearing the familiar, gravelly voice brought back many fond memories. Doc tried to blow off Aulis's concerns, but he protested too much, and the more Doc said nothing was wrong, the more Paavo sensed just the opposite.

He also realized how much, as a boy, he had loved that good man, and how much he'd missed seeing him. It was time to remedy that. Paavo spent his workday investigating suspicious deaths, so he could surely spend a week's vacation doing the same thing for a friend.

He told Angie all this, and they decided to go to Jackpot as tourists, to nose around and ask questions. Most likely, a simple explanation would be found for whatever was troubling Doc.

Angie knew this trip was important to Paavo for a variety of reasons. Yes, she had a wedding to plan, but there was no way she'd miss this.

"This place hasn't changed at all," Paavo said.

All she could do was nod as she found herself in a town she never even knew existed before a few days earlier.

They entered what appeared to be the only café—a small place with booths, wooden tables, and a long white counter. One scruffy, long-haired older man sat at the counter, while two younger fellows who were dressed for fishing in clothes that looked fresh off a Bass Pro Shop rack were seated at a table in the back.

"Sit wherever you like," the middle-aged woman behind the counter called, grabbing mugs, menus, and a coffee pot.

She poured as they settled into a booth. Her eyes skimmed over Angie, then fixed sharply on Paavo.

"You FBI?" she asked.

He looked surprised. "No."

"You look FBI. More than some." She gave a little sniff. Through the bifocals, magnified eyes darted toward the two fishermen. "Can't fool me. I've got a nose for these things."

Another sniff, this one in Angie's direction, and she marched off.

"That was weird," Angie murmured. "And it looks like Ned's not here yet." She referred to Paavo's boyhood friend, who had offered to meet them at the café.

"Not yet."

They sat back to wait.

Ned Paulson and Paavo played together as kids. His mother had been Doc Griggs's secretary. Ned was a little younger than Paavo, but a nice kid, who knew the desert well. Paavo had called Ned and told him he was coming. Ned had sounded both surprised and vaguely troubled, but added that he understood Doc's concerns. He wanted to talk to Paavo in person about it and suggested that they meet at Merritt's the afternoon Paavo arrived.

"If Ned's got a customer, I can see why he's running late." Angie gazed out the window at the town's one stoplight. "The town doesn't look like it gets many visitors."

"Sorry you came?" Paavo asked, reaching across the table for her hand.

She smiled, brushing her thumb over his knuckles. "Of course not. We've got a week, just the two of us. No work, no family interference, no wedding plan disasters! I was starting to feel like we were being pulled in so many directions, we forgot why we're even getting married. I thought maybe you'd decide the whole thing was a huge mistake."

His gaze held hers. "Not me, Angie. Never."

Her heart swelled. She needed this time with him.

And she still toyed with the idea of finding a unique wedding location. Not that it would happen. Her wedding plans were set in stone, but a girl could dream, couldn't she?

Her mother, Serefina, had decided the wedding would be held at Sts. Peter and Paul Church in San Francisco's North Beach. Angie's parents' and sisters' weddings had all taken place there. They'd booked the church, but Angie couldn't help but think about finding a place that was different, unique, and memorable.

Looking around now, Jackpot was definitely different, unique, and probably memorable. If only she'd known about it —and Paavo's attachment to it—months ago.

"You ready to order?" The waitress loomed over them, pad in hand.

Angie blinked. "Uh, turkey and Swiss wrap."

"Chiliburger," Paavo added.

The food came fast. They ate in silence, scanning the café door. No sign of Ned.

Paavo tried Ned's number again. Voicemail.

"How about dessert?" the waitress asked, staring at Angie like she was a stain on a white tablecloth.

"No, thank you," Angie said coolly. "We'll be leaving soon."

"Passing through?" The woman's gaze narrowed.

"We're staying at the Ghost Hollow Guest Ranch," Angie said.

"Is that so?" Her brows lifted, then smoothed. "Nice place. Not too many guests lately…"

"Oh?"

"LaVerne Merritt," the waitress added. "I've owned this café since before Ghost Hollow was a guest ranch. Back when it was Hal Edwards' home."

Angie perked up. She glanced at Paavo. Hal Edwards' death was the reason Doc Griggs was upset.

"His home?" she prompted.

"I thought everyone knew that." LaVerne pursed her lips. "Hal Edwards used to be the richest man in all of Arizona. Owned all the Halmart stores—from Yuma to Flagstaff. He claimed Walmart stole its name from him. The house was beautiful. Everyone still calls it the hacienda. You'll see why."

She frowned and then added, "Now it's going to his worthless son, Joseph Edwards. Everybody calls him Joey."

"The resort used to be a hacienda?" Angie asked, excitement sparking.

A beautiful hacienda... had she found a destination-wedding venue after all?

"You didn't know that?" LaVerne sniffed again. "What brings you here anyway?"

"We're here to fish," Paavo said smoothly. "Our contact suggested Ghost Hollow. He was supposed to meet us here."

"Fishing? You, too? So, your contact must be Ned Paulson. Are you waiting for him? I could call him for you, see what's keeping him."

"No need," Paavo said. "I've tried his number. No answer."

LaVerne raised an eyebrow. "Those cell phones don't always work out here. People go missing for hours. I'm pretty good at tracking folks down, though. Just being helpful."

"Thanks, but we'll wait," Angie said, lifting her mug. "No pie."

LaVerne lingered, then sighed and shuffled back to the counter.

They were just about to give up waiting when a woman burst through the doorway. She seemed to be in her early thirties, with olive skin, shoulder-length black hair, and striking almond-shaped green eyes, her umber-and-turquoise print dress should have been bold, but on her, it looked oddly somber.

She scanned the café, frowned at the older man at the counter, then zeroed in on Paavo and Angie. She hurried over.

"Are you Paavo?" she asked, tucking a strand of hair behind her ear.

He stood. "Yes."

"I'm Teresa Flores," she said, offering her hand. "Ned told me about you."

Angie couldn't help but notice LaVerne, openly eavesdropping from the counter, or the scruffy guy at the bar, who suddenly got up and left, a hand suspiciously shielding his face.

Teresa turned to Angie. "You must be Paavo's fiancée."

"Yes, I'm Angie."

They barely exchanged pleasantries before Teresa asked, "Has Ned been here?"

"No," Paavo said. "I've been trying to reach him."

"I see." She rubbed her arms as if cold. "We ... had a misunderstanding. He's not answering my calls. I thought maybe if I saw him here…" Her voice trailed off, while her brow furrowed. "I should go."

"You'll work it out," Angie offered kindly.

"Should we tell him you came by?" Paavo asked.

Teresa hesitated. "It wouldn't hurt." She glanced at Angie's hand. "That's a beautiful ring."

"Thank you," Angie said, letting her admire it.

"When's the wedding?"

Angie hesitated. The question always made her flinch ... the date was fast approaching, and she still had this concept about a fascinating "destination" wedding. "In two months."

"How exciting. You're lucky. Both of you." Teresa stood as a shadow crossed her features. "I'm surprised Ned isn't here yet. But I'm sure it's nothing. I have to get back to Maritza's. That's my family's restaurant—named after my grandmother who still runs it."

She gave a wan smile, then those exotic green eyes rested on Angie's diamond ring once more before she hurried out the door.

Angie stared after her.

Something about the visit felt ... off.

Very off.

2

————

About four miles from town, Paavo turned onto a rutted gravel road. The landscape gradually rose as they angled northwest. As they neared the Colorado River, the terrain grew less arid—still far from lush, but scattered with scrub, cacti, rough grasses, and even a few cottonwoods and tamarisk trees. In the distance, mountains loomed, dark and stern, with the indifferent permanence of time.

"This land is quite different from what we came through to get to Jackpot," Angie said, gazing out the window.

"The greenery is from a creek that runs through here." Paavo pointed to the left. "Out that way."

"You remember a lot, don't you?"

"I'm surprised how much," he murmured. A flicker of vulnerability crept into his voice—the child he once was, surfacing for an instant. "I guess I enjoyed it here more than I thought."

She smiled, touched. But even as she did, she saw the inspector slip back behind his familiar mask. His hands tightened on the steering wheel as the Mercedes bounced along the road.

They climbed steeply. At the crest, an unexpected valley opened before them. It looked like a scene from a model train set: one large house surrounded by cottages and small buildings. Hal Edwards' personal estate—his "hacienda," as LaVerne Merritt had called it—lay spread out below.

Near an open gate in a barbed-wire fence, Paavo slowed. The SUV clattered over a cattle guard, the metal rattle jarring. A weathered sign read: *Ghost Hollow Ranch. Guests Only.*

Paavo's jaw clenched with determination.

"Relax," Angie said. "With that look, no one's going to talk to you. Even the coffee shop gal thought you were FBI. Remember —you're a tourist, not a cop."

"Right." But his expression didn't budge.

The SUV rolled to a stop in front of a small adobe building with a trailer behind it. A sign above the door read *Ranch Office.*

Angie stepped out. The sun pressed down, heavy and still. Even so, she could barely get over the scale and beauty of the place.

"This is amazing," she said. "I never would've expected something like this way out here. The Spanish architecture—the adobe, the wood, the plaza—it looks like a Mexican villa."

In the center of the plaza, a reddish clay fountain with a tall spire spewed water. Beyond it rose a sprawling white adobe home, two stories tall, with wooden balconies and a red tile roof —the hacienda.

A newer, one-story building with similar styling stood off to one side.

"It's like something out of a travel brochure," Angie murmured, heading for the fountain. Just listening to the water splash made her feel cooler.

"Hal Edwards had good taste," Paavo said, eyes scanning the grounds.

"Definitely." She turned toward the office—and froze.

Three of the ugliest, largest birds she'd ever seen stepped out from behind the trailer. They stopped walking and gawked at her as if just as startled as she was.

She'd seen pictures of such birds before, and maybe one or two in a zoo, but never out in the open. They must have stood over six feet tall, and Angie was only five-two. "Ostriches!" she shouted. "Paavo, look! They're ostriches! Should we run?"

Paavo turned, his jaw dropping. "They're just looking at us, and one is backing away."

"I was expecting cows and horses," she muttered, still wary, "not gigantic birds."

At that moment, a grizzled man of medium height burst from the trailer. "Goddamn!" he bellowed, flailing his arms at the birds. "Get your mangy, ugly, smelly, soon-to-be-cowboy-boot hides outta here!"

The ostriches retreated in long, loping strides but didn't go far.

The man turned to them, ignoring the birds. "Welcome to Ghost Hollow Guest Ranch. They won't hurt you none. Just don't startle or corner 'em." He was wiry and weathered, with long, unkempt gray hair and a bristled, pockmarked face. Red, watery eyes studied them. "Name's Lionel Edwards. I manage the place."

Angie picked up on the name "Edwards," most likely a relative of the famous Hal Edwards the waitress had talked about. Angie and Paavo shook his hand. The sour reek of whiskey on his breath nearly made Angie gag.

One of the ostriches broke from the others and approached. It had bluish skin, gray-brown feathers, and huge black eyes. A single tuft of feathers on its head bent forward, very much like a cowlick. It paused behind Lionel and leaned over his shoulder, staring.

First at Angie. Then a long beat at Paavo. Then back to Angie.

She didn't like the way it looked at her. Its eyes narrowed and long lashes blinked once… twice… slowly.

"Nice birdie," she said, her voice wobbly. *Are ostriches friendly?*

Lionel's head whipped back, and he jumped away from it. "Damn useless beasts! Watch it doesn't go for your earrings, ma'am. They like shiny things."

Angie clapped her hands over her ears—but then she noticed the creature's black eyes zero in on her engagement ring.

With a grumble, Lionel flapped his hat, shooing it away.

"Why do you have three ostriches?" she asked once he faced her again.

"Three? We got twenty. All females too."

"You have twenty female ostriches and no males?"

"That's right. And if you figure out why, let me know."

She waited, confused, but he didn't elaborate.

He pointed across the plaza. "That two-story house was Uncle Hal's. The new building has a dining room for our guests, plus a common room with a bar and pool table. Happy hour at five, dinner after. Behind it, you got the stables, cookhouse, workers' cabins, maintenance. But those are off-limits to you."

They nodded.

He gestured behind them. "Those are the guest bungalows."

Ten adobe cottages, charming and well-kept, curved in a semi-circle facing the plaza.

"I'll take you to yours."

As they walked, Paavo asked, "Are we the only guests right now?"

"Yup. The winter folks, we call 'em snowbirds, come down here to get away from the snow back home. As we move toward summer, the desert gets way too hot for tourist types, so they all clear out. I like the break. But this year, after Uncle Hal turned up dead, I closed up earlier than ever. Hal's ex-wife, Clarissa, a.k.a. Hell-on-Wheels, and his son Joey are here. You two are the only paying guests. I only took you in as a special favor to Ned Paulson and Doc."

"What do you mean by 'Hal turned up dead'?" Paavo asked.

"Oh yeah. Guess you are new. Couple weeks back, some Injun found Uncle Hal's body in a cave. Rich old guy like that—what a way to go. You just never know, huh?"

"How'd he die?" Paavo asked, all innocence. Angie knew he'd heard Doc's theory already.

Lionel shrugged. "Who knows? By the time he was found, animals had got 'im. Coroner figured heart attack or stroke. He'd been in rough shape for years."

"How long was he missing?"

"A little over three months."

"Three? You didn't search for him?"

"We searched some, but everyone figured he'd taken off again. Last time, he was gone five years—lived like a hermit in Mexico, best anyone can tell. Then he comes back here, goes to the caves, and ends up dead."

Angie and Paavo exchanged a look. This was exactly the kind of local intel they'd hoped to hear.

Lionel unlocked their bungalow and handed over two keys. The interior had a warm Mexican flair—colorful tiles, hand-carved furniture, soft terra cotta hues. It included a living room, bedroom, bath, and a full kitchen.

"This is lovely," Angie said, turning to Lionel with bright eyes. "Everything is. And about your uncle—I'm sorry for your loss."

"Yeah, thanks." He offered to help with their luggage. Paavo headed back out, Lionel following—but before stepping outside, the man glanced back at Angie.

"Glad to hear you don't mind staying at a ranch where the owner's body wasn't found 'til it was nothing but a skeleton. That's kind of rare in a woman." He hesitated. "That, and the other stories about this area."

Other stories? "What other stories?"

Rheumy eyes met hers. "This place *is* called Ghost Hollow, you know."

A chill crept along her spine. "And I'll bet you're going to tell me why."

"It's because of the stagecoach." Lionel crossed his arms. "Years back, a stagecoach and its passengers all disappeared. The coach was carrying a shitload—I mean—a lot of money. Cash. Local folks said their ghosts could be seen out here at night, near the caves, still searching for the lost stagecoach and their money."

"I see." Her voice caught. *Not that I believe in ghosts...*

"Uncle Hal was found not far from where people figure that stagecoach kind of ... vanished. Glad to hear none of that'll bother you none." He stepped outside the bungalow with a tip of his hat. "I'd better go help your man with the bags. Looks like he's got a lot of them there."

<hr>

"What was Lionel saying to you?" Paavo asked as he finished hauling in his one suitcase and Angie's three Louis Vuitton bags, plus her makeup case and hatbox.

As she'd told him before they left San Francisco, she had no idea what clothes she'd need at the resort, and needed options.

"He was trying to scare me off," she said, pouring two glasses of ice water. "But it had the opposite effect."

"That's not good," Paavo said, accepting the glass. "We'll need to be more cautious than I expected."

"I know." She didn't want to think about Lionel's warnings or poor old dead Hal Edwards.

In the bedroom, she pulled out a box of See's chocolates from her carry-on. Life was easier with chocolate. Considering the hard-drinking manager, the six-foot-tall birds that wanted her jewelry, and tales of ghosts and skeletons, maybe she should've brought the two-pound box.

"The good news is you've already had two people mention Hal Edwards," she said, searching for a chocolate cream. "This town's an open book. Finding out what really happened to him will be easy. Trust me."

As she raised the chocolate to her lips, she looked up—and found Paavo leaning against the doorway, arms crossed, those sky-blue eyes fixed on her.

Her breath caught, and in that moment, the realization struck that they were hundreds of miles from friends, coworkers, and anyone who might interrupt.

It was just them.

She put down the chocolate as their eyes locked, and she started slowly walking toward him.

He was way more scrumptious than chocolate.

3

<hr>

After testing the bed's comfort with Paavo, Angie showered and changed out of her wrinkled linen dress into a casual, comfortable but somewhat dressy chiffon pants outfit. Now she was ready to face the guest ranch's happy hour.

She and Paavo were crossing the plaza hand-in-hand when she spotted a few more ostriches pecking at the rocky ground. The wind shifted, carrying a gamey bird odor to her nose.

One of the birds—the one with the cowlick—lifted its head and stared straight at them. It waddled closer, and Angie could swear its entire expression softened, and her eyes turned downright moony as she gazed at Paavo.

He even has that effect on ostriches. Angie was a little bothered by that thought, she had to admit.

Paavo didn't notice.

She kept glancing over her shoulder at the bizarre creature as they continued into the common room.

The space was vast, dominated by a kiva-style fireplace in one corner. To the left, a full-size billiards table sat in front of a wall of bookshelves. On the right was an inviting lounge area with overstuffed chairs. A modest bar occupied the far corner opposite the fireplace. Double doors led to the dining room.

The manager, Lionel, now freshly shaved and in a clean shirt, stood behind the bar. Now that he had cleaned up, he didn't look as ancient as Angie had first assumed—maybe in his fifties or so? In any case, he was the only one there.

"Greetings!" he called, lifting a half-filled glass in salute. "Join me. I'm told I pour with a generous hand."

"Do you have any white wine?" Angie asked as she reached the bar.

"I do now that Hell-on-Wheels is here," Lionel muttered.

Angie's eyebrows rose. Before she could respond, voices came from the doorway. Lionel's face soured.

An older woman entered, followed by a man who bore a faint resemblance to her. Angie watched, intrigued.

The woman didn't walk—she swept into the room. She seemed to be in her late sixties or so and was still striking. Tall and lean, she wore elegant beige linen slacks, a billowing silk top, and massive turquoise and silver jewelry in Navajo designs. But it was her face that demanded attention: angular, perfectly proportioned, with pale blond hair lacquered into stylish waves. Her mouth was full and firm, her nose long and slightly hawkish, and her sapphire eyes cold but razor-sharp.

That's trouble, Angie thought.

The man was also tall and lean, but where she stood commanding, he slouched. His brown slacks and white long-sleeved shirt were plain, though he wore black, ornate cowboy boots with silver tips on the toes and heels—one piece missing. His posture was slumped, his hair oily, his mouth sulky, and his eyes looked as if they held a lifetime of resentment. He was perhaps a little older than Paavo, but he moved like a man twice his age.

"Who are these people, Lionel?" the woman asked, her tone making it clear no answer would be good enough.

Angie stepped forward. "We're guests. I'm Angelina Amalfi, and this is my fiancé, Paavo Smith."

"Oh yes," the woman said, nostrils flaring. "The guests Ned Paulson imposed on us."

Imposed? Angie thought, suddenly speechless.

"He said this was a good place to stay," Paavo replied evenly. "Was he wrong?"

Instead of answering, the woman shot Lionel an icy stare.

"This is Clarissa Edwards," Lionel said flatly. Clarissa extended her hand with visible reluctance, first to Angie, then Paavo. "And that's Joey, Hal's son."

"His name is *Joseph*," Clarissa snapped.

The widow, Angie thought. *Definitely Hell-on-Wheels.* She suddenly sympathized with Lionel, trying to manage a place with that tyrant watching him. She noticed Joseph's outstretched hand and shook it, finding it soft and clammy.

"The family's here waiting for the will to be read," Lionel continued, undeterred. His smirk widened as Clarissa shot him a glare sharp enough to cut glass.

"That's hardly of interest to outsiders," she snapped. Then she turned to Angie and Paavo with a tight smile. "This week is the ranch's annual cookout, a beloved tradition. Despite Joseph's father's unfortunate passing—Hal was my ex-husband, by-the-way—we're committed to making this year's event bigger and better than ever. Isn't that right, Joseph?"

Angie's ears perked up at the *cookout*. This could be useful. But Joseph was too busy eyeing the liquor to notice.

"Uh huh," he muttered, after a beat too long.

Clarissa's lips thinned. "Pour some wine, Lionel. The Domaines Schlumberger Gewürztraminer."

Lionel grumbled as he set out a glass. Clarissa snatched it up and inspected it like a forensic scientist.

Grinding his teeth, Lionel opened the wine, poured a splash. She tasted, nodded. He filled the glass.

"You may serve your cousin Joseph and our guests as well," she declared.

When Lionel handed his cousin a glass, Joey downed it in one gulp.

As Angie sipped hers, she had to admit: Clarissa might be a terror, but she knew wine. "This is excellent," she said, trying to lighten the moment.

Clarissa gave her a cool glance. "It should be. It's not exactly Gallo."

Angie wasn't about to let that slide. "A crisp Gewürztraminer is rare," she said, swirling her glass. "Wonderful spicy nose. Too often they're sweet and flabby. Honestly, this is better than most late-harvest Rieslings—which, in my opinion, are overrated. Don't you agree?"

Paavo bit back a grin.

Clarissa raised a thin brow. "How unexpected—to find someone in this area who knows wines."

"I've learned from some of the world's best sommeliers," Angie replied.

"I've learned from my own palate."

Angie smiled tightly. "You mentioned the annual cookout. When is it?"

"Saturday. Will you be staying that long?"

"We plan to stay through next weekend," Paavo said.

"What's the cookout like?" Angie asked, doing her best to contain her excitement. This could be her way into the kitchen —*and* into learning why everyone here was so weird. "Have you always helped organize it?"

Clarissa gave a brittle laugh. "Hardly. I've done my best to avoid it. Years ago, Hal ran it as a thank-you to the town after the snowbirds left. When he was gone, Lionel miraculously managed to keep it afloat. This year, Joseph will preside."

Joey looked pained and poured himself a shot of bourbon, ignoring the wine Cousin Lionel offered him.

"It sounds like a wonderful tradition," Angie said.

"If you like beer, beans, and barbecue," Clarissa sniffed. "I've recruited some women from the Mexican restaurant to help, but I'm not expecting much."

Now was her chance. Angie gazed questioningly at Paavo. He couldn't help but glance heavenward, then nodded.

"I'd be happy to help," she offered.

Clarissa blinked. "Help? How?"

"I studied at Le Cordon Bleu in Paris. I've been a restaurant critic in San Francisco, and I've worked on cooking shows on television and radio. I know food."

Clarissa studied her with renewed interest. "You're serious?"

"Absolutely. I'd enjoy it."

A flicker of genuine delight touched Clarissa's face. "Ah! *Très bien!* My prayers have been answered! A competent food person —what a novelty. I can't abide barbecue. This is a splendid offer, Miss... er, what—"

"Call me Angie."

Clarissa didn't. Instead, she paused as if recalibrating. "You'll have the full kitchen staff at your disposal—and Lionel, of course. Just tell him what you need. I might even invite a few friends from Bel Air. They have refined palates."

Angie could hardly contain her smile. This was perfect. The kitchen was always the heart of a place—and where secrets simmered.

"This should be fun," she said brightly.

"Let's freshen our glasses," Clarissa said. "Then find a quiet corner to talk logistics."

With Angie and Clarissa deep in culinary plotting, Lionel pulled out whiskey. Still, the room grew heavy with silence between the men. Weather, politics, baseball, even movies—nothing sparked a real conversation.

Lionel grew busy drinking toward oblivion. Joey sulked into his glass and watched Clarissa out of the corner of his eye.

Paavo waited, certain that if he stayed long enough—and let the drinks flow—someone would let something slip about Hal Edwards.

Joey's glass emptied. When Lionel didn't notice, Joey grabbed the bottle and sloshed whiskey into it, overshooting the rim by quite a bit.

Whiskey landed his boot and the hardwood floor.

"Want a rag to wipe that off?" Paavo asked.

Joey didn't move. "Who cares? They're already ruined."

"Damn it!" Lionel came around with a washrag to wipe the floor. "Can't even clean up your own mess? You don't own this place yet, Joey. Might never."

Joey stuck out his foot. "Since you're down there..."

"Like hell," Lionel muttered, returning to the bar.

Joey stared at his boots—cognac brown, hand-tooled shafts, lizard-skin vamp. Expensive. Dressy. Damaged.

"This terrain's rough on boots," Paavo offered.

"You a shoe salesman or just got a fetish?" Joey said then knocked back his drink.

Lionel snorted.

Paavo remained stone-faced. "You visit here often?"

Joey stared Lionel down until the bartender refilled his glass. "From time to time."

"He comes a lot," Lionel cut in. "Joey likes it here. Don't you?"

Paavo nodded slowly. "Must be nice—family ranch, warm winters..."

"He's a regular little snowbird," Lionel said with a smirk.

"Especially since he's hoping a certain miss might warm up to him."

Paavo sensed something bitter underneath.

"Lionel," Joey snapped. "I doubt this stranger cares about my itinerary."

"Just making conversation, *cousin*."

Joey turned to Paavo. "What do you do?"

"I work for the city of San Francisco."

"Doing what?"

"My agency handles social and behavioral issues."

"A social worker," Joey said with disdain. "No offense, but that sounds soul-killing."

"I suppose," Paavo replied mildly. "So, I heard your father once took off for five years and no one knew where he went. That's quite a trick for such a wealthy fellow."

Joey looked uninterested. "He pulled it off."

"Strange that no one worried. Thought he was dead? Maybe kidnapped?"

"Hell," Lionel interrupted. "Clarissa's first move was to get her lawyers to work on declaring him dead. She and her boy, here, wanted control of the ranch. It was the only thing she *didn't* get from the divorce."

"Oh?" Paavo said.

"Everyone knew Hal was nuts," Lionel muttered. "He said he was going, and then just... did. But after a couple years, when he started pulling cash from his accounts, we knew he was still alive."

"Curious old coot," Joey muttered. "I think his strange actions came about because he had a stroke in his early fifties. Totally unexpected. Mom ran the Halmart stores while he was in the hospital and then going through rehab. No one thought he'd come back from what had happened, but he did—even though it took him nearly ten years. He wasn't good as new, but damn close. And *that* was when Mom divorced him. She took over his business—the Halmart chain. Joked she should rename them Clarmart stores. Maybe that's what broke him. Or maybe he was always broken."

Joey's expression shifted, unexpectedly sad.

"I'm sorry to hear that," Paavo said.

"Yeah, she took him for every cent he had, just about. That's why he turned our home into a guest ranch. It was doing well enough. I thought he was fine, but then one day, he just left. It took a year or so before we learned he was alive and in Mexico."

"Who ran the guest ranch during all that?" Paavo asked.

"Lionel kept it going, but it's been downhill, frankly."

"Hey, I tried!" Lionel mumbled.

Joey poured himself more bourbon. The more he drank, the more he seemed to enjoy talking—maybe because Clarissa wasn't around.

He took a long swallow and continued with his story. "After five years of being away, my father suddenly returned, and even brought a bunch of ostriches to raise—something new and classy, I guess, I really don't know. Anyway, people said he seemed glad to be back here, even happy. But then, once again, he disappeared. Everyone guessed he'd gone back to Mexico. Turns out he'd gone into a cave—a place way out on the edge of the ranch land. Didn't find the body for months." He drained his glass. "Sad ending for a once powerful man."

"How old was he when he left the first time?"

"Sixty-five."

Paavo turned to Lionel. "When Hal came back, did he ever explain why he took off?"

"Not to me."

Paavo looked to Joey.

"I never even saw him," Joey said. Then he stood abruptly, belching. "Got a headache." He held out his hand.

Lionel sighed and handed him an unopened bottle of bourbon.

"Tell my mother not to worry," Joey ordered. "And when the food comes, have a girl make up a plate and bring it to my cottage."

He stalked off without a backward glance.

"Gets lotsa headaches," Lionel said into his glass. "Kinda delicate. Just like his old man."

4

———

Angie and Paavo ate dinner alone. Clarissa, like Joey, had opted to eat in her cottage, and Lionel looked more interested in his bottle than in food. Someone—an invisible yet clearly talented cook—had laid out a delicious spread of enchiladas, refried beans smothered in cheese, Spanish rice, and green salad on the dining room sideboard. They served themselves without ceremony.

While Angie got ready for bed, Paavo tried calling Ned again. He'd expected to spend the evening with Ned, then speak with the other guests at the ranch to dig into Hal Edwards' death. But nothing had gone according to plan. Odd that Ned hadn't shown up—he'd seemed eager to talk to Paavo before Doc could.

First thing in the morning, Paavo planned to go out to Doc's home. For now, he decided to walk the grounds alone, see the place unfiltered—no distractions, no watching eyes.

Angie slipped into a sexy black teddy and climbed into bed, expecting Paavo to soon join her.

Instead, here she sat. Alone.

No TV. No radio. Just silence and shadows. She didn't want to fall asleep alone on the first night of her vacation. How unromantic was that?

She opened the nightstand drawer. As expected, a Bible lay inside. But beneath it, she found a map of Arizona and a yellowed pamphlet titled *Jackpot, Arizona—The Town Hal Edwards Made Famous*, published by the Arizona Historical Society.

She fluffed the pillows and settled in with the sepia-toned booklet.

Clearly written to lure tourists, it was filled with maps and grainy photographs of Jackpot's past—dusty streets, stone buildings, stern-faced men in hats, women in high collars. The town had once been a rough-and-tumble outpost of the Old West, built on hard living and harder drinking.

Most of the booklet read like dry toast. But one story stood out: a mysterious event in 1893.

A stagecoach had departed Phoenix en route to the Pacific, aiming for a fledgling town called Los Angeles. Somewhere near Jackpot, it had vanished without a trace.

She sat up straighter, her eyes scanning the names of the missing passengers:

—Hoot Dalton, cousin of the infamous Dalton Gang of train and bank robbers

—Daisy Lane, a singer and actress

—Willem Van Beerstraeden, chef at New York's Waldorf Hotel

That name caught her attention.

How interesting. She hadn't realized the present-day Waldorf-Astoria had once been simply *The Waldorf.*

Turning the page, she found a section on Hal Edwards himself.

In Jackpot, a young Edwards had opened a general store. The business quickly expanded—hardware, ranch supplies, foodstuffs, even pharmacy and optometry services. Before long, "Halmart Stores" dotted the state.

Keeping with the Old West theme, a sepia portrait of a young Hal took up the next page. Wearing a cowboy hat and bolo tie, he was startlingly handsome, with deep-set dark eyes in an intelligent face. He looked like a throwback to a movie-star cowboy from the 1940s and '50s, not John Wayne, but more of a Gary Cooper type.

If he had been popular with the ladies, Angie could understand why.

The write-up detailed how Edwards had built a sprawling hacienda just outside of town and became Jackpot's generous benefactor. He gave freely to the townsfolk and helped transform the dusty outpost into a winter refuge for snow-weary tourists.

Then tragedy. A stroke at age 50, when he was far too young.

But, the booklet claimed, "In keeping with the strong, can-do Edwards spirit, Hal recovered. Travelers to Jackpot can now visit and stay on his property. Called the Ghost Hollow Guest Ranch…"

Angie's eyes began to glaze. "…it is renowned for its beautiful grounds and lovely guest cottages…"

Her eyelids drifted shut.

The booklet slid from her lap to the floor as her head lolled back. But the words lingered, images stirring behind her eyes.

She dreamed.

Flickering visions floated to the surface: her first visit to the Waldorf-Astoria with her parents at fourteen, dining at "Oscar's Restaurant"—named for the famous maître d'hôtel, Oscar Tschirky. He'd invented the Waldorf salad, Eggs Benedict, and Veal Oscar, among other popular dishes, despite never having worked as a chef. That night, she'd realized she could build a life, even a reputation, around her passion for gourmet food.

The dream shifted.

Now everything was in black and white, like an old movie.

Oscar Tschirky appeared, dressed in dapper 1890s tails and top hat as he strode down Jackpot's dusty main street, a six-shooter strapped to his hip. The sun blazed high, as if it were noon.

From the far end of the street came a second figure. Young, strong, healthy—Hal Edwards. His boots kicked up dry dust as he walked toward Oscar, arms loose at his sides, ready.

On the corner, Hal's son, Joey, sat on a stoop, strumming a guitar, a whiskey bottle at his feet. He sang in a slurred voice, "Do Not Forsake Me, Oh My Darling…" from *High Noon*. Even in sleep, Angie felt unease ripple through her.

She turned restlessly.

The dream sharpened. White-hot sky. Sage and tamarisk rising from gravel beyond the clapboard buildings. Heat waves shimmered like spirits.

"Where's my chef?" Oscar demanded of Hal.

Hal turned, looked at Angie, and shrugged as if he had no answer for Oscar. But then, he smiled at her. Brilliant. Disarmingly handsome, his image shimmered, distorted like a mirage. "Angie," he whispered softly. "Angie, are you asleep?" he asked, his voice warping into another tone.

Abruptly, she opened her eyes.

Paavo sat on the edge of the bed, silhouetted in the soft lamplight.

Relief filled her. "No," she whispered, brushing the dream away. As she shifted toward him, the covers slipped from her shoulders, revealing the black lace of her teddy. "I'm not asleep at all."

5

Angie had thought the two-lane road from Jackpot to the Ghost Hollow Guest Ranch was rough—until the next morning. The narrow, rutted track they were on now, heading toward the Colorado River reservation, made that earlier route feel like a cruise down Fifth Avenue.

The car jolted hard, forcing her to grip the overhead strap with one hand and brace against the dash with the other. Her stomach churned. Now she understood why Paavo had insisted that even if she wanted a Mercedes as their rental car, that it have all-wheel drive.

Eventually, he turned onto a driveway. In the distance stood a sprawling white ranch house.

"That's a large home for one man," Angie said. "Doc lives alone, right?"

"He does. And he has every inch crammed. He's a collector of interesting things."

"I think someone's standing on the porch."

Paavo smiled. "That's him."

As they pulled up, the man rushed out to greet them.

Angie's nerves fluttered. Paavo had endured countless meetings with her family—each relative studying him like a specimen. She'd never experienced that kind of scrutiny herself. When she met his guardian, Aulis, it had been long before she and Paavo were a couple, and she'd immediately liked the kind old man.

But this was different. This was Doc. She wanted him to like her—for Paavo's sake. She smoothed her light green jacket, adjusted the white tank top beneath it, and plucked a nearly invisible speck from her jeans. Her new gray, hand-tooled Justin cowboy boots completed the outfit she hoped was properly outdoorsy.

Now, she wasn't so sure.

From the name "Doc," she'd imagined a toothless Gabby Hayes type. But this Doc was a tall, solid man with the rugged presence of Clint Eastwood or Sam Elliott—thick, gunmetal gray hair, a long, weathered face, penetrating blue eyes, and a lean, firm mouth. He wore black slacks and boots, a crisp white shirt, and a black string tie. He moved with surprising strength and purpose for a man of seventy.

"So what the hell you doing still sitting in the car?" he called, his voice deep and edged with a drawl. "Come on out where I can see you."

Paavo and Angie climbed out. Doc enveloped Paavo in a crushing bear hug.

"Goddamn! It's good to see you, boy!" Doc stepped back and gripped Paavo's shoulders, eyes scanning him with pride. "Grown some since the skinny brat I last saw. Guess I can't threaten to take you over my knee anymore."

"I never dared give you trouble back then," Paavo said with a grin. "Still wouldn't."

They laughed, their bond unmistakable. Angie smiled at their playfulness, glad that someone who had been close to Paavo was going to be part of their life. That mattered.

"Smart kid. Always told Aulis that." Doc's eyes shifted to her, and he winked. "Looks like you're doing all right for yourself, too. Good job. Beautiful fiancée. I'm glad for you."

"Thanks," Paavo said. "Let me introduce Angie."

"Shame on us for ignoring your lovely lady." Doc extended a hand. "Doctor Loomis Griggs. I only answer to 'Doc.' Welcome to my home."

"Angelina Amalfi," she said, shaking his hand. "But I only answer to Angie. Thank you for inviting me."

As their hands touched, she felt his scrutiny—taking in her makeup, hair, skin, nails, clothes. For the first time, she understood exactly how Paavo must have felt under her family's microscope.

"Let's go inside," Doc said.

She followed, but his glance told her she hadn't passed muster. It had to be the clothes. Why hadn't she worn her sophisticated DKNY pantsuit?

At the front door, Doc paused, scanning the landscape with sharp, assessing eyes. In that moment, Angie saw past the jovial front. He was no charming eccentric. This man was hard-edged, serious, and guarded.

But if Paavo and Aulis trusted him, he was worth knowing.

Inside, Doc asked after Aulis as he led them into a spacious, masculine living room dominated by a floor-to-ceiling stone fireplace. High-backed leather chairs draped with Navajo blankets and a massive couch piled with pillows filled the space, along with rustic tables and an enormous rolltop desk. Books lined the walls—some in Greek and Latin.

The scent of smoke and pipe tobacco lingered in the air. There was no sign of a woman's touch. Angie's curiosity stirred. Why was a man like Doc—handsome, strong, independent—living alone?

Well, not quite alone. Two German shepherds came over to check out Doc's visitors. They were well trained and well behaved, even as Doc sent them outdoors.

There were layers and layers to Doc Griggs, she thought, and it was going to be interesting to delve into them.

"Sit wherever you like," he said, bringing in a tray with coffee, cream, and sugar. His smile was wide, but the lines around his eyes told a different story. Strain. Worry.

She knew Paavo wanted answers, but Aulis had warned them—Doc would only open up in his own time.

Angie took a sip of coffee and nearly choked. It was so thick and bitter, a spoon might stand in it. She reached for the sugar.

"Like it?" Doc asked.

"It's great," she lied.

"Nothing like real coffee to get the juices flowing." He clapped his hands. "Well, I'm starving. I usually eat by now. Who wants bacon and eggs? Toast? English muffins? We need to eat before we set out."

Set out?

The phrase landed oddly in her gut—like a small earthquake, over almost before it began.

Then the booklet she'd been reading and her strange dream came back to her, along with memories from some of the culinary classes she'd taken. One of the dishes that Oscar Tschirky, a.k.a. "Mr. Oscar" and "Oscar-of-the-Waldorf," immortalized was Eggs Benedict. He had created it—if she remembered right—as a hangover cure for one of the Waldorf-Astoria's guests, a Mr. Benedict who ordered "toast, bacon, two poached eggs and a hooker of hollandaise sauce." Oscar had used English muffins and Canadian bacon, and was so impressed with the results he put it on the restaurant's menu.

In her dream, Oscar had asked, *"Where's my chef?"*

The chef mentioned in the booklet about the missing stage-coach—Oscar's chef was the missing passenger!

The connection was too strange to ignore.

Maybe she could build Clarissa's cookout menu around

dishes made famous by Oscar Tschirky? It would certainly be more cohesive than Clarissa's muddled ideas.

Right now, though, she could practically taste Eggs Benedict. Maybe she'd get lucky and Doc would open up to Paavo while she cooked.

"If you don't mind, I can make breakfast while you two talk —it'll give you some alone time to catch up," she said.

"But you're my guest," Doc replied.

"She's also a gourmet cook," Paavo said, reading her intention. "Best Italian and French food you've ever tasted—and just about everything else, too."

Doc eyed her with new interest. "Is that so?"

"I try."

"Then I won't complain."

"Have you heard from Ned?" Paavo asked.

"I'm sorry he stood you two up." Doc sighed. "I don't know what's gotten into him. He's been distracted, troubled. I can't get to the bottom of it."

"What's it about?"

"He won't say. Clams up worse than you do." Doc scratched his chin. "It seemed to start when Hal Edwards came back."

"I'd like to hear about that," Paavo said.

"It goes back a ways," Doc warned. "You know Hal used to have it all—wealth, prestige. Then came the stroke, the divorce... He lost nearly everything but his land here. Thanks to me and some good ranch hands, he recovered. Turned the place into a profitable resort. But he never got over the fury at Clarissa for taking his Halmart business, or at his son, Joey, for going along with his mother instead of taking his side. Eventually, he became paranoid. I don't know why. Then, he left without a word."

"He never told anyone he was leaving?"

"Oh, he ranted about it. Made threats. Nothing specific. We didn't know where he was until he wired his bank for money. He stayed away five years. Then, this past February, he returned. He was here for only eight days—just long enough to have female ostriches delivered to the hacienda. And then he vanished again."

Paavo shook his head. "Five years gone, then back with ostriches?"

"You got it," Doc said flatly. "Everyone suspected he went back to Mexico—until his body was found a couple weeks ago. Now, I think he was killed after those eight days, but we might never know for sure. Or know who did it."

"And no one looked for him?"

"They looked a bit. Like I said, we all thought he'd returned to Mexico."

Paavo didn't buy it. Why bring the ostriches if he didn't plan to stay? It didn't make sense. "Where does Ned fit in?"

Angie walked in with Eggs Benedict. From her expression, she hadn't missed a word.

After praising Angie for the breakfast she'd cooked, Doc continued his tale. "From the time Hal returned, Ned changed. I don't know why."

"Did they get along?" Angie asked as she refilled the coffee cups—this time with her own brew.

"Not well. Whenever Hal's name came up, Ned looked decidedly unhappy."

"Even before he left for five years, or only when he came back?" Angie asked.

"Hmm. Actually, it was before he ever left the first time. Something about Hal just seemed to rub Ned the wrong way." Doc splashed Tabasco onto his eggs.

Angie visibly flinched.

Paavo saw her brace herself, gulp some coffee, and try to

ignore the desecration of her carefully prepared and seasoned Hollandaise sauce.

"These eggs are delicious," Doc said.

"Thanks," she murmured, trying to stop any palpitations as he reached for green chili sauce.

"So, what's Ned like?" she asked, forcing herself to act composed.

Doc's face softened. "He's a good man. Lost his dad young. His mom brought him here, raised him in the country. She remarried when Ned was sixteen, moved to Phoenix. He stayed with me to finish school."

"So when Paavo knew him, it was just him and his mom?"

"That's right." Doc glanced at Paavo. "Two boys who'd already known loss. It forged a bond. They didn't care about petty things. They valued honesty, friendship. Still do."

"He absolutely does," Angie said, reaching for Paavo's hand.

Doc nodded, pleased. "Ned started his own business. Struggled, but he's doing well now. He's got heart—and that matters. Maybe it's what matters most."

"We met Teresa Flores yesterday," Paavo said. "Seems there's something between her and Ned."

Doc frowned. "Ned's loved her since high school. But she's always wanted more than this town. She paid no attention to him for years, but he wouldn't give up hope. For a while, just recently, I thought he'd finally gotten through to her, but then it seemed to end. He'd be better off if he could forget about her. Find someone else."

"When did it end?" Paavo asked. From the way Teresa had acted the day before, their relationship might not be over.

"I remember everything was fine at Christmas. Teresa's mom, Lupe, even invited Ned and me over for dinner. But about a month later, I remember Ned saying there'd be no Valentines that year. He was quite bitter about her."

"So, December all was fine," Paavo said. "In February, Hal returns—"

"With ostriches," Angie added.

Paavo nodded and continued. "Also in February, for reasons unknown, Ned is upset, and the romance is over again."

"That's right," Doc said, his gaze glancing at the silent phone on his desk.

Angie tried to shift the mood by changing the subject. "I heard there's an interesting Ghost Hollow legend. Something about a stagecoach?"

Doc waved it off. "Wildly exaggerated. Hal just used it to draw tourists."

Bummer, Angie thought. But still, most stories like that have a reason to get started. First chance she got, she planned to find out what it was—especially given the Waldorf-Astoria connection.

They had finished breakfast and cleaned up the kitchen when there was a knock on the door. Doc opened it to an older man that Paavo immediately recognized—Joaquin Oldwater.

He was compact and sturdy, with weathered features, white hair tied back, and strong cheekbones that hinted at his heritage. His worn jeans, a red plaid shirt, and scuffed boots had clearly seen decades of use.

Paavo stood. "Remember me, Joaquin?"

"Course!" Joaquin's expression creased into a slow smile. "Taught you to ride. Taught you to shoot. You were a good kid. Why don't you come down anymore?"

"Big mistake. I let myself get too caught up in work," Paavo said, then introduced Angie.

Joaquin studied her, then nodded. Angie brightened—she'd passed the first test.

"Ned's still missing, I take it?" he asked.

Doc nodded. "This has gone on too long. No one's seen him. Neighbors said his home was empty this morning; his business is locked up; and his motorcycle's gone. He wasn't arrested, and wasn't in the hospital. I'm thinking about calling the sheriff."

"Fat lot of good that'll do," Joaquin muttered. "We still going?"

Doc turned to Paavo and Angie. "Joaquin's taking us to the cave where Hal Edwards' body was found. You'll be interested, Angie, to learn it's near where the stagecoach disappeared. I'd forgotten about that."

"Scene of the crime," Paavo said.

"Exactly. Something's going on, Paavo. I can feel it. There were two break-ins last week—my home and at the clinic. My records were rifled."

"You think someone's after the Hal's will? You're the executor, right?"

"There isn't one. That's not what worries me. It's Teresa."

"She's in danger?" Angie asked, alarmed.

Doc nodded. "Strange things happened around her. Ned was worried about her as well. Over the last few months, her car brakes failed. Someone tried to run her off the road late at night —it was too dark for her to see the make or model of the truck. Someone mugged her, stole her purse, hit her head hard enough to knock her out. She says they were random attacks—wrong place, wrong time. I don't believe her. What's weird is they started when Hal returned, then stopped, and now they've started again. Teresa's mother, Lupe, is worried sick. Teresa still pretends all is well, but it obviously isn't."

"That's what you meant when you told Aulis strange things were happening?" Paavo asked.

"Yes. And one more thing. Not only were there break-ins at my office, there was one at the church."

"The church? Was anything stolen?" Paavo asked.

"Not that Father Armand could tell. He found the doors to the sacristy and records area open. None of the chalices or anything of value was taken, but since Father Armand is fairly new here, he just doesn't know. For all he knows, the break-in might have been simply vagrants, illegals, even some old prospector looking for food or warm shelter for the night."

"But you don't think so," Paavo said, realizing the break-in was similar to what Doc had experienced with his records.

"No." Doc shook his head. "I don't."

Paavo nodded, then said, "You've told me no one knows the cause of Hal's death—that the body was too decomposed to find decent forensic evidence—but what's the official explanation?"

"Hal had a history of a stroke, so the coroner took the easy way out and said the death was from 'natural causes.'"

Paavo asked the question uppermost in his mind, "Do you think Hal was murdered?"

Doc and Joaquin traded glances. "Yes," Doc said, "I do. Don't ask who or why. I've given it a lot of thought, but I just don't know."

"Enough talk," Joaquin grunted. "Ready to ride?"

Doc retrieved a gun and holster from his desk. Paavo had a feeling it wasn't mountain lions Doc feared.

Doc's eyes shifted to Angie. "Can you ride?"

She hesitated. "I've ridden."

Uh, oh, Paavo thought. He knew that look. "Probably pony rides when she was a girl. I don't think—"

"That's not true, Paavo," she protested. "I'll be just fine."

"You never told me you knew how to ride," he said. And she'd told him almost everything ... except about old boy friends, which she kept a deep, dark secret.

She shrugged. "The subject never came up."

He was ready to argue that that had never stopped her before, when Doc said, "I've got a mare up in years—like me.

She's gentle and forgiving. We could take my pickup, but it's tougher to drive over that terrain than it is to ride."

"Believe me," Angie said, smoothing her colorful designer's idea-of-Western-garb outfit. "I know all about riding horses."

Doc and Joaquin glanced at each other.

Paavo knew what they were thinking: clothes like Angie's shouldn't be allowed within five hundred feet of a horse. He hated to think of how her fashionable boots were going to look after a simple jaunt to the stables. "The lady says she can ride." He looked at the men and nodded. "Let's go."

"Oh—wait!" Angie cried. "I'd better get my cowboy hat. It's still in the car."

6

———

Soon, three tall, beautiful horses stood saddled and ready to go. The fourth, an old roan mare with a gray muzzle and bald patches, was much smaller than the others. The mare's hooves splayed outward—the opposite of pigeon-toed—and one ear stood upright while the other was bent forward.

"This is Ophelia," Doc said, patting the mare's neck. "You two should get along swell."

Angie wasn't sure how to take that. She knew Ophelia was the crazy girlfriend in *Hamlet* who drowned herself. The mare gazed at her, head cocked, like she was sizing up Angie's qualifications.

She'd told the men she could ride. She hadn't told them her only experience came from two lessons when she was nine. As she eyed the mare, she plunked a red-dyed Ralph Lauren Western straw hat onto her head—a prized find from a boutique in San Francisco. Just the thought of how difficult it had been to find that hat in San Francisco made her appreciate it all the more.

Ophelia now wore an expression of complete amusement.

Angie drew a breath, squared her shoulders. No way was she missing a ride into the desert. Not if she could help it.

Still, the idea of bowing out to help Clarissa with the cookout had its appeal. She'd much rather be cooking than pretending she belonged in the Wild West.

With one foot in the stirrup and both hands on the saddle horn, she tried to mount—just as Ophelia began to stroll. Hanging on, Angie found herself suddenly taking impromptu hops around the yard. Seeing her dilemma and trying to keep his face straight, Paavo held the mare still and boosted her up.

Once seated high, very high, off the ground on the massive beast, all the reasons she'd quit after only two lessons hit her like a sledgehammer. But she'd been about nine years old at the time. She was an adult now; she could handle this.

She gripped the saddle horn rather than the reins and tried to remember how to steer. She and Paavo both gaped in amazement as Ophelia made backward figure eights. What was this? Angie wondered if she'd been given the figure skater of horses.

This time, Joaquin came to the rescue and gave her a quick lesson, assuring her that Ophelia would follow Doc's horse, Achilles, and Angie would be fine.

She doubted it, but nodded.

Once everyone mounted up, they rode out. Angie lagged behind until she started to get the rhythm. Eventually, she relaxed enough to notice just how hard the saddle was—and how much she ached.

They headed across open desert toward the foothills. It was spring, and delicate orange and yellow wildflowers peeked through creosote and jojoba scrub. Higher up, saguaro cacti rose like sentries, their L-shaped arms stretching skyward. Not a tree in sight. In the sand, she saw long, wavy lines.

"Snake trails," Joaquin said. "Could be rattlers. Keep watch."

Rattlesnakes? Angie's head bobbed like a ping-pong ball on alert.

Lizards darted past, and in the far distance a roadrunner streaked across the plain. The sky stretched overhead, high and bright blue. Heat shimmered across the land in fleeting mirages that always hovered just ahead.

Doc and Joaquin rode with purpose. Paavo—handsome in the black Stetson Doc had lent him—looked surprisingly at ease. Angie had no idea he was good on a horse.

For her, though, this was slow torture.

Before coming to Jackpot, she'd flirted with the idea of a full Western wedding—maybe even a rodeo theme. Not anymore. The most rustic she'd go now would be a coach pulled by Clydesdales, beer commercial style.

Lost in wedding thoughts, she didn't notice where they were headed until a flicker of light and shadow across a rock formation brought her back to the present.

The land was eerily beautiful, but it could be deadly. She couldn't help but contemplate the stagecoach lost in this barrenness and the terror a Dutch chef must have felt to be stranded out here with his few fellow passengers. A cold chill, almost a premonition, rippled through her as she thought of another person who was missing—Paavo's boyhood friend, Ned.

As Joaquin, Paavo, and Doc reached the shadows of a rock wall, they stopped, and Joaquin pointed toward some rises. Angie caught up to them in time to hear Paavo say, "... watching us now?"

She didn't like the sound of that. She followed Joaquin's gaze but saw nothing.

"We've been watched all day," Joaquin said calmly. "I spotted a glint—could've been binoculars, maybe a rifle—back on the desert floor."

Doc looked anxious. Paavo scanned the terrain with cold precision. Angie's pulse kicked up. The hills were rugged, the shadows long. Whoever was out there could be anywhere.

"You won't spot him," Joaquin said. "But he's there. I feel him."

"I've had this feeling before," Doc murmured, brow tight.

"Are we in danger?" Angie asked, her voice low.

Paavo shook his head. "I don't think so. We've been out in the open for hours."

"I hope you're right." She tried to edge closer to him, but Ophelia focused on a prickly bush instead. The air shifted, and the beauty of the desert was now tinged with menace.

"The watcher is a watcher," Joaquin said. "Not a shooter. Not today."

<hr>

Everyone dismounted at the bottom of the rocky incline, all too conscious of the secret observer.

"There are several caves up here," Joaquin said. "Only one's large enough to matter." He pointed six feet up, where a crevice hid behind a scraggly brush.

That's the cave? Angie thought. *No way I'm going in there.*

Joaquin pulled two flashlights from his saddlebags, gave one to Paavo, and led them upward. Up close, the opening was larger than it had looked. He clicked on the flashlight and ducked inside. Paavo and Doc followed.

Angie hesitated, then curiosity overcame her. She crouched to enter, her eyes wide, scanning for spiders or snakes. Thankfully, she saw none.

The cave walls were smooth and surprisingly high. Even Paavo could stand upright—though the ceiling dipped lower toward the back.

She wasn't claustrophobic, but knowing a body had been found here made her hope this visit would be short. The smell of death and decay still seemed to linger, just past the edge of perception.

"Why would Hal have come here?" Paavo asked.

"That's the question," Doc said.

"Maybe to hide something," Joaquin offered. "But what, I don't know."

"How'd you find him?" Paavo asked.

"This is Hal Edwards' land. Goes for miles. I saw Hal's nephew, Lionel, out here once. I was curious about why. A few days later, I came back and followed tracks to this cave. Found the body."

"Anyone ask Lionel what he was doing here?"

"The sheriff did," Doc replied. "Lionel said he was being a good manager, checking the property. Claimed he never went inside the caves. Maybe true, maybe not. But the sheriff bought it. "

Joaquin's beam settled on a dark patch near the far wall. "That's where Hal was. I recognized his ring and belt buckle."

At the realization as to *why* the ring and belt buckle were all that Joaquin could use to identify an old friend, Angie shuddered and backpedaled toward the entrance.

As the three men bent forward like fortunetellers reading tea leaves to scrutinize the ground where a dead body had lain rotting on the way to becoming nothing but a skeleton, the walls closed in on Angie. Visions of bones danced in her head like something from a macabre Halloween celebration. With a shudder, she backed toward the entrance.

It was hot. Above, buzzards circled in lazy arcs. She wondered what they'd found—and immediately told herself she didn't want to know.

A large, chair-shaped boulder sat just above her. Compared to the cave, it looked inviting. She climbed up, grateful at least that there were no ostriches in sight.

She watched the buzzards and waited, wishing Paavo and the others would hurry.

"What are you doing up there?" Paavo called, one hand shading his eyes.

"I'm guarding you!" she shouted back. "Like a sentry. If that watcher showed up, I'd have spotted him."

"See anything?"

"Not a thing," she said, starting down.

"Did you fall?" Joaquin asked sharply, scanning the dirt.

"Me? No," she said, puzzled.

"Something happened up there." Joaquin studied the slope, then moved higher.

His expression made the hair on the back of Angie's neck stand up.

Joaquin half-walked, half-climbed up the steep, dusty slope, following a trail only he could discern. Paavo and Doc glanced meaningfully at each other and climbed up the hill to Angie's side.

She was beginning to get a real bad feeling about this. "Be careful!" she yelled.

Joaquin kept going.

"He's part mountain goat, Angie," Doc said, but looked decidedly worried himself.

Paavo's mouth set in a grim line as he continued to follow Joaquin's progress. Joaquin climbed on steadily and without hesitation. Their relief when he stopped on more level ground was short-lived. Joaquin walked back and forth, halting and kneeling, and then disappeared.

"Joaquin?" Doc called. No answer.

"I'm going up," Paavo said.

Angie looked at the steep slope, the buzzards, then back at the cave. Something was terribly wrong. "I'm going with you."

"Me, too," Doc said. "Lead the way."

The climb was much rougher than Joaquin had made it

appear. The sun beat down relentlessly. Sand and gravel were stirred by their scrambling, and Angie gulped in mouthfuls of dust kicked up by Paavo just ahead of her. Earth and sweat formed a film on her exposed skin and over her new clothes. Behind her, she could hear Doc coughing, cursing, and sliding.

Finally Paavo, then Angie, reached the level ground of the ledge. They turned to Doc as he struggled the final yards to them. He was red faced and wheezing as he lurched and fell his way up. Paavo took his hand and pulled him the last few feet.

They all moved forward, deeper into the mountain. She saw Joaquin at the same time as the others. He was kneeling by some rocks, his head bowed with grief.

Suddenly, all her instincts told her what had happened. Why he hadn't spoken, hadn't called out. Still, she prayed that it wasn't what she feared.

Paavo told her to wait there. *He knows as well,* she thought, even as her heart begged that she was wrong.

Doc froze. Dread shadowed his suddenly pale and haggard face.

Paavo stepped closer to Joaquin, then stopped. His body stiffened. When he turned, the pain and sorrow in his blue eyes confirmed their worst fears. Angie's hope died.

Doc's head bowed as he moved slowly and mechanically forward, like a man in a trance.

Down below, the horses continued to calmly eat sprigs of tender brush near the cave. The hot sun still beat relentlessly on the hillside. But here, Angie felt nothing except the coldness of death.

7

———————

A plume of sand spiraled into the air as two vehicles tore across the desert toward the ridge where the four waited. Remarkably, Paavo's cell phone had worked. He'd called for help nearly an hour ago.

Since the discovery of Ned Paulson's body, time had hung in a stunned, aching silence.

Doc had tried to hide his tears, but eventually let them fall. Paavo sat beside him, an arm around his shoulders, head bowed.

Angie had stayed with Paavo until she noticed Joaquin standing off to the side, shoulders hunched, eyes red. He sniffled quietly and rubbed at his face with the back of one hand. Her heart ached for him, and she moved to his side.

Without looking at her, he said softly, "I watched Ned grow up, Angie. I loved him, too."

"I know you did." She gently touched his arm.

She mourned for them all: for Paavo, who had looked forward to reconnecting with a childhood friend; for Joaquin, who had clearly been a steady guide as Ned grew into the man Doc had so proudly described; for Doc, who had become a father in every way but name. But most of all, she grieved for

Ned himself—for the promise in Doc's voice when he'd spoken of his future, now forever lost.

Watching their sorrow, her own eyes welled with tears.

In the distance, the vehicles grew larger, closer.

"They're almost here," Paavo said, rising to his feet. "Two of them."

"Two?" Doc pushed himself up, wincing. "Then the sheriff must be dragging Deputy Buster along."

"Deputy who?"

"Also known as Wallace Willis," Doc said dryly. "He's deputy and likes to be called 'Deputy Buster.' Apparently, Buster alone sounds like a kid's name to him. Don't know that 'Deputy Buster' is much of an improvement."

Below, the vehicles rolled to a stop—a massive Hummer and an old Jeep, both fitted with flashing red beacons and antennae snapping in the breeze. The Hummer had to be a good fifteen or more years old, but it was as shiny and unblemished as the day it came off the assembly line.

From the Hummer emerged Sheriff Schwartz, wearing an oversized beige cowboy hat, a bulky jacket and khaki slacks over surprisingly short legs, and a heavy-set body. A utility belt sagged with a phone, gun, and nightstick.

From the Jeep, Deputy Buster leapt out, taller and looking almost skinny next to the sheriff. He began furiously swatting dust from his uniform, that even from a distance appeared crisp and well ironed.

"You all got a body up there?" the sheriff hollered in a voice peculiarly high and sharp.

The four called back variations of "Yes!"

"We're coming up!" came the reply.

Angie couldn't help staring as the two began their ascent. The sheriff cursed and wheezed, sending dust and pebbles flying—much of it into Buster's face. The climb grew steeper, and more than once, Buster boosted the sheriff upward with a firm shove to the rear. Near the top, Paavo and Joaquin clambered down to offer their hands and hoisted the sheriff, then Buster, onto the ledge.

The sheriff yanked off the hat and shrugged out of the jacket. Angie gaped.

The sheriff was a woman.

Somewhere between ages forty and sixty, Angie guessed—short, broad, and solid. Her straight brown hair, streaked with gray, was pulled back in a rubber band. No makeup. A red, sweaty face with pale, nearly invisible brows and lashes. Her mouth was tiny; her nose pert and upturned—and oddly delicate for such a stout frame.

With the khaki uniform, she wore heavy combat boots, a badge and a glower that could have been carved in stone.

Deputy Buster might have been a decent enough looking man, mid-thirties, with large blue eyes and wavy brown hair, if not for his dull expression and protruding lower lip. To Angie's surprise, the collar and front placket of his shirt were edged with maroon piping, and his hat had a small yellow feather stuck in the band. She couldn't help but stare.

As soon as he spotted her, he gazed back with equal fascination.

"Where's the body?" the sheriff asked between gulps of air, eyes watering from the climb.

They pointed. She marched off.

"Buster!" she barked. He jolted, then followed. Moments later, dry heaving echoed from behind the brush.

Paavo cringed. Angie knew exactly what he was thinking—*they're trampling all over the crime scene.*

Doc glared after them. "Our delightful sheriff is the orneriest cuss west of the Mississippi. She got the job because nobody could match her in meanness or stubbornness. It's a toss-up which is worse—her temper or Buster's incompetence."

The words had barely left his mouth when the sheriff reappeared.

"Damnation, he's dead," she wheezed, hands on hips, jowls trembling. Her eyes darted over them as if deciding who to blame. "What the hell's going on around here? I didn't take this job expecting people to drop like flies!"

"That's Ned! Show some respect!" Doc snapped. Paavo put a restraining hand on his arm.

"Don't you think I know who it is?" she sneered, her face tight.

"Listen here, Merry Belle—" Doc started toward her, furious, but Paavo's grip held firm. Doc turned away, eyes glittering with unshed tears.

Merry Belle? Angie's head tilted. *Did I hear that right?*

"You don't yell at the sheriff," Deputy Buster said weakly, wiping his mouth with a white handkerchief embroidered with royal purple *WW*. "You okay, Aunt Merry Belle?"

"Of course I'm okay!" Merry Belle barked, thwacking Buster's chest with the back of her hand. "Better than you! Now get down there and radio the county coroner. See if we can get a chopper from Yuma to lift the body. Might not be able to land, but they could drop a line."

She paused and glanced sheepishly at Doc. "Cool off, Doc. I'm sorry about Ned, I truly am. But I don't know what the hell's happening out here. Looks like an accident ... but up here?"

Doc said nothing. He turned and walked away, shoulders heavy.

The sheriff looked around, trying to make sense of the scene. When her gaze swung back toward her deputy, her eyes narrowed.

"I still see you," she snapped.

Buster hadn't moved. He was staring at Angie.

"Have your legs failed you, boy?" Merry Belle growled. "Or do I have to shoot?"

"I'm going," Buster muttered. Then, pointing to Angie, "But who's she?"

"I'll do my investigating once you're gone!" she shouted, exasperated.

"I like her red hat," he mumbled before turning to make his way back down the ridge.

8

Much later that day, Angie found herself back at the guest ranch—alone. She'd taken the Mercedes and returned while Paavo did some investigating on his own.

He clearly had no confidence the sheriff would handle the case properly, or anytime soon. It had taken all his restraint to keep her and Deputy Buster from disturbing the crime scene further. He'd told Merry Belle he was a homicide inspector from San Francisco and offered to assist. She bristled at the suggestion, not buying that he was vacationing in Jackpot "just by chance."

When Paavo discovered Doc had an extra set of keys to Ned's house and business, he decided to take matters into his own hands.

Angie figured she'd only be in the way. Better to give those who knew Ned space to mourn his loss together in their own way.

Now she stood in the shade of the porch outside her cabin, fishing through her purse for the key.

"Junior!" Clarissa's voice cracked across the plaza. "Junior Whitney, get over here right now!"

Angie glanced up to see what was going on.

Clarissa stood on the veranda outside the common room. The man she'd called Junior Whitney had been trudging toward the stables. Angie wondered if he was yet another relative.

He slunk closer. His hair was long and unkempt, his clothes wrinkled and grimy. Maybe in his late fifties, early sixties, tall and stringy. Dust coated his jeans and boots, and dirt smudged his hands and face. Even from a distance, his face looked too red and puffy. But for some reason, he seemed vaguely familiar.

"Where have you been?" Clarissa snapped, stomping toward him. "I haven't seen you in two days! Lionel's got work for you."

"Now?" he groaned. "I been helpin' out at Hal's cattle ranch. I'm worn out."

"Now!"

Junior spun on his heel, muttering something under his breath—Angie could've sworn it was "too damned cheap to hire enough help"—as he headed toward Lionel's trailer.

Clarissa turned and noticed Angie watching. "Now you see what I deal with," she said crisply. "Help is egregious these days! Oh, and I haven't heard what you plan to prepare for the cookout."

She said it as if Angie were nothing more than unreliable help herself. Angie bit back the urge to stick out her tongue and felt an unexpected pang of sympathy for Junior Whitney.

A memory sparked—Junior had been in LaVerne's diner the day she and Paavo arrived. And he'd ducked out the moment Teresa walked in. She'd found that suspicious at the time, but now, already learning how strange everyone was acting around here, she became immediately curious as to why he'd done that.

She turned back to Clarissa and gazed unwaveringly at her. "I've been busy."

"Well, pardon me for asking!" Clarissa sniffed and swept back into the common room.

Angie shook her head in disgust and stepped inside her cottage. The weight of the morning had settled on her, casting a gray tint over everything. Even the little space felt overly quiet and dreary.

She peeled off her dusty clothes. They were no longer stiff and stylish—more worn and weathered now, like something Joaquin Oldwater might wear. She used the bootjack to remove her Justins. They were scuffed and scratched, but she was grateful for them. They'd held up through horseback rides and rocky climbs.

What a day.

What a *sad* day.

Heading toward the bathroom for a quick shower, she paused. Something flickered near the bedroom door—just a mote in the eye, maybe. Still, a chill danced down her spine.

She crept into the living room.

Nothing. Everything was exactly where it had been. Just her imagination.

After a brisk shower, she slipped into soft, loose drawstring Capris and a matching hoodie. Barefoot, she curled up on the sofa with a notepad and pen.

Last night, while speaking to Clarissa, she'd learned Clarissa wanted a special dish for her family and any guests she might invite. The specialty couldn't be beef or pork since they would be plentiful at the barbecue. Angie made several suggestions, and Clarissa finally agreed to a cracked black pepper salmon roulade with white leeks and cucumber sauce.

Now it was time to finalize the accompaniments. If nothing else, it might keep Clarissa off her back—though Angie suspected the woman would find a reason to complain, regardless.

Her breathing slowed as she relaxed into the sofa cushions.

She yawned, her body heavy with fatigue from the early morn-ing, the ride, the hike, the heat—and the sadness. But no matter how she tried to focus on food, her thoughts kept circling back to that ledge. Doc's sorrow. The sheriff's cold dismissal. The deputy who gawked at her so weirdly...

Her eyes shut and soon she was asleep until ...

A tickle brushed her foot.

She shifted slightly.

Another stroke—like feathers on her ankle.

Her eyes flew open as the sensation that woke her crept higher... inching along her calf.

With a gasp, she sat bolt upright, heart pounding. She looked down and saw movement—just a slight ripple beneath the loose fabric of her capris.

Oh no, oh no! Panicked, she gripped her pant leg tight at the thigh to block whatever it was from climbing any higher up her leg. With her other hand, she gingerly lifted the pant fabric, inch by inch.

A black, hairy spider that was at least three inches wide, clung to her knee.

The two stared at each other, both equally frozen.

Her throat closed. No sound came out.

The spider recovered first. It darted down her leg, across the sofa, and onto the floor.

That broke the dam, and the sound Angie had held came out loud and long at the same time as she sprang up so that she was standing on the sofa. Immediately, she doubled over to inspect her skin for a bite, and then rubbed her hand hard over her leg to brush away the "feel" of the spider.

The spider scurried across the floor and vanished behind the rolling TV stand.

Without thinking, Angie grabbed the thick, heavy Phoenix telephone book—at least ten years old—sitting by an even older rotary telephone. She shoved the stand aside and slammed the book down with a thud.

Then she bolted outside—and ran straight into Lionel.

"There's a spider in my room!" she gasped. "Huge. Black. Hairy!"

"I thought I heard some screechin'. Hairy, you said?" He steadied her by the shoulders, trying to stop her shaking as he looked her in the eye. "Sounds like a tarantula. Real dangerous. Once they get in, it's hard to find 'em. If you wanna leave now, I unnerstand. Won't even charge you none extra."

"Leave?" she echoed as suspicion crept over her. "No. I don't want to leave. I think I killed it."

Lionel went inside to check.

And, in fact, she had.

Paavo stood on the dock peering out at Ned's boat rental fleet—a couple had motors, but most were rowboats and canoes for use on the lake. His boyhood friend had been building himself a good business.

The dam-created lake was a decent size, although not nearly as large as he'd remembered.

Foolishly, he found himself scanning the water for Ned. Many times as a child he had run to the lake to see a tanned, towhead boy out there waving skinny arms and telling him to "Come on in, the water's warm!" And it was. They'd splash around in it for hours of fun and laughter.

Paavo turned away.

It wasn't hard to see why this business had become Ned's world. His trailer home sat directly behind the small shop where the boat rentals were made.

Both doors were locked. A "CLOSED" sign hung in the shop

window. A truck sat idle in the driveway. Two dogs barked and darted around, but other than that, all was still.

Earlier, Joaquin Oldwater had confirmed that Ned's motorcycle was missing.

Paavo unlocked the shop and stepped inside. Regret hit him hard. He regretted never calling Ned, not visiting, not keeping in touch. Regret for not continuing to join Aulis on visits as he grew older; regret for not finding time to visit after he left the Army, or even while he was a cop.

Ned had been an important, joy-filled part of his childhood. But he knew nothing of the man his friend had become, and that was the worst regret of all.

The shop was neat—surprisingly so for a place full of boat parts and grease. That had always been Ned. Even as a kid, he'd preferred tinkering with appliances to playing with toys.

A memory flashed: young Ned surrounded by radio parts on Doc's floor, Doc pacing behind him, exasperated—until the radio worked again.

But no more.

Everything here was strictly business. Paavo moved on to the single-wide house trailer.

It was sterile. Old furnishings from Levitz, kitchenware from Target, everything inexpensive and practical.

"Every penny he made went into the business," Joaquin said, stepping in behind him. "He wanted it to grow. To make real money for—"

He stopped.

"For Teresa?" Paavo asked.

Joaquin gave a small nod, followed by what looked like an exasperated shake of his head.

The trailer had one large room in the middle—living, dining, kitchen—and a bedroom and bathroom at each end, one of which had been converted into an office.

Paavo checked the landline phones first. He'd already

discovered that cell phones worked sporadically, at best, in this area. No saved numbers. No redial history. Nothing useful.

The answering machine was full: Doc. Teresa, tearful and apologetic. Paavo himself. Even LaVerne from the coffee shop. A message from Sanderman Stables wondering when Ned would return Lightning.

"Lightning's his horse," Joaquin explained. "Bet you'll find the bike at Sanderman's." That answered the question of how Ned got to the caves.

Paavo nodded and searched for Ned's cell phone. The sheriff had checked—although phones frequently showed "no service" in this area, people still carried them. But the phone hadn't been on his body. It was missing.

"You knew him well," Paavo said. "What do you think happened?"

Joaquin stared out the window at the lake. "He was... troubled. About Teresa, I think. Wouldn't say why. Just clammed up. That wasn't like him. He was usually open. Friendly. Liked helping people. Maybe too much."

There was little more to add.

In a drawer, Paavo found a small carved obsidian piece—some kind of dog or wolf.

He held it up. "You know what this is?"

Joaquin looked, stiffened a moment, but then shrugged and turned away as he replied, "Just a charm. Tourists love that stuff. Worthless."

Paavo shot him a sharp glance. Why was Joaquin lying? The carving was crude, yes—but his evasiveness was unmistakable.

In the den, photos lined the walls: Teresa alone, Teresa and Ned together, Doc and Ned, and even one of Ned, Paavo, Doc, and Aulis—all four together, smiling for some forgotten photographer.

That one stopped Paavo cold.

He had tried to treat this like any other murder case. But it wasn't.

Ned had been his friend.

He was reviewing Ned's email when Joaquin called him to the bedroom.

Paavo found him on the floor by the closet, holding a box filled with newspaper clippings—stories about Hal Edwards' body being found.

"I heard talk in winter—February—when Hal returned to town," Joaquin said. "That Ned hated him, even said he wished Hal was dead. Didn't make sense. Their paths hardly crossed. Then Hal disappeared. I never told Doc. Don't think anyone did."

Paavo scanned the headlines. "Yet, Ned went back to the place Hal's body was found—and that's where he was murdered."

"Is it true villains return to the scene of the crime?" Joaquin asked, scanning through the stack of yellowing articles.

"At times. What we need to do is find out why he saved these, and what he was looking for out there," Paavo said quietly. "Whatever it was, I think it killed him."

9

Angie rushed over to Doc's house. She'd much rather wait there than risk another encounter with the tarantula—especially if it turned out to be a family man. Not that she had much to fear. From the common room, she'd called her doctor in San Francisco, who assured her that tarantula bites were painful but rarely very serious. Since she hadn't felt anything, she clearly hadn't been bitten.

Tarantulas were burrowers, dwellers of soil and shadow. To find one inside a cabin was not just unsettling. It was unnatural. They would rather run than fight, and attacked only if provoked. By the time the doctor finished talking to her, she felt guilty that she'd killed it.

She needed to talk to Paavo. Now.

Expecting to sit outside until the others returned, she rang Doc's doorbell just in case. To her surprise, the door opened.

Doc stood there.

He looked like he'd aged ten years since morning.

"Hi," Angie said gently. "Is Paavo back? I thought I'd stop by, see how you all were doing. Maybe help out."

"He's not back yet," Doc said, his voice flat with exhaustion. "I'm heading into town. You can wait here for him if you want."

"To town?" She studied him—haggard, drained, barely upright. "Doc, are you sure that's a good idea? Maybe you should rest."

"Rest?" He let out a bitter snort. "Only rest I've got coming is the eternal kind. No, I've got to be the one to tell Teresa. Ned would've wanted that. I just ... I don't know how."

He rubbed a hand across his face and turned toward the door.

"Wait." Angie's heart wrenched. As much as she didn't want to, she knew she couldn't let him go alone. "I'll go with you. I'll drive."

"No need," he said, jaw stiffening. "I've done this sort of thing before. Comes with the job. Anyway, you never even met Ned."

"I know—but I've met you. And Teresa. This isn't something you should do alone."

He looked at her for a long moment, eyes dull and far away. Then he nodded, weariness overriding pride.

And just maybe he didn't want to be alone either.

They decided to leave the Mercedes for Paavo and take Doc's car—a 1990 black Cadillac Coupe de Ville parked in the garage. Doc, she decided, would get along famously with her father, who still drove his red Lincoln Towncar like it was royalty.

As they headed toward Jackpot, Angie realized Doc was someone not so different from herself. When upset, he sought company, conversation, comfort. She encouraged him to talk, and in that short drive, something unspoken but solid grew between them.

The irony wasn't lost on her. She understood this near-stranger's need for connection better than she did her own fiancé. Paavo, when hurting, shut down. He sought silence.

Doc talked about Teresa's family restaurant, named after her grandmother, Maritza Flores. He expected Teresa to be there, working.

"So, we've got Teresa, Lupe, and Maritza—daughter, mother, grandmother, right?" Angie asked, double-checking the family tree.

"That's it."

Angie mentally filed it away. If Flores was Lupe's maiden name, and both she and Teresa still used it, that probably meant Lupe was unmarried—or had taken back her name after a divorce. And ... she had noticed something in the way Doc had said her name. A softness. A lilt.

Doc explained how Maritza had started the restaurant as a young widow, serving food out of a retired dining car. When it grew popular, Hal Edwards loaned her money to build a permanent location downtown—incorporating the original train car into the front of the building.

Once again, Hal Edwards. His name seemed woven through every corner of this town.

When they arrived, Angie was charmed by the place. The old railcar gave the restaurant a character all its own. Inside, remnants of the original diner—stools, counters, appliances—lined the walls. Mexican blankets and pottery added splashes of color. Framed photos documented the restaurant's evolution, and in the corner, above a carved wooden chest and high-backed chair, hung a painting of Our Lady of Guadalupe and a crucifix.

"This is odd," Doc murmured.

"What is?" Angie asked.

"Maritza isn't in her chair. She always sits right there"—he pointed to the corner—"all in black, scarf over her white hair. She's not as sharp as she used to be, but she still loves greeting her guests, as she calls the restaurant's customers. Everyone knows Maritza."

The hostess spotted them, her welcoming smile faltering

when she saw Doc. Her eyes widened. Without a word, she turned and hurried away.

Seconds later, an elegant woman in a tailored blue dress appeared. Her long black hair was braided and pinned at the nape of her neck. With wide dark eyes and olive skin, she bore a striking resemblance to Teresa.

Her anguished face met Doc's, stemming the words from his lips. Angie knew he wouldn't have to deliver the bad news. This woman had already heard of Ned's death.

"Doc, I can't believe it." Her voice broke. "I'm so sorry."

"Lupe," he whispered hoarsely as his tears brimmed. Angie had expected the two to give each other comforting hugs, but they held themselves ramrod straight. All comfort was given with their eyes, which—as Angie read them—spoke volumes.

"I came to tell you and Teresa," Doc said finally. "But it seems you already know."

"Yes." Lupe dabbed her eyes. "LaVerne heard from someone at the sheriff's station. She rushed over—said it sounded like someone killed him. Doc, please, tell me that's not true."

"It may be," he said, voice low.

Her breath caught. "My God."

Doc introduced Angie.

A pair of diners entered. Lupe pasted on a forced smile. "Welcome. Your hostess will be right with you." She turned back to Doc and Angie. "Come with me."

She took Angie's arm as they walked through the restaurant. Lupe wasn't tall and slim like Teresa; she was closer to Angie's height, with a softer, rounder build.

"Teresa told me about meeting you and Paavo," Lupe said. "Thank you for being here with Doc. This is ... it's hard for him, more than he'll admit." Her eyes flicked to Doc with such a mixture of warm affection and yet sadness it pierced Angie's heart to see it. "He's a tough, stubborn old bird."

"I've already learned that," Angie murmured.

Lupe glanced at her with somber eyes, then nodded. She led them into a small office with a desk and four chairs.

"Where's Teresa?" Doc asked.

"She went home with her grandmother. I'm worried about her. Strange things have been happening around her lately, and now to have Ned..." Lupe bit her lip to stop her words, her face fierce with unspoken anger and distress. "I considered closing the restaurant, but figured you might come. And I doubt you've eaten all day."

"He hasn't eaten since breakfast," Angie said, sitting near Doc.

"Food's the last thing on my mind," Doc muttered. "Ned was filled with hope, Lupe. He finally had money coming in. I thought he and Teresa might fix things. Now, it's all gone."

Lupe said nothing, but her lips tightened and she gave a slight nod.

"Should I see her?" he asked softly.

"Yes. But only after you eat." Lupe crossed to the door. "I'll bring you both plates, then we'll go together. I'll call and let her know you're coming. Maybe you can give her something to help her sleep tonight."

"I'll do what I can."

Lupe sent in Carta Blanca beer and an appetizer of crisps—light, crispy tortillas baked with cheese, chilies, garlic, and salt.

Angie had eaten crisps before, but never like these. They were spicier, yet more delicate. She loved them.

Then came the stew—Maritza's famous creation.

She didn't think she could eat... but once the first spoonful hit her tongue, resistance was futile.

Chunks of pork, black beans, poblano and Anaheim peppers, garlic, onions, tomato sauce, lime juice... and jalapeños for zest. Served over rice, topped with cheese, sour cream, olives, and salsa verde. The flavors melted in her mouth.

Delizioso, she thought—and didn't care that the word was Italian.

As she ate, Paavo walked in. His eyes flicked from her to Doc, checking his condition. When he and Joaquin had found Doc's place empty, Joaquin made a single call and pinpointed his location.

While Joaquin returned home, Paavo had come here.

Lupe greeted him warmly, telling him she remembered him as a boy. A waitress brought him stew, and the way he devoured it, Angie knew she'd have to learn how to make it—it was destined to become a Smith-Amalfi family favorite.

Lupe hovered near Doc as he ate, urging him to take another bite. Angie watched the two of them—drawn together by something magnetic, yet holding back.

Lupe wore no wedding ring, and Angie's earlier speculation about her unmarried state appeared accurate. Which meant that Angie couldn't imagine, since the two so obviously cared for each other, what was keeping them apart.

10

─────────

Maritza Flores opened the door of the ranch-style house. Her short white hair framed a serene face, though deep creases spoke of long years and hard truths. Her onyx eyes were clear but weary. Leaning on a cane, she gave Doc a small, sad smile.

"*Buenas tardes*, Maritza," Doc said.

"*Mi amigo*." Her gnarled hand clasped his. "Come in, everyone, please." She led them into the living room. "My heart is filled with tears. I pray for Ned."

"I know you do," Doc said in a thick, sad voice.

"So much evil in this world." She shook her head, the weight of it all bowing her shoulders.

Doc introduced Paavo and Angie.

"I'm happy to see friends of Doc," Maritza said, then turned her gaze to Paavo. "Paavo ... I remember you when you were a boy. Not so long ago, I think. You came here with the Finland man." Her eyes glistened. "And you would play with Ned."

"I'll tell Aulis you remember him," Paavo said gently. The surprise and emotion in his voice made Angie glance at him—he was visibly moved.

"Aulis, he loved my stew! I still cook it ... I think." She rubbed her forehead, frowning in confusion, then turned her warm gaze on Angie. "And your fiancée. Angie, welcome. I'm sorry it's such a sad time."

"Me, too," Angie said softly, touched by the older woman's kindness.

A voice cried out from the hallway. "Doc."

Teresa stood in the doorway, her face streaked with tears. She didn't acknowledge anyone else—her eyes were locked on Doc.

He crossed the room and folded her into his arms. They clung to each other, silently sharing a grief that words couldn't hold.

Lupe leaned toward Angie. "I'll take my mother to bed," she whispered. Gently, she guided Maritza from the room.

Only when Doc and Teresa stepped apart did Teresa seem to realize they weren't alone.

Angie and Paavo offered their condolences.

Teresa's gaze lingered on Paavo. "Is it true?" she asked. "Ned was murdered?"

His face was grave. "That's how it appears."

Her hands balled into fists. "You're a homicide detective. Find who did this."

"I will."

"I'm just an old man," Doc said hoarsely. "But my new life's work is justice—for Ned. And for Hal."

"Yes. Hal." Teresa's eyes clouded. She shook her head sharply, as if trying to banish a memory. Then she sat beside Doc on the sofa.

Paavo and Angie took the loveseat across from them.

"You and Doc knew Ned better than anyone," Paavo began. "I have some questions—if you're up for them."

"I am," Teresa said, though the rigid line of her shoulders suggested otherwise.

"Do you have any idea who might've done this? Someone Ned had trouble with? Anyone who threatened him?"

A pause. Then: "No. No one. Ned was a good man. Everyone liked him."

Paavo gave a neutral nod. He'd seen it before—murder victims and killers both polished into saints in the eyes of the grieving. "You know he died near the cave where Hal's body was found. Any idea why he would've gone there?"

"No," she said too quickly.

"He seemed very interested in Hal's death. Do you know why?"

She flinched. "I have no idea."

Just then, Lupe reentered and sat quietly in a corner.

Angie shifted in her seat. Something about Teresa wasn't right. Yes, she was grieving—but there was something else. Fear? Guilt? Or just the weight of too much loss?

Doc had mentioned suspicious accidents. Now her lover had been murdered. If she was frightened, it made sense. But if she was hiding something...

"Did Ned mention plans to meet anyone yesterday?" Paavo asked.

"Only you and your fiancée," she replied.

He continued his questions—had Ned seemed worried? Was he troubled by anything? Problems with neighbors? Friends? Finances? Addictions?

Teresa's answers were short and flat. Doc watched her, concerned, but didn't interrupt beyond nodding.

Eventually, Paavo circled back. "Let's talk about Hal Edwards again. It might be a coincidence that Ned was killed near where Hal's body was found, but I doubt it. We need to find a link. Do you agree?"

Instead of answering, Teresa's gaze drifted. She seemed to slip into some distant place.

"I think she's had enough," Lupe said quietly.

"I'm very tired." Teresa rubbed her forehead. "Could we continue tomorrow?"

Paavo didn't stop. "What was your relationship with Hal Edwards?"

A shadow flickered across Teresa's face. "I used to work at the hacienda. His nephew, Lionel, was supposed to help him manage the Guest Ranch. But he..." she hesitated. "He didn't do a good job."

"When was that?"

She cast a quick glance at Lupe. "I started working there when I was eighteen. Just part-time—three days a week. It was fun. Got me away from the restaurant." She folded her hands, eyes downcast. "At the ranch, I met people from all over the country, some from far away places. I had time to talk to them, not just take their dinner orders."

Lupe stood abruptly.

"You liked working there?" Paavo asked.

"Yes," Teresa said, and for the first time, her voice gained energy. "Eventually, I became the manager. I helped modernize the cabins, the common room—even the kitchen. Hal was a generous employer. A generous man."

"Teresa," Lupe said firmly.

Teresa rose. Doc stood with her, placing a hand on her back. "She's had enough, Paavo."

Paavo rose too, but pressed one more time. "Did you see Hal when he returned to Jackpot last winter?"

"No, she didn't," Lupe cut in. "Doc, can you give Teresa something to help her sleep?"

As Lupe and Doc guided Teresa from the room, Angie and Paavo exchanged a glance.

The interview had ended—abruptly, and strangely.

On their walk back to the cabin, Angie told Paavo about her encounter with the tarantula.

He agreed with her doctor—it was unlikely to be dangerous. But Lionel's frightening words to her—almost a warning—made no sense. Paavo lapsed into a brooding silence.

He remained quiet as he showered and dressed for bed. Angie, now in Paavo's pajama top, slid under the covers, while he, wearing the bottoms, stood by the window, staring out at the desert night.

Finally, he spoke. "I think you should go back to San Francisco."

She sat up, sleeves pushed to her elbows, eyes flashing. She might usually wear satin and lace, but deep down, she really did love flannel. "I'm not going anywhere."

He sighed. "Listen. I thought this was going to be a simple inheritance squabble. Instead, we've got two murders, break-ins, a hostile sheriff's office—and who knows what else brewing out here."

"You need me here," Angie said.

"So I can worry about you?"

"I can take care of myself."

"Really? Like when a serial killer tracked you to Wings of an Angel? Or the time I found you trapped in that church basement by a lunatic who thought he was a demon?"

She folded her arms. "And what about the time I stopped a publisher from shooting you? Or saved you from being blown up at the Legion of Honor? Or dragged you from a watery grave on the day of our engagement party?"

But then, she smiled. "Things always worked out, didn't they?"

He frowned. "Barely."

"That was then. This is now. And Doc needs me."

"He does?" He looked skeptical.

"You know he wanted us here to keep an eye on the vultures

—Clarissa, her son Joey, and Hal's nephew Lionel. Now, Ned's death makes it even more important that I stay. That's why I'm helping with the cookout."

"Undercover Angie."

She smoothed the blanket, giving him a sultry smile. "Well... I *am* under the covers."

He grinned, stepping toward the bed.

"Besides," she said, "you know I'm good at finding things out. I'm staying."

He sat beside her. "It could be dangerous."

She looped her arms around his neck. "Pooh."

He raised a brow. "How am I supposed to argue with 'pooh'?"

"You're not. Not with this, either." She kissed him.

It was long, lingering.

When they pulled apart, Paavo chuckled. "No fair."

She grinned. "Ah, but all's fair—"

"The last words many a man's heard before being led to the slaughter."

"You may be many things, Paavo, but you're no lamb. Now tell me I'm staying."

He tossed back the covers and stretched out beside her, pulling her into his arms. "You're staying ... at least for now."

11

───────

aavo welcomed the brisk morning air as he walked to the sheriff's station, having dropped Doc and Angie at the mortuary. He was grateful Angie had offered to go there with Doc since he had no idea how to help Doc with the funeral arrangements.

Last night and again this morning, they'd searched the cabin for more tarantulas. They found none. Still, he wasn't sure he should have let Angie stay here. But the thought of facing this alone... Selfishly, he wanted her with him, wanted her warmth in a world that suddenly felt hollow and so very cold.

The streets were quiet as he passed through town. Despite everything, Jackpot looked much the same as it had in his youth —some new pavement, a few more cars, a couple of motels and trailer parks near the lake. But at its core, it was unchanged.

That only made Ned's absence all the more jarring.

Even seeing how completely gray Doc's hair had turned had hit him hard.

They'd both called home the previous evening. Angie had phoned her mother, her best friend Connie, and at least one sister. He'd talked with Aulis, filling him in on all that had happened. Aulis reminded him that he'd met Teresa years ago—a shy girl clinging to her mother's skirts, yet fascinated by the big-city visitors. Aulis's words brought back more of Paavo's memories of summers in Jackpot, memories he was glad to have had awakened.

Ahead, the sheriff's station came into view—a squat, pale yellow building straight out of *Mayberry RFD*. In San Francisco, the sheriff's department mostly acted as bailiffs and jailers. Here, with no local police, the sheriff was the law.

He needed to know what Merry Belle Schwartz had uncovered in the investigation of Hal Edwards' death, and how she intended to handle Ned's.

Inside, sea-green walls in need of fresh paint gave the space a tired, utilitarian feel. Behind a gray metal desk sat Wallace "Deputy Buster" Willis, his feet propped on an open drawer like it was an ottoman. The desk held only a landline phone, a computer monitor, and a 3x5 notepad. In the corner, three plastic chairs formed a waiting area, angled toward a small TV. Paavo blinked at the screen. *Eagle Crest*, a soap he hadn't seen in years, played silently.

Through an open office door, he glimpsed a hallway and a single jail cell—empty.

"Is the sheriff in?" he asked.

"Yup." Buster's gaze lingered on the TV as he slowly stood. "Your fiancée go back home already?"

"She's in town," Paavo said. "I'd like to speak with—"

"Sit back down, Deputy!" Sheriff Schwartz's voice boomed from her doorway.

Paavo turned. Her pinprick blue eyes fixed on him, cheeks flushed with anger. She stepped back into her office.

"Come in, San Francisco. I want a word with you."

He ignored the jab. Her office was cramped. Two stiff-backed wooden chairs faced a massive oak desk and a high-backed leather swivel chair. She shut the door behind him, motioned for him to sit, then circled to her side of the desk. Neither of them sat.

"You interfered with my investigation," she said. Her voice shook. "I'm considering filing a complaint with your superiors."

"I don't know what you mean," Paavo replied, calmly.

"The hell you don't." She planted both palms on the desk. Her hands and wrists were surprisingly small—delicate—compared to her thick forearms. "You went to Ned's house and his business. You looked at his things. Talked to neighbors. The stables. That's my job."

"I know how to handle a crime scene, Sheriff."

"That's not the point!"

"There was no tape. No posted deputy. Doc had a key and gave me permission." He held her gaze. "We can pool our findings or waste time arguing jurisdiction."

She dropped into her chair with a grunt and stared at him.

"I haven't gotten out there yet," she muttered.

Paavo blinked, and then he took the seat she'd offered earlier. "You haven't?"

Her lips pressed into a tight line as she straightened papers on her desk. "I've had other priorities. The house and office aren't going anywhere."

"They might not," he said sharply. "But the killer might. Clues don't last forever, Sheriff."

"Nothing's missing, is it?" she snapped. "I know what I'm doing, Smith."

Do you? he wondered. She was flailing, and she knew it—that's why she was angry. She couldn't dismiss this death as an accident, not like Hal Edwards'.

"This is a sleepy town, I get it," he said, more gently. "But this is what I do. I can help."

"All right, San Francisco," she sneered, "tell me what you saw."

"Ned was digging into Hal Edwards' death. That much is clear. He also had a small wolf carving. Black. A charm, supposedly. I was told it's a tourist trinket, but I've never seen anything like it."

Merry Belle's eyes narrowed. "Everyone in Jackpot is fascinated by Hal's life and death. That's old news. As for that charm…" Her chin jutted out. "Tourist junk. Doesn't concern this office."

He kept his expression neutral, though the investigator in him filed away her too-casual dismissal.

"When is the autopsy scheduled?"

"It's done." She folded her arms. "It's not like the coroner has a waiting list."

"Cause of death?"

"Blunt trauma to the brain. Ned's head was bashed in—just in case that escaped your keen detective senses."

"Time of death?"

"Two days ago." She looked pointedly at him. "The same day you rolled into town asking questions."

He let the sarcasm slide. "Do you have any suspects? Anyone who threatened him?"

"No one's come forward."

Her voice had the brittle ring of evasion that gave Paavo his answer.

"I've heard Hal and Ned argued. Have you looked into that?"

"Why?" She sneered again. "Think Hal's ghost did it? Is that how you work cases in San Francisco?"

"Let's talk about Hal Edwards, then."

She stood abruptly. "Forget it." She stormed to the door and threw it open. "I've wasted enough time with you. Stay out of my investigation."

He didn't flinch. "As a public officer, much of your work is open to public inquiry. I'd like to see Hal Edwards' case file."

"That is *not* public."

He left her office, then turned back to face her. "I can get a lawyer to explain the finer points of the statute to judge. Or"—he held her gaze—"you can save time and hand it over. And while you're at it, I'd like Ned Paulson's autopsy report."

Her eyes burned. "Deputy!"

Buster jerked so hard he nearly fell off his chair.

"Give him the Edwards and Paulson files," she snapped. "They're in the cabinet. No copies. Nothing leaves this office." She spun on Paavo, jabbing a finger an inch from his nose. "And stay the hell out of my office."

She slammed the door.

Buster retrieved the files—both disappointingly thin—and slouched back toward the TV, where Rhonda Mulholland was lounging seductively across a velvet chaise.

Paavo took a seat at the desk and opened the folders.

Ned Paulson's report was exactly as Merry Belle described.

The Hal Edwards file was another story.

Death occurred 80–90 days before the body was found. Cause: uncertain, due to desiccation. But a nick on the rib cage —possibly made by a bullet—looked different from the animal bite marks. If it *was* a bullet, Hal had been shot through or near his heart.

And the sheriff had apparently done nothing with that detail.

The file included interviews with Dolores Huerta, the long-time cook-housekeeper; Sherman Whitney, Jr., aka "Junior" Whitney, a ranch hand; Ralph Dittersley, foreman of Hal's cattle ranch; and several others—maintenance men, gardeners, and part-time housekeepers. No one offered anything useful.

There was no record of interviews with Clarissa or Joseph Edwards. No indication they were in Arizona at the time of Hal's reappearance at the ranch, or his death.

No forensic work. No crime scene analysis.

Paavo could imagine Merry Belle and Deputy Buster stomping around the guest ranch, barking questions, then leaving when no one confessed.

But Hal Edwards *had* been murdered.

And the sheriff had missed it.

Angie was accustomed to going to mortuaries.

As a little girl walking through North Beach with her mother, Serefina, they would often stop at mortuaries in the area. Serefina always wanted to see if any of the Italians she knew had gone to their great reward and she'd somehow missed it. When Serefina would find someone she knew vaguely (she'd already know about the death of anyone she knew well, as well as their relatives and friends), she'd cry out, *"Poverino,"* or *"Poverina"* as appropriate, and sign the guest book.

Probably, Angie thought, you had to be Italian to understand.

Because of those childhood visits, mortuaries didn't creep her out the way they did some people. Still, when she and Doc stepped from the drab building into the bright sunlight, she was thrilled to see Paavo waiting for them.

Doc remained convinced that everything somehow revolved around Hal Edwards. He wanted to meet with Hal's attorney next. Paavo agreed to go with him.

Angie bowed out. She could handle dead bodies, but not

lawyers. Instead, she asked Doc to point her toward Jackpot's library. She was curious about the lost stagecoach and the Waldorf chef, and this gave her an opportunity to look into them.

As she followed the route Doc had given her, a voice called her name. She turned.

Teresa Flores approached with a tentative smile. "Hi! I saw you leaving the mortuary. Do you have time for a cup of coffee?"

Angie wouldn't have turned her down for anything.

LaVerne Merritt's face lit up like she'd hit the jackpot when the two women walked into her café. As they slid into a corner booth, she snatched up the coffee pot and hurried toward them so fast Angie half-expected her to hurdle over tables like an Olympian.

"I heard your man's a cop from San Francisco," LaVerne said as she poured Angie a cup.

"News travels fast," Angie said.

"It's a small town. Nothing gets past anyone here." LaVerne leaned in, voice lowering, eyes flicking to Teresa. "Except murder."

"LaVerne," Teresa warned.

"Don't try to stop me," she snapped. "I've been quiet too long."

Teresa rolled her eyes toward the ceiling—as if "quiet" wasn't a word anyone had ever used to describe LaVerne.

The café owner bent forward and jabbed the table with a bony finger for emphasis. "Your man needs to find out why there was never an inquiry into Hal Edwards' disappearances. The man was famous. *Rich.* And we're supposed to believe he just walked off and left his worthless nephew in charge? Lionel couldn't run a toy train on a circle track!"

She slapped the table.

"Then Hal suddenly comes back, says he's going to raise

ostriches, and next thing you know—*poof!* Gone again? And then we find out he's been dead for the past three months, rotting up in a cave on his own land? No way. I was born at night, but not last night! If the sheriff was doing her damn job, someone would've gone looking. But nooooo. Hal winds up dead and we're supposed to pretend it's natural causes? Ha!"

"LaVerne," Teresa said, exasperated. "Hal did die of natural causes. The coroner said so."

"Sure." LaVerne straightened, crossing her arms. "And I've got beachfront property just down the road to sell you." She gave Teresa a sour glance, then leaned toward Angie again, her lazy eyelid drooping low. "If that's all there was to it, then why's the FBI sniffing around? Or maybe it's the DEA. Or Homeland Security? I don't even know anymore. We're not far from the border, you know."

She dropped her voice to a whisper. "Terrorists and drug traffickers still find ways to sneak across at all hours. A few weird men showed up here in winter, but after Hal disappeared, so did they. I think they were terrorists! I think they captured Hal and killed him when he wouldn't pay up!"

Angie pushed back in her seat. "My goodness." She blinked. "Terrorists? I thought all I had to worry about were tarantulas."

"You can laugh," LaVerne growled, "but somebody better find out what's going on. First Hal. Then Ned. For all we know, we'll all be killed in our beds! And Merry Belle Schwartz's gonna chalk it up to 'natural causes.' Natural causes, my ass!"

With that, LaVerne spun on her heel and stalked toward the kitchen, leaving Angie gaping.

Teresa leaned in, voice low. "She's crazy. Don't listen to her."

"She definitely has ... a different outlook."

Teresa stared out the window for a moment as if collecting herself, but Angie noticed how her gaze tracked every passerby, every car. There was something wary in her expression—something unsettled.

Angie touched her arm gently. "How are you doing today?"

"I'm all right." Her eyes met Angie's, tired and sad. "I don't know why people make such a fuss over me. It's not like Ned and I were ... engaged or anything. He was just a friend."

"A friend?" Angie hesitated. "I thought it was more than that."

Teresa's eyes teared up, but she blinked quickly, steeling herself. "I tried to discourage him. Since he was close to Doc, my mother would invite him to the house for dinner—always with Doc. That's all."

"That's not how I heard he saw it," Angie said softly.

Teresa rubbed her forehead. "It's ... complicated. Look, I never told him I loved him. Never. I can't help what he imagined."

"But did you love him?"

She dropped her gaze. "What does it matter? Love isn't enough. All I have to do is look at my own family to see that."

Angie wondered if she meant her father—whoever and wherever he was. She wanted to ask, wanted to say that love *was* enough, that it could be real and lasting. But one look at Teresa's guarded face told her such words wouldn't be welcome.

Angie opened her mouth to say something encouraging when LaVerne suddenly reappeared.

She placed a plate in front of each of them with a wedge of something dark and dense that looked vaguely like fruitcake.

"I heard you're a gourmet cook," LaVerne said to Angie, beaming as if their previous conversation hadn't happened.

"Yes," Angie murmured, wishing LaVerne would go away. She wanted to get back to talking with Teresa, who clearly needed someone to listen.

"I'm a bit of a gourmet myself," LaVerne went on proudly. "Not here in the diner—folks come here for comfort food—but when the occasion calls for it, I make something extra special. This is an old family recipe." She pointed at the cake. "Had it in the freezer, zapped it in the microwave to defrost. Don't worry —it's not hurt none. Eat up."

Teresa didn't move.

Angie, desperate to get rid of her, picked up her fork, cut a large bite, and placed it in her mouth and chewed.

In an instant the food seemed to turn into a giant sucking machine that drained all the liquid from her mouth. Her cheeks were pulled inward, while her tongue stuck against the roof of her palate. She tried to open her mouth to spit it out, but couldn't.

"Mmmurf," she cried.

"Ah, she loves it!" LaVerne cooed. "Listen to her mmm's of joy."

"Mmurf, mmmurff!" Angie voiced again.

Teresa gawked at her.

"Her eyes are even starting to tear up with joy." LaVerne's hands were clasped near her heart. "I never dreamed a big city gourmet cook would find something I made so delicious."

Angie reached for her water and somehow managed to pry her lips open wide enough to gulp it down. Chewing and drinking, she somehow managed to swallow the cake, then gasped in much needed air.

She looked at LaVerne with something akin to horror. "What in the world is in that?"

LaVerne stood tall, head high and proud. "You don't eat something like that every day, do you? Kind of makes your mouth tingle, doesn't it?"

Angie finished her water. Her lips and tongue felt numb, and she hoped the "cake" wasn't doing to her stomach what it had done to her mouth. "It's unique, all right."

"It's cactus," LaVerne whispered, as if giving away a state secret.

Angie glared at the offending slice. "You mean like prickly pear fruit?"

"No, no. I mean boring a hole in a saguaro and pulling out the inside pulp, then mashing it up good, and mixing it with pinyon nuts and figs—all good desert food. I call it my Desert Surprise Cake."

"It certainly is," Angie said, her throat and mouth now feeling like they'd been stuffed with cotton. "I think I'll just take the rest with me. Better to enjoy it when I'm not so full."

Smacking her still deadened lips, she was reaching for a napkin when Lupe Flores burst into the coffee shop.

"Teresa! What are you doing? You said you were going home!"

"It's just coffee," Teresa said, already standing.

"Go!" Lupe snapped. "We'll use my car."

She gave LaVerne and Angie a tight nod as she hustled Teresa out. "Excuse us."

Angie blinked after them. "What was that about?"

LaVerne shrugged dramatically. "Who knows? That family's always been strange. All *I* care about—" she broke into a hip-swaying dance, pumping her fists in the air "—is that I've got a *winner* with that recipe! I'm gonna enter it in the Pillsbury Bake-Off!"

13

Paavo glanced at the painting above the mirror that spanned the length of the bar. Then he looked again.

The bartender noticed. With a chuckle, she sauntered over to his table. She was well up in years, a big woman with big hair, one side clipped with a silver medallion holding a spray of turkey feathers. She wore jeans, a fringed cowgirl shirt, a bolo tie with a turquoise slide, and scuffed boots. A cap gun with "Hopalong Cassidy" engraved on the handle rested in her holster.

"What's the matter, cowboy?" she asked, her voice deep and loud. "Never seen a picture like that before?"

"Never," Paavo said honestly.

She let out a smoky laugh. "That's what happens when a gal like me owns the only saloon in town. Name's Jewel."

"Paavo Smith. Pleased to meet you."

Her warm greeting to Attorney Jack O'Connell and the affectionate smile she offered Doc Griggs told Paavo they were regulars—and favored ones at that. He alone was asked what he was drinking.

The Stagecoach Saloon was every city slicker's idea of a Western watering hole—sawdust on the floor, wagon wheels on the walls, a gallery of John Ford movie posters. The bar itself was aged oak, rich and dark, with a long brass rail along its base. Behind it, a mirrored wall held shelves of bottles gleaming in the dim light.

And over it was the aforementioned painting.

Forget the buxom beauties that usually graced bars, this was a portrait of a nicely muscled man lying on hay, buck naked except for a cowboy hat, boots, and spurs ... and with a thickly coiled rope covering his privates. The only other thing he wore was a large and knowing grin.

Paavo gave a quick shake of his head, then shifted in his chair to face Doc and the attorney. "Let's talk money. Who profits from Hal's death?"

"Good question, Inspector," O'Connell said. "And damned if I know. His land's valuable, and he had solid cash and investments. But he was so bitter about Clarissa taking the Halmart stores, he didn't want her or Joey getting a dime. Still, I could never get him to make a will. He'd tell me he was working on it, but never gave me anything to write up and file. Doc was his executor, and he didn't give anything to Doc either."

"That's right," Doc muttered.

The saloon doors opened. The two fishermen Paavo had noticed at Merritt's on his first day in Jackpot entered and glanced his way before taking seats at the bar.

Jewel greeted them politely, but with none of the warmth she'd shown earlier.

Paavo remembered LaVerne's warnings. These men dressed the part of harmless vacationers, but they were always watching. Always listening.

He kept them in his peripheral vision as he turned back to the lawyer. "So with no will, does that mean Joey inherits everything?"

"Not so fast," O'Connell said. "I never filed one, but that doesn't mean Hal didn't leave something behind. He was paranoid as hell. For all I know, he could've scrawled out a dozen wills, each naming someone different."

Paavo nodded slowly. "And that's why the estate hasn't been settled?"

"His property is valuable," Doc said before O'Connell could reply. "But other than Joey, his only other relative was his nephew, Lionel. And he's less than worthless. It'd be awful for either of them to get Hal's money. They don't deserve it."

O'Connell chimed in. "As his lawyer, I wanted to give anyone who might know about a will a chance to come forward. Like Hal, I'd hate to see that ungrateful son of his walk away with it all. I told Clarissa and Joey they'd have to wait until after the cookout to find out what—if anything—they're getting. I swear, if no one finds a valid will, I'll be tempted to write one up myself!"

***

"Hello, Miss Angie."

Angie nearly jumped out of her skin and whirled around.

She was on her way to the library, so lost in thoughts of Teresa she hadn't heard Deputy Buster come up behind her. His uniform was spotless with creases sharp enough to draw blood. The feather in his cowboy hat was red today, not yellow.

"You sure look pretty today," he said with a slow grin. "Prettiest thing to hit Jackpot since forever. Is that what you call a designer outfit?"

She blinked. That question was not what she'd expected.

Glancing down at her zigzag pastel sundress, she said, "It's a Missoni."

"I've heard of that." He pointed to her four-inch lime green wedgies with ankle straps. "And those?"

"Manolo Blahnik. Why?"

"Why?" He chuckled. "Do you realize how awful people would look without clothes?"

She stared.

"I mean, imagine all these folks runnin' around in just their underwear—or worse! So, since we gotta wear something, might as well make it beautiful, right?"

She couldn't disagree.

"Hard to find good fashion in Jackpot," he added, hands on his narrow hips. "Anywhere in Arizona, really. Though I did see some nice things in Scottsdale. Clarissa Edwards wears some decent stuff sometimes, but I steer clear of her. Want some company on your walk?"

"I'm just heading to the library," she said, disoriented by the conversation but oddly curious.

He fell into step beside her. "My pleasure."

She gave him a sidelong glance. "That maroon trim on your uniform is very nice."

He beamed and patted his collar. "Thanks! Did it myself. Got a checkered maroon handkerchief to match, too. Used to wear it in the chest pocket—Gentlemen's Quarterly style—but Aunt Merry Belle hated it. Said it was too fancy."

"You sew?" Angie asked, startled.

"Sure do. Got myself a Singer Quantum XL-6000 off eBay. Thing does everything. I love lookin' at clothes—gives me ideas. Only problem is, Aunt Merry Belle won't let me touch her stuff. And my past girlfriends didn't like me dressin' better than them."

Angie was speechless for a moment. Then she changed the subject. "Did you know Ned well?"

"Not really. We went to school together, but he was a year ahead. I was held back a couple times."

"What do you think happened to him?"

"Damned if I know. The only person I ever saw him argue with was Teresa Flores."

They reached the library steps. Buster stopped. "Guess this is where I say goodbye. All them books give me the willies."

"I'd like to find out about the stagecoach that disappeared in the 1890s," Angie said after introducing herself to the librarian, Doris Flynn.

The public library was very small, but charming, and situated in a back bedroom of a private home that had been converted into Jackpot's City Hall. The library walls had floor to ceiling bookshelves, and several freestanding ones crowded the middle of the floor. Books that couldn't fit on shelves were stacked against them.

"We've got a wonderful collection about it," Doris said, leading her to a back corner. "Best in the state. A lot of newspaper coverage at the time—one of the passengers was famous."

"I read something about an actress," Angie said, recalling the old booklet.

"Actress?" Doris chuckled. "That was just a polite way of saying what she *really* was."

Angie mouthed an "Oh." She got the message. "Then it must've been the chef from the Waldorf Hotel."

"The Waldorf? No one out here knew a thing about that. No, it was the third passenger—Hoot Dalton. There were only three passengers, and two drivers. Anyway, every one of them knew about the Dalton Gang—they were big news at the time. It was well known that the Daltons had robbed a bank in Coffeyville, Kansas, in 1893. All were killed except Emmett, who got locked up. But Hoot, their cousin, supposedly gathered the loot and made a run for it." She grinned. "'Hoot stole the loot' was the saying of the day."

Doris pulled two oversized scrapbooks off the shelf and set them on the only clear table. "The best guess about what happened to the stagecoach, is that the drivers or someone else recognized Hoot Dalton and figured he had the loot with him. So, it's assumed the drivers, or whoever, turned on Hoot and robbed him."

"Okay...," Angie said. "So if that's what happened, why is there any mystery about the stagecoach?"

"Because no one from the stagecoach was ever heard from again!"

That caught Angie's attention. "None of them?"

"Nope. And those drivers had big families. Maybe they died. Maybe them and the passengers turned on each other for the Dalton money. No one knows. All we know is, *no one on that stagecoach was ever seen again.*" Doris stated the last few words slowly, with dramatic emphasis, then nodded.

"What about natural causes?" Angie asked. "Flash floods? Or an ambush?"

"Nope. By then we had treaties with the local tribes. And if there'd been a flood, something would've turned up."

Angie's breath caught. "*Nothing* was ever found?"

"Well, there were bits of clothing, odds and ends near Ghost Hollow. Some near the creek, others in caves."

"The same caves where Hal's body was found?"

"Exactly. Those caves are said to be haunted."

"I've heard."

Doris flipped to the back of one volume. "Here we go— letters sent to the sheriff and mayor from relatives and friends looking for answers." She pointed. "Most are from the drivers' families. But here—these are about the chef you mentioned. I'm afraid, though, no one ever heard of him."

Angie stared, awe-struck, as all her student-of-culinary-history juices stirred. The letters were from the famous Oscar

Tschirky, himself. Hand-written, no less. And signed. Her heart pounded at the sight.

The first, dated September, 1893, was a short inquiry as to the state of the investigation. On the second line, it was written that if Mr. Willem van Beerstraeden's journal or recipe notebook were located, they should be sent to Tschirky immediately, in care of the Waldorf Hotel.

"Look at that!" Angie cried. "My God! Oscar Tschirky!"

"Who?"

"The recipe notebook mentioned in this letter," Angie said, "was it ever found?"

"I don't believe so," Doris replied. "You'll see more inquiries, but then I suppose the letter writer gave up."

Angie thought a long moment before she tossed out a quick, "Thank you."

Doris recognized a woman deep in the grip of discovery and quietly walked away.

Angie read through the three remaining letters from the famous Oscar Tschirky. Each became increasingly desperate to find the recipe book, saying things like "the family name and honor" were at stake, and that "it should not get into the wrong hands."

Why would those recipes cause such a reaction? The family name and honor...?

Her mind raced. What could he possibly have meant about "wrong hands"?

How she'd love to see that notebook! This part of Arizona was a desert. Things could be preserved forever in this type of climate. Look at the Dead Sea Scrolls, for example. Original recipes from one of the first chefs of the Waldorf Hotel ... recipes that Oscar-of-the-Waldorf himself wanted ... might still be buried right around here somewhere!

She read the letters again, word-by-word. Then she read them a third time.

With painstaking care, she closed the album and sat back in the chair. A thought struck her. A completely jarring, earth-shattering, mouth-dropping-in-amazement thought.

Her heartbeat quickened. Her stomach fluttered. And suddenly, it all came to her like a bolt of lightning.

Eyes shining, face flushed, she smiled until she couldn't stretch her face any further.

14

____

After the meeting at the Stagecoach Saloon, Paavo and a feeling-no-pain Doc Griggs made their way to the library, where they found Angie hunched over a computer, completely absorbed in an article about some New York City chef.

It made no sense to Paavo, which, where Angie was concerned, was nothing new.

As they headed to the rented Mercedes, Angie was just starting to explain her latest discovery when Sheriff Merry Belle Schwartz came barreling toward them.

"Hold on, you all!" she thundered.

Her belt—crammed with a cell phone, holster, mace, night-stick, and God knows what else—bounced wildly as she waddled forward, short legs and wide hips working overtime.

Deputy Buster trailed behind like a guilty dog.

"What's the problem?" Paavo asked.

"I got some info for Doc," she said, scowling.

Buster sidled up to Angie with a grin. "Say, did you bring any other designer outfits, or just that Missoni?"

Paavo gawked. Had he really just said that?

"Shut up, Buster!" Merry Belle barked. "I got business."

"What's your news?" Doc asked, swaying slightly on his feet.

"Ned's horse turned up out at Hal's cattle ranch," she said. "Foreman called it in."

As she spoke, Buster circled Angie, studying her dress and shoes from every angle. Paavo stepped closer and wrapped an arm around her shoulders, glaring at the deputy.

Buster didn't notice—or didn't care.

Doc muttered, "This is mighty odd."

"What do you mean?" Paavo asked.

"It doesn't make sense, the horse showing up way out there. It's all wrong."

The sheriff planted her fists on her hips. "Mind talking to *me*? I'm the law around here."

"Don't trouble your blood pressure, M.B.," Doc said lightly. "Just thinking out loud."

"If you've got questions, ask *me*," she snapped.

"Try this, then," Doc said. "The cattle ranch is some twelve miles from where Ned was killed. Most of that's high, rough terrain. If the horse had bolted, it would've headed across the flatland. Easier going."

"You think like a horse now?" she jeered.

Doc shot her a glare. "Better a horse than a jackass!"

Before things exploded, Paavo stepped in. "Doc may have a point about the horse, Sheriff."

Merry Belle narrowed her eyes at him.

"That's right!" Angie chimed in, a little too loudly.

The sheriff folded her arms across her chest. "So now I've got a whole stampede of city-slicker experts. Must be something in the air."

"But isn't that what *you* said earlier, Aunt Merry Belle?" Buster asked.

"*Shut up!*" she snapped. Then, to the others: "Maybe I don't know. The horse was spooked. It ran. That's what they *do*."

"Or," Doc said, "it was taken."

"Who's to know?"

"Might be worth looking into," Paavo said.

She squinted at him. "Maybe I'll give the horse the third degree."

"I wish you could," Paavo said coolly.

Her jowls twitched. "The investigation is progressing thoroughly and professionally, *Inspector*. Pleasure chatting with you all." She turned on her heel. "Buster!"

The deputy reluctantly left Angie's side and followed.

Angie took the Mercedes and headed back to the guest ranch, while Paavo went with Doc to retrieve Ned's horse. As she fished for the key to unlock the bungalow door, her mind buzzed with excitement. Paavo was going to be thrilled when she told him about her discovery—*Oscar Tschirky!* What luck! What—

"Well, speak of the devil!"

Angie turned. Clarissa Edwards stood on the veranda, arms crossed, lips pursed.

"You didn't give me a *single* detail about finding Ned Griggs!" Clarissa said. "I had to hear it from LaVerne Merritt."

"There wasn't much to tell."

"That's not what I heard." Clarissa stepped into the shade, her voice turning dramatic. "The whole town is buzzing."

This town was even smaller than Angie thought. "Yes, I—"

"Such a pity. He was a young man, wasn't he? Oh well. Life goes on. Now, we've got a cookout to plan. Have you done *anything* at all?"

"I've given the meal a lot of thought, actually," Angie said, standing straighter. "And I just learned that, around the turn of the century, a famous chef from New York's Waldorf Hotel went missing near here and—"

"Turn of the *century?*" Clarissa interrupted. "You mean the one before *last,* not the twentieth? That doesn't sound very modern. Or exciting. Oh well, if that's all you've got, I'll have LaVerne Merritt help you."

Angie gawked. "*What?*"

"That's right. She says she's a gourmet cook. Her restaurant's dull. I've never eaten there myself. I told her all about you, and she'd be *thrilled* to help. She's even agreed to prepare some special dishes for me."

"You want LaVerne Merritt to help me? The woman who makes *poisonous cactus cakes?*" Steam practically shot from Angie's ears. "Look, I'm sorry, but LaVerne's help won't be needed. At all. As I was saying about Oscar Tschirky's relative—"

"I'm afraid I don't know the man," Clarissa said briskly. "Perhaps he doesn't frequent my circle."

"He's *dead!*"

"That explains it." Clarissa exhaled heavily. "Let me show you the kitchen. Maybe it'll inspire you."

Angie gave up and followed. They walked around the main house and across a small herb and vegetable garden to a wooden building Clarissa called the *cookhouse.* The outside was plain, but inside it was a professional-grade kitchen—granite countertops, shiny appliances, and a well-stocked pantry.

A chef's dream, really.

"Teresa Flores did a wonderful job here," Angie said, running a hand along the counter. She remembered Teresa mentioning the updates.

"Teresa Flores?" Clarissa asked.

"Hal's manager."

"Oh, yes. I vaguely recall her. Her grandmother runs that little Mexican place, right?" Clarissa adjusted a perfectly lacquered curl. "I don't believe she was a manager. A house-keeper, more likely."

A middle-aged woman appeared at the doorway carrying a grocery bag. At the sight of Clarissa, she froze, bobbed her head nervously, and looked ready to back out.

Angie stepped forward. "Hi, I'm Angie Amalfi."

The woman looked startled, then greeted her by mumbling her name.

Dolores Huerta was broad-shouldered, medium height, with strong, capable hands and short curly black hair streaked with gray. Her eyes had a gentle, but serious, appearance.

Clarissa announced, "Dolores, along with a few helpers, will handle the traditional fare for the cookout."

Angie nodded and caught Dolores' eye. The woman seemed competent and kindly—rather the opposite of Clarissa. Angie felt they should get along just fine.

Dolores cast one last, rather anguished look at Clarissa before hurrying away.

Clarissa took over, pointing out where supplies were kept and offering bits of commentary that revealed she had absolutely no idea what actually happened in a kitchen.

15

———

Hal Edwards' cattle ranch lay northeast of town, where the land rose into high pasture. As far as Paavo could tell, it was miles from the caves—the reason Doc Griggs had been so surprised that Ned's horse had turned up out there.

The foreman had found it just east of the ranch—hungry, thirsty, but otherwise unhurt. The saddle and bridle were gone. The foreman had loaded it onto a trailer and brought it back to the stables, but when he heard about Ned, he called the sheriff.

The missing saddle and bridle troubled Paavo. So did the missing cell phone—likely still tucked inside a saddlebag. There were no gashes or cuts on the horse to suggest the tack had been torn away. Someone had removed it.

He wanted to find that saddlebag. But where to start?

———

"Want to see what you'll ride on at the cookout?" Lionel called out.

Angie looked up from the rocking chair in front of her

cottage. She'd just left Clarissa and was lost in thought—considering what to serve with salmon roulade—as she waited for Paavo's return.

"What do you mean, *ride on?*" she asked warily.

"Didn't nobody tell you? The cooks ride in on the chuck wagon, just like the old West. Tradition." He grinned like he'd struck gold.

He led her to a large garage filled with a truck, tractor, and old farm equipment. Parked near the back stood a rickety chuck wagon, something straight off a movie set. She stared at its high bench seat, incredulous.

"It looks ancient."

"That's 'cause it is," he said proudly. "A genuine antique from the cattle drive days. Chuck box and all. 'Course, it can be dangerous."

He guided her around to the rear, where a hinged lid dropped down to form a work surface. Inside sat the chuck box —large, wooden, with shelves and drawers for spices and utensils. Dutch ovens filled the boot. A water barrel, hooks, brackets, a coffee grinder, and an assortment of tools lined the sides.

Angie ran her hand over the sun-bleached wood. "It's like history come to life."

Everything here was. Jackpot itself felt like a step back in time. Her thoughts flicked to the missing stagecoach, the caves, and van Beerstraeden's recipe journal—the journal Oscar Tschirky seemed so desperate to find. A thousand reasons had already come to her as to why—and she could only hope someday she'd find out the real reason … along with finding the journal itself.

"This chuck wagon reminds me of that stagecoach you talk about," she said to Lionel. "I heard some belongings from it were found near here."

"Sure were," Lionel said, scratching his belly. "Mostly down at the creek, not too far from the caves where Uncle Hal died.

You can head over there anytime. Might find something yourself."

"Do you really think so?"

"Why not?" He gave her a twinkling look. "Just be careful. Treasure hunting's tricky business. Gold fever takes hold, you'll end up wandering these hills like some old prospector with a pickax and a mule."

"I know why I'm here!" Angie cried the moment Paavo walked into their cabin. She threw her arms around his neck and kissed him.

"What's this about?" he asked, startled.

"I couldn't wait to tell you!" She spun away, practically dancing. "It came to me at the library. Paavo, I *know* it—this is what'll make my name in the culinary world!"

"Angie—"

"Don't *Angie* me in that tone. I mean it this time."

He sat on the sofa, wary. "Okay…"

She perched on the arm beside him. "It's about Oscar Tschirky."

"Who?"

She gave him the abridged version: Oscar was one of the first hires at the Waldorf Hotel in 1893, before it merged with the Astoria. Though not a chef, he became famous for signature dishes such as the Waldorf salad, Eggs Benedict, and Veal Oscar —despite never cooking a thing himself.

Paavo looked like she'd told him leprechauns ran the White House.

She leaned in. "Now, listen. Willem van Beerstraeden—our vanished chef—disappeared in the *same summer* as the Waldorf opened. What if that's not a coincidence? Oscar was a maître d', not a cook. So how'd he become known for all those gourmet recipes?"

Paavo's eyebrows rose.

She dropped her voice, conspiratorial. "Everyone always wondered how Oscar pulled it off. But what if... what if he didn't?"

"What are you saying?"

She leaned closer, gripping his shoulders. "What if *Veal Oscar,* for instance, wasn't his invention? What if it came from *another man*—a real chef who vanished on a stagecoach in the middle of the Sonoran desert?"

"You're serious?"

"Dead serious. If I can prove that Oscar Tschirky stole those recipes, it could turn the culinary world upside down."

He stared.

"And if I *find* those recipes," she went on, "I'll publish them. *Willem's Lost Cookbook.* I can see ads for it already: 'The Top Ten Reasons to Buy Angie Amalfi's Cookbook.'"

He raised an eyebrow. "You've come up with a list?"

"Not yet. But I will." She stood, energized. "First step is finding that recipe book. Lionel says people still find things from the missing stagecoach."

He made no response, but she caught his look. "What? You think I'm joking?"

"No. Not at all." He pulled her onto his lap. "I think it's a great idea. Just be careful. Take Lionel or someone with you."

She narrowed her eyes. "What am I missing?"

"Nothing," he said, a little too quickly. "Nothing at all."

As they headed to the dining room, Angie practically danced with excitement, shooing ostriches out of her path. She rattled off plans to recover the lost cookbook, one more elaborate than the next. Paavo smiled, secretly relieved. If she was focused on culinary treasure hunts, maybe she'd stay out of his investigation.

But as soon as they entered the common room, she dropped the subject. Not that it mattered—no one was there to overhear it.

Dolores served T-bone steaks, baked potatoes, squash, and a green salad. A local pinot noir paired beautifully. Paavo savored the thick, juicy steak. This was cattle country, no doubt.

Clarissa and Joey had again opted for dinner in their cottages. Lionel and Junior Whitney ate in the kitchen with Dolores.

Just before dessert, Lionel and Junior wandered into the dining room. Junior looked like he'd been rolling in cow manure again. The two men glanced at Angie and Paavo almost shyly, but lit up when Dolores entered with a cheesecake covered in huckleberry preserves.

"Are we all having dessert together?" Angie asked.

"Sure," Lionel said, eyes gleaming. "Guests go first, though. This one's special—sent over by LaVerne at Merritt's Café. She's quite the gourmet."

Angie's smile faltered. "So I've heard."

Paavo watched the exchange carefully.

Dolores served slices to Angie and Paavo, then joined the men, waiting. Paavo noticed Junior, clearly tipsy, sidling up to Dolores. She took a none too subtle step away.

Paavo bent near the cheesecake and recoiled. It was the strongest goat cheese he'd ever smelled. What was LaVerne thinking?

To his surprise, Angie took a small bite with her fork.

"Mmm. Cheesecake *au chèvre*," she said brightly. "This is a special cheese. It's wonderful in *bûchette charùtiere*—pancetta-wrapped bites with chives, sautéed. Also great in tarts."

Lionel and Junior stared, mouths open.

She took another small bite, eyes half-lidded. "Marvelous. Too bad I'm so full after that steak."

"Cheesecake-oh-sheve?" Lionel echoed.

"All the rage in San Francisco," Angie said as she lifted a napkin to her mouth, and then finished her wine.

"I'll try some," Junior said eagerly.

"Me too," Lionel added.

Dolores cut big slices for all three and joined them. Angie whisked Paavo from the room.

As they left, he saw the others take big bites … soon followed by the sound of coughing, gagging, and spitting … and then Angie's soft cackle.

———

The last customers had gone, and Teresa Flores stepped into the dark parking lot outside Maritza's restaurant. She'd gone there to get out of the house, to be around people who could still laugh, still enjoy a good meal.

She'd once been that way, an eternity ago.

Tomorrow was Ned's funeral.

The thought made her chest tighten. She shoved a strand of her long black hair behind her ear and quickened her pace toward the car. But Ned's face hovered in her mind—those intense blue eyes, full of hopeless longing. If only she'd loved him more. If only her life had been different. If, if, *if*…

Would he still be alive?

Would Hal?

Was it all her fault?

She walked faster, striding across the lot toward the back where she always parked. But something stopped her cold.

A whisper in the gut.

A voice in her head.

Turn around. Go back.

She shook it off. She didn't believe in intuition, or "second sight," or any of the superstitions her mother and grandmother swore by.

Still, her heart pounded. Then—she ran.

She didn't know why. Only that she had to get back to the restaurant.

Behind her, an engine roared to life.

A truck.

No headlights.

A black monster barreling out of the dark.

She flung herself toward the restaurant steps, grabbed the handrail, and pulled herself up onto the stairs just as the truck tore past below.

Chest heaving, she turned to the shadows, searching.

Had it been real?

Had it come that close?

Or—once again—was it just her imagination?

ngie and Paavo were alone in the dining room, sipping coffee and picking at waffles from the break-fast buffet when Lionel walked in. At the sight of them, he faltered, half-turning to leave.

"Join us," Paavo said, his tone making it clear it wasn't a request.

Lionel hesitated, but after a moment, poured himself some coffee and sat at their table.

"Guess your fishing plans fell through," he muttered. "You folks heading out soon?"

"No. We'll stay," Paavo said. His voice was low. Firm.

"It's nice here," Angie added, trying to keep things light. "Even with the ostriches and hairy spiders. Turns out tarantulas aren't nearly as dangerous as you said."

"Really? I got bit once. Hurt like hell." Lionel sipped his coffee. "Just figured, after you found a dead body, you'd be long gone. Sort of a busman's holiday, ain't it?"

Paavo didn't smile. "I want to know why Ned was out at those caves. Any ideas?"

Lionel looked genuinely surprised. "Me? Hell, no."

"Strange," Paavo said. "Ned was found near where your Uncle Hal died. Did Ned ever talk about him?"

"Ned and me didn't talk about nothing." Lionel loudly slurped his coffee. "He was kinda uppity. Had his own business. Guess I wasn't his kind."

"Weren't Ned and Hal friends?"

Lionel let out a chuckle. "Ned and Hal? Nah. Hal couldn't stand the guy."

"Really? Why not?"

Lionel shrugged. "Beats me."

"Did they see each other when Hal came back?"

Lionel raised an eyebrow, lowering his voice. "I'm surprised nobody asked me that before. Then again, ol' Mighty Butt didn't ask much at all."

Mighty Butt? Angie wondered... then she got it. M.B.

"I saw Ned and Hal going at it right out there on the veranda." Lionel gestured toward the windows. "Though that don't mean much. Hal argued with everybody."

"Ned was here?" Paavo asked sharply. "What about Teresa Flores? Was she out here too?"

Lionel shifted in his seat. "Hell, course she came around. Trying to get her old job back, for one thing. She knew Hal had an eye for a pretty woman, and didn't care she was young enough to be his daughter—hell, his granddaughter, maybe. But in time my uncle would have figured her out. She was a gold-digger. He run her off once. I knew he'd do it again."

Angie's eyes widened. That was new.

"When did he run her off?" Paavo asked.

"Five years back—the day before he took off for Mexico." Lionel scratched his chin, suddenly looking uneasy. He glanced toward the door. "Well, I got work to do." He downed the rest of his coffee and left in a hurry.

Once they were alone, Paavo leaned back, his eyes narrowing. "If Lionel's telling the truth, Teresa lied to us. And Ned lied to Doc—or Doc would've told us Hal and Ned had a falling out."

Angie met his gaze. "The question is: Why was Ned lying then? And why is Teresa lying now?"

"I think it's time I had a word with the sheriff." Paavo stood. "You want to stay here or head into town?"

"I still need to finish the cookout menu," Angie said. "Then I might take a walk down to the creek."

"Be careful," Paavo warned.

Angie smiled. "Don't worry about me. Around Mighty Butt, you're the one in danger."

<hr>

"There's no evidence of squat," Merry Belle grumbled as Paavo sat across from her desk, sifting through reports. Beside her was a massive cup of caffè mocha, topped with whipped cream. Jackpot didn't have a Starbucks. She'd bought a Saeco espresso machine and set it up in her office.

Expensive taste, Paavo thought. Saecos weren't cheap. Neither were top-of-the-line Hummers outfitted for police work, even if it was bought used. It raised the question of how Jackpot's sheriff afforded them.

He skimmed through the forensic reports: fingerprints, blood, fibers—gathered from Ned's home, his office, the caves, and the ledge. None of it matched anything. No surprise, once Paavo learned Deputy Buster had done the analysis himself using basic CSI kits.

If there'd ever been solid evidence, it was gone now.

"You should've sent the samples to Phoenix for proper analysis," he said, unable to hide his frustration.

"Oh, and have them tell us we can't use the fancy kits they gave us?" she said, sipping her coffee. "We used them just fine.

It's just, lots of folks been through those areas. Could've been anyone's prints."

"The skill comes in separating the ordinary from the critical," Paavo said. He tapped the fingerprint reports. "You've got hundreds, and they aren't even marked by location. Do you know where they came from?"

Merry Belle yanked the reports back and shoved them into a folder. Out of sight, out of mind. Her glower dared him to say more.

He bit back a sigh. No use pointing fingers now. "Have you requested Ned's phone records?"

"Oh … phone records." She rolled her eyes and opened the office door. "Buster! Did you get Ned's phone records?"

"No, Aunt Merry Belle."

"Well, why not? Get 'em!"

"You didn't say nothing about—"

"Do your job, Buster!" She slammed the door shut. "Satisfied now, San Francisco?"

Paavo took a long swallow of plain black coffee. It was going to be a very long day.

<hr>

Angie went to the cookhouse to review supplies and spices. She was proud of the menu she'd created.

Alongside grilled salmon, she planned to serve a liver pâté with poached apples, a beet, orange, walnut and arugula salad, and shaved fennel with mushroom and parmesan. Vegetables included butternut squash timbales and a gingery orange dal of crushed lentils. Dessert would depend on Clarissa's approval.

She needed to ask Lionel to shop for ingredients. Some, like pâté and fresh fennel, might require a trip beyond Jackpot.

Dolores Huerta was washing breakfast dishes, looking sheepish.

"Sorry about that cake last night, señorita," she said. "Lionel said it'd be a good joke. But the joke was on us."

"It's all right," Angie said. "I guess LaVerne tries."

"She is very trying," Dolores muttered, and they both laughed.

As Angie made her list, she chatted with Dolores.

The woman had worked at the ranch for over forty years, from the time she was sixteen years old. Never married. When Hal first built the hacienda, he gave her a room off the kitchen to call her own. She lived there until the hacienda was closed up after Hal's death. Now, she had a cabin in back of it. When Hal ran the place, the staff had filled the workers' quarters. All were gone except for Dolores and Junior Whitney. Winter help was hired, as needed, when guests were at the resort.

"Did Junior Whitney live in one of the rooms like you?" Angie asked.

"No. He's got an old RV. Mr. Hal never liked him much, but he put up with him. Mr. Hal was a good man," Dolores said.

Just then, Clarissa entered. Dolores pressed her lips together and went silent.

"I've just come from my morning ride," Clarissa said, grabbing a bottle of Perrier, ignoring Dolores. "I heard you were in here. Come up with any new ideas for the cookout?"

"I've come up with a menu. Would you like to see it now?"

"I'm sure it's fine," Clarissa said. "It's hot today—let's go have some chilled wine." She grabbed a body from the wine cooler and one glass, then headed to a shaded area outdoors.

Angie rolled her eyes, found a glass, and waved goodbye to Dolores as she followed.

Outside, the sky was a vault of brilliant blue. Even the smelly ostriches looked majestic against the desert backdrop.

"Do you ride often?" Angie asked.

"Every day, when I'm here," Clarissa said. "This used to be my home."

"You lived here?"

"Twenty-five years. And now it's an ostrich farm." She shook her head. "If someone hadn't beaten me to it, I might've killed Hal myself for filling this land with those wretched birds."

It was the first time anyone had spoken so plainly about Hal's death.

"What did he plan to do with them?"

"I don't know and don't care."

"I'm surprised you didn't get the house," Angie said, changing the topic. "Usually the wife does, especially with a child involved."

"I wanted to go back to California. I took the business instead."

"That's unusual."

"After his stroke, Hal couldn't run anything so huge and complex. I thought I'd made a smart choice." She gave a dry laugh. "Was I ever wrong. Joseph's been struggling, and put his trust in a manager who was even worse. By the time we fired him, we'd lost more stores than I can count."

Clarissa poured chardonnay like a pro.

"That's awful," Angie said.

"It is." She handed Angie a glass. "I've made do with investments, but I worry about Joseph. That's why I want the reading of Hal's will over and done with—assuming there is one. Hal had money. Look at all those stupid ostriches. They're expensive. And I hear he was planning to buy breeding males—more money down the drain. Do you know male ostriches are between seven and nine feet tall? Can you imagine?"

Angie couldn't. She didn't want to think or talk about the birds. "You must've had a difficult divorce."

"Acrimonious." She drained her glass. "It was so bad Hal had our marriage annulled by the Catholic Church. Can you imagine?"

"But … you had a child."

"I'd been divorced before, so the Church found it easy to annul Hal's marriage to me." She refilled her glass. "Hal used religion when it suited him."

Angie toyed with her engagement ring. "I'm sorry to hear that."

"Don't be. Just remember, love doesn't last. Someday, you'll thank me for the warning."

"I don't believe that."

"Realism is an asset in marriage. The biggest one."

"So are love, trust, and perseverance."

Clarissa scoffed. "Let's revisit this in ten years." She downed her wine then stood. "I need to wash off the horse smell."

As she walked away, Angie watched her go, torn between frustration and pity for the lonely, bitter woman.

When Paavo learned that Ned's best friend was Johnny Lightfoot, a handyman from the Colorado River Indian Reservation, he had Merry Belle show him the way to Lightfoot's trailer, out near the lake.

Lightfoot was outside sanding a coffee table, a strong, capable man around Paavo's age. When Paavo asked if he had any idea who might've killed Ned, the response was as expected: Ned was "nice" and no one could imagine hurting him.

But Paavo pressed on.

"If Ned got involved in something shady," Lightfoot said, indignantly, "it was because of that bitch Teresa—pardon me, but that's how I feel. He was crazy about her. But she thought she was too good for him. Ned just didn't see it."

"What kind of 'something'?" Paavo asked.

"I don't know," Lightfoot said. "He wouldn't tell me. But I think it had to do with Hal Edwards."

"Why do you think that?"

"Because he started trying to learn everything he could about ostriches."

Paavo paused, then asked, "Did Ned ever show you a charm—black obsidian, carved like a dog or a wolf?"

"It was a coyote," Lightfoot replied, brow furrowing. "No idea why he had it. Some people say it has to do with drug cartels. But I know Ned never got involved with them. If he had one, he found it somewhere. It doesn't mean anything."

But Paavo wasn't so sure.

17

Angie was looking for Lionel to get directions to the creek where remnants of the stagecoach had been found when she noticed Junior Whitney scrubbing out the plaza's center fountain. Clarissa had insisted it sparkle for the cookout.

Several ostriches loitered nearby, fascinated by the sloshing and swirling.

The second time Junior jabbed one with the mop handle, Angie stepped in.

She'd read up on the beasts since she was now neighbors with them and learned they weren't as free-ranging as she'd first thought. They were herd animals, usually sticking close to one another. As long as a mound of feed was maintained behind the workhouses, they mostly stayed put. But they were curious. And since they had long, fast legs, it only took a few steps before they wandered into the plaza.

They were generally good-natured. But startled, they bolted —blindly and ran in straight lines. That meant crashing into trees, buildings, or people. And when cornered, their powerful legs could kick a man clear into next week.

So, Junior had no need to hit them.

When another ostrich approached, Junior raised the mop again.

"Is that bird being stubborn, or is it just you?" Angie called out, striding toward him. "She'd probably follow a trail of corn kernels if you bothered to try."

He scowled. "You herd ostriches in San Francisco, do you?"

"No, but I've watched Lionel do it."

"He don't know nothing."

As Junior moved toward the bird, Angie grabbed the mop handle. "You don't need to do that."

The look he gave her made her wonder if *she* might get a taste of the mop next. But then his gaze shifted past her, and something in his face twisted—white, then flushed red, then dark with fury. He shoved the mop at her and stomped off.

She turned to see what had set him off. Lupe was walking toward them.

"Are you all right?" Lupe asked, eyes fixed on Junior's retreating back with thinly veiled hatred—and something else Angie couldn't place.

"Fine," Angie replied, surprised. "Didn't expect to see you out here."

"I need to talk to Paavo. It's important."

"He's off somewhere with Merry Belle, I think."

Lupe's hands clenched. "Someone tried to kill Teresa last night."

"What?" Angie stiffened.

"She says I'm overreacting, but I *saw* it. If she hadn't turned back, a truck would've hit her."

"Whose truck?"

"I don't know. It was too dark. No headlights. But I *know*..."

"You know what?"

Lupe shook her head. "I'll go back to town. Try to find Paavo."

"Give me a minute to grab my purse and phone," Angie said. "I'm coming with you."

———

Paavo stood at the base of the rocky hills, eyes scanning the terrain near the caves. He was searching for Ned's saddle and saddlebags.

He tried to think like the killer.

Whoever had done this probably planned it, lured Ned to that ledge, knowing the odds of anyone finding the body were slim. Vultures, coyotes, wind and time… Nature would take care of the evidence.

But the horse? That was a loose end.

The killer couldn't leave the animal behind. Too obvious. So they'd led it back into the desert, stripped it of gear, and spooked it into a gallop. A strong horse like Ned's could run for miles before tiring. Long enough to disappear.

That meant the saddle and saddlebags had been stashed somewhere nearby. Paavo was betting on that.

As he waited, listening, he noticed how unnervingly quiet it was here—so still he could hear Ranger, the roan gelding, breathing beside him.

It gave him an idea.

He pulled out his cell phone. Oddly, there was reception. No idea why, but he wasn't going to question it.

Chances were slim Ned's phone would be anywhere nearby. Still… worth a shot.

He dialed the number.

It rang once. Twice.

Then, to his astonishment, a voice answered. "Hello?"

———

Angie tried calling Paavo while Lupe drove, but her phone had no service.

How did people exist in an area where they couldn't be reached any time of the day or night?

Hmm... come to think of it, that sounded sort of nice.

When they reached the restaurant, Teresa was there—refusing to engage, brushing off Lupe's concern, and denying anyone was out to harm her.

Then she stormed off.

Seeing the distress on Lupe's face, Angie offered to stay, but Lupe shook her head. "I want to talk to Doc."

Angie took the hint and left.

Paavo had to admit, he was surprised when Ned's phone was answered. And even more surprised that the fellow who answered it was chatty. Because of that, he now found himself in a situation that could have been straight out of an old-time Western movie.

The talkative fellow now handed him a dark brown bottle. Paavo opened it and sniffed the liquid inside. Immediately, his breath caught and tears stung his eyes.

"You call this medicine?" he croaked, gave back the bottle of *Wainwright's All-Genuine Medicinal Elixir*. "It's criminal."

Lucius Wainwright, a florid-faced man with too much cheer, capped the bottle. "It most certainly *is* medicinal!" he said, cooking himself dinner. He turned the wieners on a spit over a butane heater, his lips smacking.

They sat in lawn chairs in the shade of his van, which was painted with a covered wagon and the name *Lucius Wainwright, Esquire* in flowery script.

"My elixir relieves headaches in men, and for the ladies—

whatever ails them," Wainwright declared. "Women have a great many ailments, you know."

Paavo raised his brows.

"My great-grandfather sold Lydia Pinkham's Compound for female complaints. Made a fortune. It's a family tradition."

"Tradition of selling eighty-proof booze?"

"Now, sir," Wainwright said solemnly, "you should know that twenty percent alcohol, at minimum, is common in herbal tinctures. The alcohol disperses the medicine. Especially to uterine tissue. Where, as you might imagine, the little ladies suffer most."

"So that rockgut is only forty-proof?"

"Eighty, actually," Wainwright admitted. "But it's excellent for depression, especially in bleak places like this."

"I'm not with the FDA," Paavo said. "I don't care what you're selling. I just need the saddle and saddlebags you found."

Earlier, Wainwright had explained how he'd found them. When he heard a cell phone ringing, he answered it out of curiosity.

"Finders keepers," Wainwright murmured as he removed the frankfurters to buns. He offered one, which Paavo declined. "That's the way of the West."

"This is a murder investigation," Paavo replied. "That phone is evidence."

"Damnation! Every time I find something good, someone wants to take it away." He sighed. "Not that anyone would call me, anyway. Is it worse to have a phone that never rings, or to have no one to call?"

Paavo didn't answer. "Have you found anything else interesting?"

Wainwright took a bite of his hotdog. "Depends. You mean, like the boat rental guy poking through the caves before he died?"

Paavo sat up straighter. "You saw Ned?"

"Sure did. Same day he died. Two horses out there, so I guess he wasn't alone. I didn't see the other guy, though," Wainwright went on. "If I'd known what was coming, I might've stuck around. Maybe gotten a reward." He popped open an ice chest. "Want to talk about it over a drink?"

Paavo took the beer he was handed. "Sure."

Wainwright lifted his bottle. "Cheers."

Angie stuck her head into the sheriff's office. Merry Belle was gone, but Buster looked up from his desk.

"Oh my God!" he cried. "Is that a *Dolce & Gabbana* dress?"

"You know your designers," she said, startled.

"I *love* their clothes." He twirled her around. "Casual, funky, classy."

"Well—"

"I'd love to go shopping in San Francisco sometime. Maybe when you're back...?"

Angie raised her eyebrows.

"Or not," he said, suddenly sullen. "I understand. No one wants to be bothered by the weird guy in the office. Only me and Teresa know how dull this place is. We're like rats in a cellar."

"You and Teresa?" she asked, incredulous.

"Not as a couple. She never liked me that way." He sighed. "But she *was* into Joey."

"Joey? You don't mean Hal and Clarissa's son, Joey."

"I do. Teresa worked for Hal, remember? Lived at the hacienda. Happiest time of her life, I think. And Joey comes every winter. He was everything she ever wanted, namely, rich."

"Teresa and *Joey*," Angie whispered, stunned.

"Clarissa would've gutted her if she found out," Buster said.

"So Teresa settled for Ned. I think she was just trying to make Joey jealous."

Angie's thoughts raced. "Do you know if Joey was here when Hal returned this past winter?"

"Could be. Joey comes and goes all the time. I never pay attention." He brightened suddenly. "Enough about that! Have you ever met Manolo Blahnik?"

The waitstaff gasped as Doc grabbed Lupe by the arm and hustled her out of the kitchen. She stared at him, startled.

In her office, door closed, he turned to her. "What's this about Teresa almost getting killed?"

Lupe folded her arms, turned her back. "I'm scared. So scared for her. I told myself I was imagining things. But when I think about Ned—"

He spun her around, then froze. They were close. Too close. Her scent—roses and spice—filled the space between them. The tension that had always simmered beneath their friendship flared.

"I lost Ned," he said softly. "I won't let you lose Teresa. Talk to me."

"I'm not sure."

"You trust me?"

"I do." Her eyes glistened. She touched his chest lightly— whether to hold him back or draw him in, he didn't know.

He pulled her into his arms.

"No!" she said, pulling away. "I made promises. I have to keep them."

He shoved his hands in his pockets to stop himself from reaching for her again.

"Send Teresa to my place," he said. "No one will know. She'll be safe."

Lupe nodded slowly. "That's a good idea. I'll ask her." She stepped closer. "Doc..."

Her eyes were full of sorrow. He knew if he reached out this time, she'd let him. But she'd made her reasons clear. If he ever broke her resolve, he suspected it would mean losing her completely.

This time, *he* had to be the strong one.

"I'll be waiting," he said, and walked away.

Angie was in a foul mood.

She'd spent the whole evening with Deputy Buster, who clung to her every word about clothes and shopping like a castaway to a life raft. *She* had nearly drowned in boredom.

When Paavo finally returned to the cottage, he was cheerful. He'd spent the night drinking beer and swapping stories with a humorous snake-oil salesman. Angie wasn't impressed.

Still, he'd recovered Ned's cell phone and saddlebags. A call had come in the morning before Ned's death—from "Hal Edwards." That was the last call Ned ever answered.

At the guest ranch, they discovered all the common area phones had two lines: a public one, and a secondary line. The call to Ned had come from that second line. Anyone could have used it.

As they stood in the empty common room, Angie couldn't shake the feeling of being watched.

"The ostriches like to keep an eye on all of us," Paavo said. "They've got nothing better to do."

"I think the one with the cowlick has a crush on you," Angie muttered. "It's always nearby."

He didn't laugh.

Later, in the cookhouse, Angie made him a cheese and

chorizo omelet. Afterward, as they walked back to their bunga-low, the eerie feeling returned—stronger than before.

The plaza was dark.

"Why aren't the lights on?" she whispered.

"Maybe Lionel's saving money. We're the only guests."

"He doesn't want us here," she murmured. "He's been trying to scare me."

"There's nothing to be afraid of. And you don't need to whisper."

He opened the door.

She stepped inside just as the door bumped a spring-loaded lever.

Then something dropped onto her head.

Long. Scaly. Rope-like.

It was a rattlesnake—freshly killed, still flexible—dangling from a bungee cord, bouncing as if alive.

Angie screamed.

If Lionel had been trying to scare her off … it was working.

18

———

It was the day of the funeral.

Angie headed for the kitchen, where she was going to bake a traditional favorite, a chocolate bourbon pecan pie, for the reception at the Flores' home after the funeral. With this hard drinking town, the dash of bourbon in the pie would probably be appreciated.

And after the snake episode, the reason why the town was so hard drinking was becoming ever clearer. In fact, she was sorely tempted to join the boozers herself.

Last night, she was still loudly telling Paavo what she'd like to do to whoever put the snake in their room when Joey and Lionel ran over to find out what all the commotion was about. They denied any knowledge of what had been done, and both swore pranksters from town liked to play tricks on visitors. Looked like the work of teenagers, they insisted. Harmless, they swore. The snake was dead, wasn't it?

Lionel then pointed out that if Angie was too upset to stay, he'd refund their money.

The smirk on Lionel's face as he said that was all it took to get Angie to change her mind about leaving. In fact, Paavo was the most difficult to convince to let her stay.

Now, she detoured to the common room to get her morning cup of coffee. Joey was inside, his face flushed, his eyes glassy as if he'd already been drinking more than coffee—or was nursing a horrendous hangover. "*Hola!*" he called, lifting his cup as if in salute. "Seen any snakes lately? Or tarantulas?"

"Very funny," Angie said as she served herself. "Are you going to the funeral?"

"I don't think I'd be welcome." His demeanor turned glum. "Poor bastard."

Angie decided baking the pecan pie could wait a few minutes and sat near Joey. "Did you know Ned well?" She didn't bother to ask if he knew Ned at all, as she truly believed everyone knew everyone else in this town.

"Of course. I went to school here until I was fourteen. Then my mom sent me to a boarding school in California, and before I knew it, she also moved to the Los Angeles area and divorced my dad. I hardly saw him after that."

"I thought you often came to the ranch in winter," Angie said.

"I did now and then, early on. I only came every year when Lionel was supposed to be running the place. He needed watching. Still does."

"I see." Angie remembered Deputy Buster making reference to Joey and Teresa. Looking at Joey now, Angie was even more certain that Buster was completely wrong, but some innate curiosity made her ask, "Do you think Ned and Teresa Flores would have gotten married?"

"Does it matter?" His face tightened.

"Just curious," Angie explained, then drank more coffee before saying, "It must be hard for you being here, first losing your father, and then a friend."

"Ned and I weren't exactly friends," he said. "And I hardly

knew my father." He downed his cup, and before Angie could say another word, he left the room.

Paavo had insisted on driving Doc to the funeral. This was the kind of day the doctor would get through by doing a fair amount of self-medicating, and Paavo didn't want him behind the wheel of a car.

They stopped at the Flores home. Doc wanted to escort the women to the church, and Angie wanted to drop off her pie. A few people were already there to leave flowers and food dishes.

"It's so wonderful to have another gourmet cook in town!"

Paavo turned as the sound of LaVerne Merritt's voice cut through the room.

"I brought something special," LaVerne was saying to Angie as she held up a Saran-wrapped Pyrex container. "You'll have to be sure to try it."

"What is it?" Angie asked.

"Javelina-noodle casserole." LaVerne beamed.

Others immediately began to walk away. Far away. Several left.

"What's a javelina?" Angie asked.

"It's kind of like a skinny pig," LaVerne said. "We have all kinds of pigs and wild boars in the area, you know."

"They're black and bristly," Paavo added, "with tusks. They're ugly things. Some people call them musk hogs."

"I think I get the picture." The dismay on Angie's face left him no doubt that she did.

"It's delicious. Just like pork." LaVerne licked her lips. "Wait until you try it! Lupe, can I refrigerate it?"

"Yes, of course," Lupe replied.

"I hope LaVerne's javelina is better than her goat cheese-cake," Paavo whispered.

"I'd rather not find out!" Angie added, just as all talking in the room ceased. Even LaVerne stopped in her tracks.

At the door stood Joey Edwards. He didn't appear to be in any better condition than when Angie last saw him.

No one said a word to him. His gaze searched the room until he found Teresa. With no more than a nod to the others, he approached her.

Lupe immediately left Doc's side and stepped between them. If her eyes were daggers, Joey would be dead.

Teresa put a hand on Lupe's arm, stopping her. Teresa then nodded at Joey, turned and walked out the patio door to the garden with Joey following close behind.

Lupe watched them, her face thunderous.

LaVerne interrupted. "Lupe, there's a problem with your mother. She's in the kitchen."

Lupe and Doc hurried to Maritza, Angie and Paavo following. "What's wrong?" Lupe asked.

"There's something... I can't remember," Maritza said, head bowed and resting her hand heavily against the sink. "I try, but..."

"Sit down." Doc slid a chair beside her.

"I'm sorry," Maritza said, as tears filled her eyes.

Lupe stooped low, eye level with her mother. "Sorry for what? What's the matter?"

Instead of answering her, Maritza gazed up at Doc. "Hal come. He talk to me. He give me something."

"When was this?" Doc asked.

Maritza's face contorted in thought. "Yesterday. No, not yesterday, but soon."

"She's confused," Lupe stood and patted her mother's shoulder. "All this." Lupe haphazardly waved her arm, clearly referring to the recent deaths. "The last time my mother saw Hal was at least five years ago."

"Poor Hal. Poor Ned," Maritza murmured as tears fell.

"I think it might be best if she stays home," Doc said softly. Lupe nodded.

"I want you to lie down, Mama," Lupe murmured. "This is too much for you. You stay here and keep an eye on the food. We'll be back soon."

"No. I should come. For Ned."

Doc took Maritza's arm and slowly walked her to her bedroom. "Ned wouldn't want you getting sick. You rest at home. He'd understand, I'm sure."

Maritza nodded and lay down on her bed, her tears had stopped, but her expression was dazed. Lupe kissed her cheek and walked out, quietly shutting the door behind her.

Teresa was alone in the living room, her eyes wide and sad. Joey had already left the house.

Lupe stared hard at her a moment, then turned to Doc. "Let's go to the church now."

Nuestra Señora de Guadalupe, a small version of the classic adobe and wood missions of the Southwest, held an aura of permanence and serenity. To one side of the church was a building that might be a school or large meeting hall. Set back on the other side was Father Armand's rectory. The mission wasn't directly in town, but slightly above it in the foothills—a rustic setting with a vista of the Colorado River.

The day was overcast and chilly. A film of gray covered the sun and made the surroundings as somber and glum as the people who filed into the church. They came from the town, the lake, and the reservation. Angie was amazed at how many knew who she and Paavo were. People she hadn't met told Paavo that they remembered when he came to Jackpot as a boy and would play with Ned while "the Finnish man" visited Doc.

Paavo seemed surprised and touched by their memories. He

spoke movingly with them about Ned. More than one strongly hinted they were glad "a real detective" was in town. Although the sheriff had swept Hal Edwards' death under the rug, everyone knew she couldn't do that with Ned's.

Inside the church, flowers surrounded the altar, candles had been lit, and incense burned. Paavo scrutinized the crowd, his face hard, looking much like a detective searching for a suspect. Merry Belle hovered near the door as if ready at a moment's notice to rush off in her Hummer in case there was an outbreak of crime in Jackpot.

Deputy Buster was near his aunt, and when Angie noticed him, he was watching her. He raised his hand, waggling his fingers in a slight wave in her direction. She nodded back. He pointed to her navy blue Oscar de la Renta suit and gave two thumbs up. Despite herself, she smiled.

She and Paavo remained in the back, not wanting to intrude on those who had been close to Ned all these years.

Doc was seated in the front row of the church with Lupe on his left and Teresa on his right. Behind him, was Doc's good friend, Joaquin Oldwater. Father Armand, a young priest who Doc had introduced earlier to Angie, was speaking quietly to the little group, offering consolation.

The two fishermen Angie had seen the first day she was in town, the ones LaVerne had called FBI, stood in the back of the church, perusing the crowd much as Paavo was doing. She decided LaVerne was right. Just who did they think they were kidding?

Angie then searched for people from the guest ranch, but didn't see anyone until the ranch hand, Junior Whitney, pushed his way through the crowd. As unkempt as ever, he stared hard at the mourners in the front row, then took a seat.

Almost the whole town had turned out. It was odd that Clarissa didn't have the sense to get herself and Joey there, or at least Lionel. If, as she'd said, she wanted the town to accept Joey as Hal's heir and new neighbor, she should have gotten him to clean himself up and show some respect to Ned.

The service began. But halfway through, the peace of the church was broken by the town's fire siren, its loud wail an ominous call for the volunteer fire department to gather.

Suddenly, Merry Belle's voice boomed out, "Fire! Main Street is burning!"

19

Merry Belle probably didn't mean to cause a commotion, but she did. As one, people rose from their seats, frantic.

"Go," Father Armand told them. "I will finish here."

Immediately, everyone streamed from the church. Some were volunteers who helped the town's two professional firemen; others were townspeople with businesses in the area. Whatever the reason, a problem for one was a problem for all. An unchecked fire in the dry desert could spread quickly.

"It's near our restaurant, or at it!" Teresa cried, a catch in her throat, as she scanned the horizon.

"*Dios!* We've got to go!" Lupe hurried to her car. Doc got in beside her while Teresa climbed into the back.

"We'll follow," Paavo said. He took Angie's arm, and they hurried across the parking lot. Fishing in his jacket pocket for his car keys, he found more than keys. He lifted out a small piece of paper and read it, bad grammar and all...

Ned Paulson killed Hal Edwards. So he had to die. Keep your nose out or your next.

Teresa had been right about the fire's location. Smoke streamed from the back of the restaurant.

Lupe and the others arrived in time to see the firefighters carry her mother out on a stretcher. Maritza was unconscious, apparently from smoke inhalation.

Lupe nearly fainted at the sight and tried to follow, but Doc reminded her of her other duties. She quickly steadied herself and asked Doc to take care of her mother. He got into the ambulance with the paramedics.

Fortunately, the damage to the restaurant wasn't as bad as it first appeared. None of the workers were inside; they'd all gone to the funeral service. Lupe's office was burned, and the fire had just reached the kitchen when the fire truck arrived.

Lupe's responsibility to check on her workers' safety done, she left Teresa to deal with the all that was happening in the restaurant, and headed for the medical clinic.

Seeing how distraught Lupe was, Angie stopped her and insisted on driving. Paavo would stay at the restaurant with Teresa and try to learn what had caused the fire.

"Do you have any idea what your mother was doing there?" Angie asked Lupe as she drove. "I thought she was staying at her house?"

"She was. This is crazy!" Lupe cried. "She's never wandered off before without telling me. Never!"

"She seemed confused earlier," Angie pointed out.

"She's been troubled by something lately, but can't say what it is. She easily remembers things that happened twenty years ago, but last week is another story. Sometimes, she doesn't remember that Ned is dead, or Hal. I try to watch her, Angie." Lupe fought to control her emotions. "I really do. She's never done anything like this before. I wonder if she caused the fire."

Angie had wondered that as well. "Your office seemed to be

where the fire started. If it was in the kitchen, that would make sense, but it wasn't."

"I agree," Lupe whispered. "It makes it look like, whatever happened, it was deliberate."

"Gasoline." Fire Chief Manny Gonzalez walked up to Merry Belle. Paavo and Teresa were with her. "Looks like somebody wanted to destroy the office."

"Where was Maritza found?" Paavo asked after introducing himself to Gonzales.

"In the hallway between the office and the kitchen. She must have been overcome by smoke and collapsed. The gas canister was at her side."

"You're saying she might have done it?" Merry Belle asked.

"That's crazy!" Teresa cried.

"Hard to imagine, but if her prints are on the can..." He didn't need to complete the sentence.

"Or, someone set things up to look that way," Paavo offered.

"Anything's possible." The chief looked over the building and shook his head. "I can't believe Maritza would want to destroy her own restaurant. I've gone to that place my entire life. The whole town has."

Angie and Lupe entered the waiting room of the medical clinic where Maritza had been brought. Almost immediately, Doc saw them. As he approached, Angie saw the troubled look on his face.

"It's not only smoke inhalation," he told them. "Someone hit her. She's in a coma."

"Like Ned," Angie whispered.

"Not exactly." Doc's expression was grim. "Whoever did it probably didn't want her dead—they probably hoped the fire would do that, and make us look no further for a cause of death."

"Why?" Lupe murmured, then looked ready to pass out. Doc had her sit, and Angie got her some water, but neither could answer her question. "How is she?"

"She has a hairline fracture on the back of her head," Doc said. "No surgery will be needed unless she develops an intracranial hematoma. I'm going to go back with the doctors. I want to observe as she undergoes more tests."

Lupe looked at him blankly.

"It'll be a long wait."

She nodded and watched Doc leave.

Angie sat beside Lupe. "None of this makes sense," Angie said softly. "Why would anyone do this to your family?"

"No, but thank you for staying with me, now, and for being there for Doc," Lupe said as her gaze traveled to the door to the medical offices where Doc had gone. "I appreciate you and Paavo being with him through all this. He's a good man."

"I think so, too." Angie hesitated to say more, but then added, "In fact, it's so obvious that you two care deeply about each other, I'm surprised you aren't an item."

"An item? Such an old-fashioned word to be coming from you." Lupe forced a smile before her face turned serious. "I guess no one's ever told you ... I'm married."

"Married?" Angie was stunned. "I'm sorry ... I mean, I assumed you were divorced or ... I mean, your last name ... and Teresa's."

Lupe folded her hands on her lap. "I understand. Legally, I am divorced. He divorced me, in fact, and I must admit I'm glad he no longer has any legal claim over me or my belongings. I didn't want anything to do with him, not even his name. Teresa felt the same. But that doesn't change the fact that I'm one of those old-fashioned Catholics who believes I married for life. Talk about strange, right?" Her eyes, even as she spoke those words, were calm. "I take my faith seriously, Angie. Some say too seriously—but God has sustained me though so very many harsh, bitter days, I will not turn my back on him."

Angie's mother was also a very traditional Roman Catholic —strict, one might say—in her beliefs. Angie understood what Lupe was saying.

"Where is your husband?" she asked gently.

"He's here, in Jackpot. He's here when he's not in jail, or alcoholic rehab for the umpteenth time. His life is a mess, Angie, and after years trying to straighten him out, I finally gave up."

"I see."

"His name is Sherman Whitney, but everyone calls him Junior."

Angie couldn't believe it. "Junior ... who works out at the Ghost Hollow Guest Ranch?"

"Yes. He and Lionel used to hang out together. So when Lionel took over managing the ranch, he let Junior work there when Junior's on the wagon. Then, when he falls off, Lionel fires him, and the cycle starts all over again. At least when he's working he doesn't come bothering me for money."

Angie thought of the raggedy fellow who poked ostriches with mop handles. "You give him money?"

"I can't let him starve, can I?" Lupe asked.

Might not be such a tragedy, Angie thought. She was curious about Lupe and Junior. "I guess Junior wasn't always the way he is now."

"I thought he had promise," Lupe admitted, "though my mother never saw it." At the mention of Maritza, Lupe bowed her head and paused a moment before continuing. "Anyway, Junior worked in his father's cantaloupe business, when I met him. He was a few years older than me, and a bit of a wild man. You know how lots of women fall for excitement, and hope they can tame the guy. Sometimes it works out—but a lot of times, it doesn't. When his father's business fell on hard times, Junior was no help. If anything, he was a hindrance. Finally, Sherman Senior sold what remained of the business to Hal Edwards, and left town."

"So Hal ended up with a cantaloupe farm?" Angie asked.

"Hal was involved in everything," Lupe said wryly. "Junior liked to say Hal had robbed his father, but it wasn't true."

"So Junior disliked Hal?"

"Hated him. He always said he knew Hal's dirty little secrets, and that Hal had better think twice about disrespecting his family."

"What did he mean?"

"Who knows? He's a blowhard. All talk, no substance." Her lips tightened, and when she spoke, her anger was palpable. "Pay him no mind, Angie. No matter what he says. The guy is a liar."

Angie took a moment to let the temperature lower a bit, then she asked. "Does Junior see much of Teresa?"

Lupe shook her head. "He was never a father to her, though in his way, he cares about her. I've always wondered if Junior isn't the reason she's so resistant about love." Tears filled Lupe's eyes as she said, "I feel bad about her, Angie, as if I failed in the way I raised her. Because, even though my marriage hasn't worked out, at one time in my life I truly did love him, and because of that, I have Teresa. I wish she could understand the way I feel. Unfortunately, she never has. And I doubt she ever will."

20

———————

"Buster can't lift any prints off the gas can." Merry Belle stood to make her pronouncement as soon as Paavo entered the office. "He tried, but said they were all smudged. I think he made things worse by trying, if that's possible."

"Take it away from him and send it to Phoenix." Paavo had had it with the incompetence in the sheriff's department. "If there's any evidence on it, we need to know."

"You're right." Her round face scrunched into a frown. She hesitated, then dropped back into her chair as her entire demeanor took on a weary, almost defeated air. "Smith, can we start over?" Her voice was uncertain.

"What do you mean?"

"Sit down and listen." The words were bossy as ever, but the tone softer. Something in her eyes made him curious enough to do as she requested. "I know I come on strong. I'm not big on outside cops interfering with my work."

"I understand," he said. No cop liked outsiders poaching, even if they were other cops.

She nodded and continued in what was for her a muted

manner. "I got two people dead, and now an old woman got knocked around, plus an arson fire. Too much old nasty stuff is coming to the surface."

Paavo waited.

"This isn't easy to say, San Francisco." This time, there was no sarcasm in the nickname. She took a deep breath then added, "I could use help. Another professional. You're a good homicide cop. I checked."

Merry Belle's look of embarrassment almost made Paavo smile. It figured she had vetted him, but for the first time, she did something right. She needed help. The question was, could he trust her?

"I'd like to help, but..."

"I know, I know," Merry Belle interrupted. "You think I'm corrupt." The sheriff allowed herself a sly smile. "I may do favors for campaign contributors—as a courtesy, you under-stand—but that's all." She went on in a firm voice. "I'm not bought and paid for. Don't ever think that."

To his surprise, Paavo believed her. This bellicose woman seemed to have her own goofy set of ethics.

"Look, I took this job because I needed work and nobody else wanted it. Besides, I knew more about being a cop than any ten men in town put together. I watch every police procedure show on TV, including the ones from the BBC, and every episode of CSI no matter where it takes place—New York, Miami, Las Vegas, Nome. Hell, I even wrote and told them they should put a show right here in Jackpot." Her plain features softened, her voice lowered. "I can roust drunks and testos-terone-laden teenagers with the best of them, but I never expected to deal with murders."

Paavo relented, although a part of him enjoyed Merry Belle's discomfort. Doc would probably say she was eating huge slices of humble pie. "I'll be glad to work with you."

"I appreciate that," Merry Belle said, hastily adding, "It'll be purely unofficial."

"However you want to play it. And I've got something here for us to start with." He then took out the note he'd found in his pocket, holding just one corner, and laid it on her desk. It was block printed which was considered one of the easiest ways for a person to disguise his or her handwriting. "Someone slipped this note in my jacket. I don't know when. In this warm climate, I spend more time carrying the jacket around than wearing it."

Her eyes widened as she read the note. "Someone is trying to warn you off the investigation," she murmured, and he could tell it rankled her that no one was trying to warn *her* off as well.

"It seems to be saying that Ned's death was revenge for Hal's murder," Paavo suggested.

"That's right!" Her round face lit up brighter than a full moon. "And who'd want revenge ... except his son! It's telling us Joey killed Ned!"

"I'm not so sure," Paavo said. "Look at the grammatical mistake on the note—it shows y-o-u-r rather than y-o-u-apostrophe-r-e. Any ideas who might make that kind of mistake? I'm not sure Joey Edwards would," he said.

"Mistake?" She studied the note. "Uh..."

He didn't pursue it. "Let's bag this, then I'd like you to send it to a crime lab in Phoenix for a fingerprint analysis." To emphasize his point, he added, "Don't let Buster touch it."

<hr>

"Thank the good Lord you got back!" Lionel panted, more red-eyed and scraggly than usual. He met Angie as she pulled into a parking area at the Guest Ranch. "Clarissa's raising holy hell."

"Why's that?" Angie asked.

"'Cause you ain't here, that's why!" Lionel exclaimed. "And

the cookout's in three days. Miss High 'n Goddamn Mighty wants you to give me your list of supplies."

Lionel and Clarissa's concerns were the last thing Angie cared about at this point. Maritza was still in a coma. Doc had insisted that Angie and Lupe go home while he and Teresa kept the vigil. And Paavo had to leave to work with Merry Belle and Deputy Buster.

Before each went their separate ways, however, they had gathered together at the cemetery for a brief but tearful prayer for Ned, and to put flowers on his fresh grave. The emotion at the gravesite had been heartbreaking.

"It's late, and I'm tired." Angie stifled a yawn. She was emotionally and physically exhausted. "Doesn't Clarissa know what happened today?"

"You mean about Maritza going nuts and trying to burn down her restaurant?"

"I doubt that's the real story."

"Whatever," Lionel grimaced. "You don't think Superbitch cares about that, do you?" Angie wondered if Clarissa had scared Lionel into being stone cold sober, because he was that now.

"Does she harass everyone this way?" Angie asked.

"Sure does. Dolores has been here since long before Hal had his stroke and Clarissa treats her like she don't know shit; and Junior, who's been here on and off for over ten years, is treated like he knows even less!"

That got Angie thinking. "Interesting," she murmured. "Well, goodnight. I'm going to bed."

"What about the supplies?" he demanded.

"I'll give you a list tomorrow."

"What you going to cook for us, anyway? Is it any good?"

She stopped in her tracks and slowly turned. "Is it *good*?"

"Hell, when LaVerne cooks fancy, I wouldn't give her food to the hogs."

Angie's eyes narrowed. "For you, I'm going to make something really special."

"Is that so?"

She put her hands on her hips. "Sliced rhubarb and okra in a nest of alfalfa sprouts."

"God damn," he muttered to himself as he walked off. "She really does sound like a gourmet cook."

21

———————

It was late, too late for a priest who would be saying mass at six a.m. to still be awake. But in bed after his evening prayers, Father Armand found it hard to sleep. The priest had few illusions about the desperate troubles people could get themselves into, but the web of ugly secrets, vengeful passions, and violence that gripped his small community disturbed him greatly. He felt useless—a failure. He should know his people better. He'd been here four years—an eternity in some parts of this country, but in Jackpot, he was still considered an outsider. The former priest, Father Benedict, had been there sixty years. It was with thoughts of Ned Paulson's murder and the attack on Maritza Flores that Father Armand finally drifted toward a restless slumber as he wondered if a better or more experienced priest might have been able to unravel the mysteries that lay hidden behind this trouble.

The sound of a car engine nearby, of tires running over gravel, jarred him fully awake. His eyes opened in the darkness. Uneasiness filled him. He got out of bed in the moonlit bedroom and put on his robe, slippers and glasses. Perhaps some troubled soul had come to the church in need of comfort and counsel.

The priest walked to the front room that served as his office and opened the door. The parking lot was empty. It must have been someone driving by ... or who changed his mind and left.

Okay, he told himself, his imagination had become overactive. With all that was happening in his parish, that was no surprise. He turned to go back to bed when the squeal of old door hinges being opened shocked him. He stood on the porch unable to believe that anyone would be breaking into a church for a second time in the same number of weeks. What was going on?

He headed toward the mission, baffled and angry.

It might be someone here to steal the sacred vessels, especially the silver chalices! That made him pause, but outrage overruled prudence.

All was quiet when he reached the sacristy. The door lay open. The priest stopped and looked all around. He heard no sound, saw no one. Fear for the sacred vessels filled him and he crept inside, leaving the lights off.

The moonlit room appeared empty, the storage area undisturbed, and the chalices safe. Whoever was here may have heard him and run.

Breathing easier now, he looked around and noticed that the door to the room where the parish records were archived was ajar. Soundlessly, he inched near. The windowless room should have been deep in darkness, but a small penlight flickered.

Curious, he reached inside and flipped the switch to turn on the overhead lights...

The shrill, insistent ringing broke the night's deep quiet. Paavo, shaking the sleep from his head, glanced at the nightstand clock.

He was accustomed to being awakened by the police dispatcher back home.

1:12 A.M.

He groped for his blaring cell phone. Next to him, Angie stirred.

"Smith," he mumbled into the mouthpiece.

Angie sat up in bed, flicked on the lamp, and turned towards Paavo, blinking owlishly at the light.

"Yes. Do you need anything? ... Okay, I'm on my way."

Paavo clicked off his cell phone and got out of bed.

"What's happening?" Angie asked groggily.

"That was Father Armand. Teresa's at the church. He caught her going through the archive records. He doesn't want to disturb her mother. Doc's still at the clinic and gave the priest my number. He wants me to talk to her."

"She broke in?" Angie was fully awake now. "That doesn't make sense! Did he say why?"

"I'll know soon enough," Paavo said as he began to dress.

"I'll get dressed, too," Angie announced.

"No, you're staying here."

"But—"

"I'm going alone." His voice was stern and inflexible. "You stay here with the door locked."

One glance at Paavo's hard, no-nonsense expression made it clear that any arguing was futile. "I'll stay, but you call me as soon as you find out anything."

"Angie, I'm sorry about the way this trip has turned out," he said grimly.

Her heart seemed to stop as she watched him pull his Beretta and shoulder holster from the dresser drawer. "It's not your fault," she said. "But I'm planning our next vacation."

Angie's phone remained silent as she finished a cup of coffee. Of course, Paavo never phoned when he was on a case in San Francisco, so why should it be any different here?

The night was chilly, and the coffee warmed her, but she feared the onset of caffeine nerves if she kept this up. Her mind raced, and her imagination conjured increasingly improbable scenarios for Paavo as the waiting wore her down.

Angie got up from the sofa and meandered through the rooms of the bungalow. Each time she passed the coffee table in the living room she would glare at her cell phone, willing it to ring. At the living room window she stopped and stared across the plaza toward the dark, supposedly empty, hacienda.

Something flashed. Was it her imagination or something else? *Calm down,* she told herself.

She saw it again. Was it a flashlight? Somebody was on the second floor of Hal Edwards' supposedly empty hacienda. Every muscle stretched tight as she watched the upper rooms' windows. Her eyes strained as if trying for x-ray vision. Despite her best efforts, though, she couldn't achieve Superwoman powers. It could be Clarissa or Joey ... but why wouldn't they simply turn on the lights? They wouldn't be using a flashlight unless they wanted to make sure Lionel or Junior or one of the other ranch workers didn't see them, which made no sense.

If she could only get a wee bit closer... the instant the idea occurred to her, so did Paavo's warnings about avoiding danger.

She quickly put on jeans, a shirt and her boots, then ran back to the window. The light flashed again. Her mind warred. She would phone Paavo—that was a condition of her staying after the snake incident. Frankly, though, he was too far away to help.

No excuses! She should phone him, and she would.

She picked up the cell phone and dialed. The message came back to her that the party she was calling was outside the cell area. At least she knew why he hadn't phoned. She thought a moment. If she simply waited and watched from the bungalow for whomever it was to leave, it'd be too easy to miss seeing the prowler in the darkness. She wanted to know who was sneaking around in there.

What choice did she have? It wasn't as if she had to go *inside.* Just close enough to see if someone had broken in. She'd be cautious and avoid danger, of course. That decided it. She switched her cell phone to go straight to messaging so that, if Paavo did phone, he wouldn't wonder why she wasn't answering.

She slipped out the front door. As much as she tried to tread soundlessly, the crunching of the gravel beneath her boots was like machine-gun fire. Hurrying across the open plaza, she felt safer once within the hacienda's shadows. She could only hope no one had seen her on the moonlit square. Her breathing grew heavy.

Relax, she ordered herself.

She worked her way to the side of the hacienda and froze.

A dark shadow loomed before her, then slowly moved toward the moonlight.

After a moment she let out a breath of relief. It was just an ostrich.

She darted around the corner of the hacienda to the rear. Inching along, she stayed as close to the wall as possible, her every sense magnified. The feeble breeze in the night air seemed to rush, the tiny scampering of small animals and insects sounded like a stampede, and when the high cry of an owl shrilled, she jumped, convinced Gabriel had sounded the Last Trumpet.

Steps led to the veranda. The entry door was ajar, inviting and beckoning.

Maybe if she simply went up to the opening, she could hear voices from inside. She ascended the steps. Beside the door lay a crowbar. Somebody means business, she thought.

She listened, but didn't hear a sound. What harm would one quick-as-lightening peek do? Who would even know?

With Paavo's admonitions thrumming in her ears, she touched the door. Like magic, it swung open to the kitchen, dusty and distorted by shadows cast by the moonlight streaming in through streaked windows.

The house was quiet. Had she imagined the light?

She moved past the kitchen and into the moonlit dining room. A single placemat lay atop the table. It was spooky—as if Hal had eaten there alone and would return any second. The presence of the bitter, fearful, and lonely master of the hacienda loomed over the room, and she couldn't help but contrast it with the vibrant, charitable, handsome, and clever man the historical society had written about. A surge of pity for Hal rose, followed by a deep, gnawing uneasiness. This is where a murdered man would haunt, she thought.

Outside the dining room was a hallway.

She paused.

Upstairs, soft noises could be heard. As her nose twitched from the dusty, stale air, she crept through the shadows until she reached the base of a staircase.

Clutching the banister with painful caution, she started up. Midway, a crashing sound reverberated through the house, and she came to a startled halt.

"Goddamn it!" grumbled a male voice.

"Don't curse, Joseph."

It was Clarissa! And her son! Angie's curiosity skyrocketed.

"I bumped my leg on this damn dresser."

"Stop whining!"

"This is a fool's errand," Joey cried, louder.

"Then you're acting well-suited for it! Get busy. I want to get out of this room. Look at this jewelry, these clothes. The place reeks of Hal's cheap women."

Angie eased her way down a couple of steps, but stopped to listen when they began to speak again.

"Mother, for cryin' out loud," Joey said, his voice climbing with each word, "it's clear Dad didn't hide it here. We've searched this place high and low. I'm not tearing up any more floorboards! It's not here!"

Angie didn't want to miss a word.

"If we can't find it, we might just have to burn the house down." Clarissa's voice was cold and deadly serious.

"That's crazy!"

"Don't you dare talk to me that way!" Clarissa snapped. "You seem to forget that you wouldn't have anything if it weren't for me!"

All talking stopped. *Go on,* Angie urged.

"Are you just going to stand there and rub your leg all night?" Clarissa demanded.

"It hurts, Mother. When will you get it through your head that other people have feelings, even if you don't?"

The sound of a slap rang through the dead air of the house. Angie listened, horrified, as a deep silence settled over the hacienda. Her breathing became so shallow she was growing light-headed. Her body ached from the strain of silent immobility, her nose continued to itch from the dust, but she wouldn't miss this for the world.

Clarissa's voice turned low and menacing. "You will stop acting like a vulgar weakling! You wonder why your father despised you? Why wouldn't he? You acted scared of him even when he was a bed-ridden drooling wreck."

"Stop, Mother," Joey pleaded.

"Stop, Mother," she repeated in a mocking tone. "You'd be nothing if it weren't for me, and don't you ever forget that!"

"I should never have come here."

"Listen to me." Clarissa spat the words. "If we can't find the will, I'll use his computer, his letterhead and printer, and we'll create one for him."

"But Mother," Joey said, "if we can't find it, no one else can either and I'll still inherit everything. Why are you bothering?"

"It's insurance," she said. "Who knows what your father did when he was away? Over the years I learned to never trust him. Never!"

There were footsteps as the two moved about in their search. Angie waited. If the steps grew louder or seemed to head her way, she'd run. Besides being achy and miserable, the tingling pressure in her nose was mounting, demanding an explosive release. She rubbed it until the feeling passed.

"Damn! This odious computer still won't work," Clarissa cried. "Why is nothing simple?"

"How many times do I have to tell you it's password protected?" Joey snapped.

"And how many times do I have to tell you that you ought to know how to break into it! It's your generation that deals with computers, not mine! I want to use it."

Angie's nose suddenly took on a life of its own. Twitching, wrinkling up, the need to sneeze built inexorably. She squeezed her nostrils, holding them shut, continuing to listen.

"All right, then." Angie could all but hear Joey pout. "But it's a waste of time."

The sound of a chair scraping the floor reached her, along with the 'oomph' of a weary man sitting down.

Soon after the tingling began, Angie's nose went back to normal.

Joey and Clarissa seemed to be doing nothing but squabbling, and she needed to get out of there. She started slowly down the stairs.

"I can't do it," Joey cried, his voice loud as his frustration grew at not being able to get into Hal's computer.

"And maybe I can't help you turn the Halmart stores around?" Clarissa jeered.

"For all your talk, you haven't been much of a help to me so far!" Joey's tone was beyond indignant.

"Not much help? You wouldn't even have the stores if it weren't for me! Now, get busy with that computer."

"Stop ordering me around!" Joey cried.

"Don't you dare use that tone with me!"

"I can't take it anymore!" Joey yelled.

And right then, Angie sneezed.

22

———

"What are you doing here?" Teresa stood as she saw Paavo enter the rectory's living room. She spun toward Father Armand. "You said I'd be left alone. You lied!"

"You can stay, Teresa," Father Armand said quietly, "but you refused to talk to me. You've got to speak with someone about what you're doing. What you've been saying."

She looked about wildly as if trying to decide if she should run. "I haven't been saying anything."

"Yes, Teresa, you have." The padre's tone was firm.

"What were you looking for?" Paavo asked her.

She turned away, and he looked to the priest for an answer.

Father Armand shook his head. He didn't know. "I allowed her to continue to search the records. In the end, though, she came away with nothing."

Her eyes darted from one to the other, and slowly, her face became hard and stony, devoid of all emotion.

"What's this about, Teresa?" Paavo asked.

"It's about... nothing. Everything was a lie. All that's

happened," she stopped speaking and covered her mouth with a shaky hand.

Father Armand took a chair and gestured toward the sofa. "Teresa, sit down, please. You need to tell us what's troubling you. How can we help if we don't know?"

"You can't help!" Even as she said the words, she sat dejected on the edge of the sofa. "I'm beyond help!"

"Never—"

"It's true!" Silent tears fell. "Please, leave me alone."

"Doc thought you should talk to me," Paavo said, pulling up a chair to face her. "Why is that?"

"I have no idea!" she said, trying to stop her tears.

"Yes, you do. Doc knows something or he wouldn't have told me to come."

"If he knew, he'd hate me."

"Tell us, Teresa," Father Armand urged. "Tell us together, or one of us alone. Whatever you'd like."

She stared at him a long moment, then whispered. "It's my fault, Father. It's all my fault."

"What is?" he asked.

"Everything." Her voice was grating and desperate. "Hal's death, Ned's, the attack on my grandmother. It's all because of me."

"What do you mean?" he asked. "Why do you think that?"

"I *know* it! I should be the one who's dead, not Ned! And my grandma, if she dies too..."

A sob fell from her as she ran out of the rectory. It was as if all she'd kept bottled up inside had finally broken her.

Paavo saw her stop once she was outdoors, and look up at the starry night. He knew he would somehow manage to get her home, but first, he had a question for the priest.

"Did she say anything to you that you're able to pass along?" he asked.

The padre shook his head. "She refused to say anything at all, refused even to make a confession. She said she doesn't deserve absolution. That if she died now, she'd be damned. And that she deserved it."

Clarissa froze. The sneeze had echoed through the old house. Hal was always sneezing and coughing and complaining of how tired and sick he felt. She couldn't help but look around guiltily, almost expecting him to walk through the door, accusing and angry. "Did you hear that?" Clarissa whispered.

"I think so," Joey said, his voice small.

Clarissa yelled, "Who's in here?"

"It s-sounded like a sneeze," Joey stammered.

Anger—anger at Joey for his weakness, at Hal for all he'd put her through, even at herself for her mistakes—caused her to sneer. "That's so astute, Joseph. Now, why don't you find out who it is?"

"Okay... I'm going to look around."

Duh, she mouthed, much like young people on TV. Like her own grandchildren would be doing, if she had any. "Move it, Joseph! You couldn't catch a statue!"

Slowly, she followed him down the stairs. How she hated coming to this house. It held too many memories, especially with Hal dead...

She wished she could think back to at least one time when she'd been happy here. Hal tried, she had to give him that. But he didn't hold her heart. Someone else did. She hadn't thought about him in years, not until she talked to that young woman, that Angie, so happily in love. Her hand slid along the smooth railing as regret filled her. And strangely, the regret was about Hal, of how he seemed to really love her, but she'd never really given him a chance to make her happy. She married him out of fear of her father, who hadn't approved of the man she loved and threatened to cut her off with nothing. She never could have defied her father, but how different would her life have been if she'd opened her heart to Hal, at least a little?

How different would life have been for Hal as well as for her? But time for regrets were long past. She didn't have regrets; didn't have anything at all.

Clarissa stepped out the backdoor to find Joseph on the veranda. "Why are you still here?"

"I don't know where he's gone. He was fast."

Clarissa stared into the darkness, then snorted. "He? 'She' is more like it. Look." Just then, the ostrich with the cowlick ambled toward them. "You idiot! You were chasing an ostrich!"

"I wasn't! Anyway, ostriches don't sneeze."

"How do you know?" she demanded. "It was probably standing at the door. You left it open, didn't you?"

"Well, yes, but--"

"Stop." Sudden weariness overwhelmed her. "As things stand now, you should inherit everything, but to be absolutely safe, we're going to return tomorrow and type up a will. You have all night to figure out how to do it. Once we've got it, the sheriff will declare it official. We'll be fine as long as that homicide detective doesn't get involved."

"How can you be so sure the sheriff will go along?"

"She has to." Just the thought of Merry Belle—talk about an ill-suited name!—made the words curdle on her tongue. "For years I've been a heavy, unofficial contributor to her campaign and, no doubt, retirement funds."

"So, Mother, you took money from the business to buy yourself a sheriff?"

"Some expenses are necessary. Where do you think she got that Hummer she's so proud of?" Clarissa frowned. "The problem is the homicide inspector. It's no coincidence he chose this spot for his vacation. I'll have to make sure the sheriff doesn't allow him to interfere any more than he already has."

Angie didn't believe she was fast enough to run all the way across the plaza without being seen, so, spotting some bushes to the left of the hacienda, she ran to them and dived inside.

As she crawled for cover, all the scary things she'd heard about desert creatures came back to her. She couldn't help but wonder where live rattlesnakes slept. Dead ones were bad enough!

She stopped, laid low, and listened to Clarissa's continuous berating of her son. No wonder the man was such a basket case.

Eventually, Clarissa must have grown tired of being a harridan because she abruptly said she was going to her bungalow and gave Joey a frigid "Goodnight." He said he was doing the same and slinked off to his.

Suddenly, a lot of what Angie had heard and saw made more sense. Apparently, Clarissa hated living at the hacienda so much that even now, when Hal was gone, instead of staying in it, she and Joey were staying in guest cottages. That explained the flashlights. Clarissa probably didn't want Lionel to know she and Joey were skulking around through Hal's things.

Angie decided to wait a short while to be sure the two of them were in their cottages and had retired for the night. She didn't want them to catch her.

Unfortunately, in the silence following Clarissa and Joey's departure, Angie became aware of strange noises and scurrying in the undergrowth. Hadn't someone mentioned that there were wild boars in the area? Surely they didn't come this close to the hacienda, she told herself. Or did they?

Somewhere in the brush behind her, she heard the sound of stirring, breaking branches and distinctly unfriendly snorts. Something was crashing over the terrain, gaining speed. The snorts were urgent and insistent. Angie began to scramble through the brush.

She reached the clearing and stood, listening, scarcely noticing the twigs and stickers that had attached themselves to her hair and clothes. All was quiet for a moment, but then, suddenly, the noise began again.

As if she were setting a record for the hundred-yard dash, she crossed the plaza to her bungalow. The window was open. She didn't bother with the door, but dived in, head first, then just as quickly, shut and locked the window.

Cowering behind it, she peered out to see the deadly fiend.

It was a pig, all right. But not a wild one.

It was a young piglet, probably one that had somehow broken out of the sty. Her monstrous wild boar turned out to be about the size of a chubby cocker spaniel.

23

"What's Teresa up to?" Angie asked. Although half asleep when Paavo returned, she became fully awake and alert after hearing how Teresa blamed herself for Hal and Ned's deaths and Maritza's injuries. "How could she blame herself unless she had a part in the deaths?"

"I don't think that's the case," Paavo said.

"But why else would she sound so guilty?"

Apparently, that was Paavo's question as well. He put it aside to listen with interest to Angie's story of eavesdropping on Clarissa and Joey. She left out the part about the piglet.

"I guess it's about time I saw where Hal Edwards lived," he said. "It sounds as if everyone else has. Want to join me?"

"Aside from being worried about you," she said with a grin, "why else do you think I stayed up so late?"

"Lead the way."

Quietly, they crept across the plaza.

The back door had been left unlocked.

Once inside, Paavo turned on the small penlight he usually carried, but soon found a larger flashlight near the back door—

perhaps the one Joey had used—and switched to it. They followed Angie's earlier path to the stairs, and she walked partway up. "This is where I stood."

They then continued up the stairs to Hal's bedroom.

Feminine toiletries had been pushed to one side on the dresser. Angie stared, surprised to see them. She wondered what Clarissa had made of them. In the closet was a jumble of strewn clothing, as if someone had taken everything off the hangers, and then tossed them in there.

"I don't get this at all," Angie said, looking in horror at the clothes.

"Did they do all this?" Paavo asked.

"It didn't sound like it." She went to the closet. "Why would anyone throw around Hal's things this way?"

The first garment she pulled out was a brown cowboy shirt, then a pair of Wranglers. Beneath them was a brightly patterned teal and yellow material. She lifted it high. A dress.

"Size ten." She looked at the label—Merona. "I don't recognize the designer. It's not expensive."

"Not Clarissa's, in other words?" he asked.

"Not a chance. That string bean is a size four at most."

There were two other dresses, same size and colorfully patterned, in the pile. A prickle played along Angie's spine.

"These look like something Teresa would wear," she murmured.

"Teresa? That doesn't make sense," he said.

"Doesn't it? I wonder... From the pictures, Hal Edwards was quite good looking when he was young. Maybe for an older man, he was still decent looking—and everyone said he was a charmer." Angie then shook her head. "But on the other hand, we've heard talk about Teresa and Joey. It makes sense that while Hal was off in Mexico, Joey came back here to the hacienda. Maybe he'd meet Teresa here, in this house. Maybe she'd stay with him during his visits." They exchanged looks that said it was possible.

Paavo then checked the other bedrooms. Two were practically empty, and the third had been used as Hal's office.

Paperwork was scattered everywhere, files opened and riffled, and the computer left on. Angie moved the mouse. Sure enough, a log-on screen appeared, but a password was needed to get past it.

Paavo began sorting through the paperwork quickly, Angie peering over his shoulder. It looked business-related, but old. Probably the last time Hal Edwards used any of it was five years ago.

As Paavo continued with the papers, she took his penlight to look at the dining room and kitchen. She was a cook, after all.

There were no surprises in the dining room. In the spacious kitchen, she went through cabinets and the pantry. At some point, someone had cleared out foodstuffs that could spoil or attract vermin, for which she was grateful.

The refrigerator was not only empty, but off.

From the time she'd entered the kitchen, however, she realized there was something odd about its set up.

A large pedestal table and chairs were in the middle of the room, but instead of being centered, they were so close to the refrigerator it was impossible to open the door all the way. At the same time, the far wall was empty, yet roomy enough that the kitchen table and chairs would have fit nicely. With her mind racing, she pulled the chairs out of the way and shoved the table toward that wall.

Directly under the spot on which the pedestal had stood, a large stain discolored the oak floor. It had a whitish cast, but some darker flecks seemed to have seeped through the old, porous boards.

She drew back. "Paavo!"

As soon as he reached the kitchen, Angie flashed her light on the hardwood. "What do you think happened there? It looks like someone tried to clean it, maybe using bleach."

He looked at how she'd pushed the table aside. "If blood was there, it'll show up with Luminol. I'll get the sheriff to run tests."

"It makes me wonder"—Angie swallowed hard—"if this is where Hal died."

A strange voice filled the room. "What the hell's going on in here?"

"Junior!" Angie turned and stared at the gun in the man's hand.

"Put the gun down," Paavo said. "We aren't dangerous. We're just curious."

"Curious enough to break into someone's house? I think I should call the sheriff."

"Fine," Paavo said. "There are things in this house the sheriff needs to see."

Junior snorted. "Yeah, I heard about you. You're some kind of expert, they say."

"Homicide, San Francisco."

"Homicide?" His eyes darkened. "Nobody wants you snooping around here. This is none of your damn business. Get out!"

"Who are you trying to protect, Junior?" Paavo asked.

"Nobody."

"Yourself? Or is it Teresa?"

"Leave Teresa out of this!" Junior yelled.

"Why? Because she's your daughter?" Angie asked. Now, studying Junior, Angie could see a slight resemblance to Teresa, especially in the eyes. She'd wondered where Teresa had gotten those green eyes. Now she knew, although Junior's were always so bloodshot it had been hard to discern their true color.

"She's in danger," Paavo said. "Someone tried to kill her. Two people have already died. We've got to find out what's going on before anyone else is hurt."

"I don't believe you," Junior snarled, and raised the gun.

"Put the gun down, now!" Paavo repeated in his most forceful tone. "You don't want the kind of trouble this will bring you."

Just then, Junior was knocked hard from behind. The gun flew from his hand, and he landed face first on the floor halfway across the kitchen.

Standing in the doorway, where Junior had been, was the ostrich with the cowlick. Her black eyes gazed adoringly at Paavo and the edges of her beak seemed to curl into a proud smile.

24

———————

The next morning, as Angie approached the Flores home, Joey Edwards was leaving. She ducked behind a telephone pole. Her conjecture about Joey being the reason a couple of Teresa's dresses were left at Hal's was looking ever more correct.

She needn't have worried about Joey noticing her. He seemed preoccupied as he drove off in the opposite direction.

The whole scenario suddenly became quite clear to her.

Somehow, Ned found out that Joey and Teresa were having an affair and were using Hal's house for their tryst. He saw movement in the house, broke in, and attacked someone he thought was Joey. Instead, it was Hal.

So, Ned killed Hal by mistake, and carried him out to the caves. Assuming no one would go in there, so he wouldn't be found for many years, if ever.

But then, Hal's body was found. Ned had to go back to the caves for some reason. And maybe Joey, who realized what had happened, followed Ned. They might have fought, and Joey killed him.

The note that someone had left in Paavo's jacket pocket confirmed her theory.

She was quite pleased at this point—the pieces fit together very well. Now, the search for proof!

She had to admit, she didn't really see either Ned or Joey as a murderer. But then again, if killers were obvious, Paavo wouldn't have a job.

Now that she had everything figured out, Angie decided it was time to resolve these murders—for Doc, for Paavo, and even for herself and what little was left of her vacation.

She was going to confront Teresa—woman to woman—and convince Teresa to admit to Paavo all that had been going on between her and Joey.

With firm determination, she marched up to the house and jabbed the doorbell hard.

Drapes at a nearby window fluttered, as if someone was peeking out. A moment later, Teresa pulled the door open. "This is a surprise," she said. She seemed nervous. "Are you here to see my mother? She's at the hospital."

"I'm here to see you," Angie replied. "There's something I want to talk to you about it."

Teresa invited her in. They went into the kitchen and Teresa got them both some iced tea.

"I saw Joey leaving," Angie said.

"Yes. He's an old friend." Teresa's voice and expression remained glum. "Angie, please tell Paavo I'm sorry about last night. I never should have gone through the church archives without permission. I thought it could help, could end all this quickly, but it turned out I was wrong. Everything I believed was wrong. And I was ashamed. Too ashamed to face Father Armand."

That wasn't exactly what Angie had expected to hear. "What do you mean?"

"It doesn't matter. It means nothing now."

Angie's irritation skyrocketed. She needed an explanation! She was tired of these people and their secrets. "Actually, Teresa, it means a lot." She told Teresa about the clothes she'd found in Hal's home. "They look like they're your size, your style."

Teresa sat back in the chair without speaking for a long moment, then gazed at Angie. "Yes," she said, her expression at once resigned yet almost relieved. "They're mine. I suppose you're wondering how they got there."

"I know how they got there," Angie said. "Your affair with Joey."

"Joey?" Teresa nearly laughed. "Of course not! It was Hal."

If Angie wore false teeth, they would have fallen out right then and there. *"Hal?"* She couldn't quite imagine what Teresa was saying.

Teresa sighed. "I wanted to tell, but my mother said no one would believe me—that they'd say I was just seeing him because of his money. My mother ... she's ashamed of me. I can't say I blame her. I was searching for proof." She chuckled sadly. "But I can't find any."

"Wait... proof? Of your affair?" Angie was beside herself with these riddles.

Teresa shook her head, her eyes staring at a far wall, looking lost. "Perhaps I really was as stupidly young and naïve as my mother said." She drew in her breath. "I feel like a fool saying this, but I truly believed Hal and I were married."

As Paavo headed for the sheriff's office, he saw something that made him pause.

The two "fishermen" had been parked a half block from the sheriff's station and watched it so intently they didn't notice Paavo approach their truck from behind. He tapped on the window and one man automatically reached for the gun under his vest.

"No need for guns," Paavo said. "Let's talk. You can start by telling me who you are."

"Mackenzie," the older man said.

"Cragin," replied the younger. "FBI, Tucson." They showed their badges.

"Any good at cracking computer passwords?" Paavo asked as he looked over the IDs.

"I've been known to, Inspector Smith," Cragin replied, even before Paavo introduced himself. "Whose computer is it?"

"Hal Edwards'."

"I'll definitely do it."

"Good," Paavo said, adding, "And, since you know me and why I'm here, how about giving me some information? What's your interest in all this?"

"Drugs," Mackenzie said. "Nothing more."

Paavo really hated dealing with the Feds. They wanted all the answers and gave none. "What brought you here?" he asked, trying again.

Cragin looked at Mackenzie and waited. Mackenzie nodded.

"This." He took a small, carved obsidian stone from his pocket. "Have you seen one before?"

"Yes."

"Where?"

"Why don't you tell me what it means first," Paavo replied.

"It's a coyote, but this particular one has nothing to do with illegal border crossings," Cragin began. "Years back, there were rumors that Hal Edwards was helping a cartel move drugs into the country, but we weren't involved back then. When Edwards left the country, the rumors ended."

Mackenzie picked up the story. "But then, a couple weeks ago, his body was found in one of the caves we'd heard the cartels used as a staging area for the smuggled drugs. We're here to see if his death is linked to the drug smuggling, and if the cartels are working again in this area. If so, we'll shut them down."

Cragin jumped back in. "We've learned a housekeeper still out at the Edward's Ghost Ranch, had a family member in the cartels, but that guy died a number of years back. It seems the housekeeper, herself, never worked with them. But there's still the question of who killed Edwards, and now this young guy, Ned Paulson. If their murders have to do with drugs or any cartel activities, it's federal, so we're here. Anyway, with how the sheriff was bungling the investigation, we thought we'd have to work the cases ourselves. Good thing you're here, Inspector."

"Glad to be of service," Paavo said sarcastically. "Tell me, was the housekeeper's name Teresa Flores?"

"We can't discuss an ongoing investigation," Cragin said. "But that computer you were talking about might help both of us. We'll get it cracked."

Angie nearly fell off her chair at Teresa's pronouncement. "You thought you were *married* to Hal Edwards? But he was old!" So much for her theory about Joey!

Teresa smiled, misunderstanding Angie's mortification. "Yes, I suppose he would seem old to you. Keep in mind—I married him *five years ago*. I was twenty-nine at the time, which is old to still be unmarried in this area. Hal was sixty-five. But you need to understand, Hal was very special in this town, not only because he gave people jobs in his stores and donated lots of money—until that witch Clarissa stole his stores and most of his money in the divorce—but he'd help people he hardly knew. He saved my grandmother's business and helped my mother when she was having terrible problems with my father. He was always very kind to me.

"I began hanging around the ranch when I was only fifteen, and Hal gave me my first real job at eighteen. I grew up all but worshipping him. I felt safe around him, loved, even cherished. And he was a good-looking man for his age. I worked there for *eleven* years before he ever showed he was interested in me, and by then I was in love with him—a hero-worship kind of love, perhaps, but to me, it felt like love. When he asked me to marry him in secret, how could I refuse? Does that make any sense at all?"

It did, Angie realized, because this was the only world Teresa knew, and Hal Edwards was king here. "It makes sense," she admitted. "But why did he want the marriage to be a secret?"

Teresa shook her head. "I felt part of him was embarrassed to have such a young wife. He didn't want to deal with the behind-the-back snickers and taunts. Also, he wanted to avoid Clarissa's reaction to him remarrying—or her badgering him over Joey's inheritance."

"But once you were married, she couldn't do anything about it," Angie said.

"I know that. But as time went by, I realized something more was going on, that something had scared him badly. He seemed to believed he was in real danger—that someone was after him. He began blaming and fearing everyone, me included. After only a month of being married to me, he began threatening to leave—and one day, he did. Lionel took over running the guest ranch; I stayed, running the staff until our customers dwindled so badly under Lionel, I wasn't needed any longer. I returned to my mother's home."

"I'm sorry," Angie murmured.

"All of us knew Hal was living in Mexico," Teresa continued. "I told my mother that I'd married Hal, and she tried to find our marriage certificate, but she found nothing. She convinced me Hal hadn't really married me—that the whole thing was fake."

Angie shook her head. She couldn't imagine anyone getting

married and not being able to tell the world about it. None of Teresa's story made sense to her, and especially not Hal's attitude. "In this small town, where everyone knows everything, how is it nobody figured out about the marriage? They must have suspected something."

"People knew we were close, but saw it as a father-daughter type relationship, nothing more. If anything, they suspected something between Joey and me. But Joey isn't all that interested in women or men, for that matter. He's simply a loner. And lonely. Sometimes, I think I'm the closest thing to a friend he's ever had. And that's all we are—friends.

"Anyway, Hal and I kept separate quarters on the ranch, though, obviously, a few of my things ended up in his room. Of course, the hacienda's household staff knew something was going on"—her face reddened—"but they assumed it was an affair. Hal paid them well to keep everything a secret—and they wanted to keep their jobs."

Angie's head still couldn't get around this young woman and Hal Edwards as husband and wife, secret or otherwise. "It sounds like your mother was right. There are public records and announcements of marriage you should have found."

"There's also something called a 'confidential marriage' in this state," Teresa explained. "Certain criteria need to be met, and Hal told me his friends in Yuma could arrange a marriage that was sealed from the public. They were most often used when people had lived together and told everyone they were married, and then decided to make it quietly legitimate. As I've said, I truly was young and foolish, and he was my knight in shining armor. I was proud he'd chosen me. I thought our secret marriage was ... romantic."

A secret marriage, Angie thought. No reception to plan. No wedding planner hectoring her. No caterers demanding decisions. No music that had to please three generations of listeners...

Teresa's next, bitter words pulled Angie from her daydream. "Anyway, I believed my mother—that Hal had tricked me. But then, after five years, he came back."

"What happened?"

"I'd thought I was single, and that Hal was never returning. I'd dated, but the experience left me *extremely* cautious of men and their sweet words. Still, I was warming, a lot, to Ned."

Teresa gave a deep sigh. "But when Hal showed up, he was surprised I wasn't living in luxury as his wife. He asked me to forgive him, and said to give him a couple more weeks, then everything would be fine. We would tell the world about our marriage, together. He said he could get through the restrictions on our 'secret' marriage in Yuma, but also, since we'd had our marriage blessed by Father Benedict, there was proof at the church. Hal's marriage to Clarissa had been annulled so that he could marry me. He'd done that for me. So, in the church, as well, there should be proof. That's what I was trying to find when Father Armand caught me the other night. But, in any case, I believed Hal saying we were married. That ended me seeing Ned."

Angie had to ask. "Did Ned know about the marriage?"

Teresa's mouth tightened. "I never told him. I was waiting to see what Hal would do—if he would tell everyone, or if he was lying to me about that."

"Oh, Teresa," was all Angie could say. She couldn't imagine being in such a situation.

"But then Hal vanished again." Teresa stopped speaking a long time. "I couldn't believe he'd run off again—not after the things he'd said to me, the promises he'd made when he came back. Even those pitiful ostriches were his way of showing he was starting up a new business. Apparently, there's a market for them—who knew? But when he took off once more, I could only think I'd been stupid to believe him. Or to believe any man —including Ned."

Teresa stood and walked to the edge of the pergola, looking out at a succulent garden. Angie didn't allow herself to say a word or make a sound. She only listened.

"Hal only returned long enough to turn my life upside down," Teresa said. "I could only hope he was gone permanently this time. But then, Hal's body was discovered, and now my own life is in danger. Ned saw that, even though he didn't know what was wrong. He began searching, asking questions. I begged him to stop. It was too dangerous. Someone here is crazy here."

Her tears began to fall. Angie realized what was coming next, and despite herself, she felt her own eyes well up.

"Ned and I fought," Teresa said. "He wanted answers I wasn't ready to give him. And then, before I had a chance to make amends, or explain anything to him, he was murdered!"

"My God, Teresa."

"The one man I thought I loved, I came to realize was 'hero-worship.' The other man I didn't recognize I loved, I caused to die. How am I supposed to live with being so wrong ... so hateful?"

All Angie could do was to wrap her arms around the woman and hope that time, and faith, and her family could somehow help lessen a suffering that would never completely go away.

25

Angie could scarcely believe it when she saw Paavo and Merry Belle head-to-head and side-by-side in the sheriff's office. That the two fishermen were with them, on the other hand, didn't surprise her at all. Even she knew their spotless L.L. Bean and Patagonia gear was just a cover. All four were pouring over Hal's computer and the sheets of papers spitting out of the printer attached to it.

"I don't mean to bother you," she said to Paavo. "But I'd like to return to the guest ranch. Can I take the Mercedes?"

"If you need wheels," Merry Belle quickly interjected to Paavo, "you can use Buster's Jeep."

"Great, thanks," Paavo said, and handed Angie the SUV's keys.

"Oh, by the way," Angie told them as she was about to step out of the door, "Teresa and Hal had a secret marriage. Teresa just told me about it." With that, she couldn't stop the smug satisfaction from filling her face as she sprang this major information on the professional investigators.

She then returned to the ranch. She had already made out the list of supplies for Lionel and thought she'd double-check it before giving it to him. She'd even come up with a few substitutes for her more exotic ingredients. Such as if no fennel, then leeks; if no leeks, then white onions. Somehow, she'd make this work.

She was still a few feet from the cookhouse when she heard voices coming from it.

Quietly, she approached. Peering in the door, she saw Clarissa and Dolores in deep disagreement over what Dolores would be cooking on Saturday.

Angie backed away. That was one fight she didn't want to get involved in.

"You're doing the smart thing," Lionel said behind her.

She jumped and turned around.

He smirked. "I wouldn't get in the middle of that either. There are too many cleavers and butcher knives close at hand."

"You've got a point," Angie said. She took a folded piece of paper from her pocket. "Here's the list of supplies I need. Do the best you can and let me know soon if you can't find some ingredient."

"Will do." Lionel stuck it in his shirt pocket. "Say, did you ever go treasure hunting?" He looked ready to laugh at her.

"You think I'd wander the desert talking to myself like some old withered prospector?" Angie asked.

"That depends on how interested you are in finding something from the missing stagecoach."

"Oh. Well, I am interested in that. But I haven't found the time."

"No time like the present. I'll take you."

That surprised her. "Really?" She couldn't imagine Lionel wanting to do anything more than absolutely necessary.

"We should take horses," he said.

Angie's memories of her last riding experience—the horse going backwards, sideways, and in figure eights—struck.

Without Paavo and Joaquin Oldwater's help, she didn't know if she could manage. "How about a truck?"

He chuckled and agreed.

She changed into boots and jeans, and soon, they were off.

Brimming with excitement over her good luck at finding Lionel in such an agreeable mood, she couldn't wait to see the place where some of the belongings from the missing stagecoach had turned up.

The chance that Chef van Beerstraeden's journal might still be lost out there was remote, but possible. After all, how many treasure hunters would care about a book filled with recipes? They'd probably toss it away.

She remembered how her sisters and her friend Connie had laughed when she told them she was going to vacation with Paavo in a little desert town in Arizona. Words like "tenderfoot" and "greenhorn" were mirthfully thrown at her.

Well, if her idea worked out, she'd get the last laugh, that was for sure.

And even more so if she brought them out here as her destination wedding site. She felt like Mustang Sally compared to them. And she wasn't talking about Mustang cars.

Or—considering that she was riding in a black GMC truck rather than a ranch horse—maybe she was.

At a bullet-ridden saguaro, Lionel turned off the road and onto a dirt path that was no more than a couple of ruts in the desert sand. Doc had been right when he'd warned that driving over that land was a lot worse than horseback riding. Angie feared the fillings in her teeth would rattle loose before they ever got there. She had no idea the desert was so bumpy.

In the distance, she spotted three flat rocks. The one on the bottom was the largest, the middle was in-between size, and the top was smallest. Her breath caught. The way they were stacked made them look like layers on a…

Could it be?

Small rocks covered the ground. Little whitish ones about the size of candy-coated Jordan almonds so often used as favors at a...

Yes!

The creek wasn't far, and near it she saw a willow with small, shimmering leaves covering branches that bowed low sweeping the ground much like a bride's...

Perfect!

A stand of saguaro looked like a reception line; a small distant hill was shaped like a church organ; barrel cactus looked like ring bearer's pillows.

Her heart filled. Mother Nature seemed to want her wedding to be held here. Did she dare try to move it? How would her family react to a "destination wedding"?

"I haven't quite figured out where you could find things from the stagecoach," Lionel said, "but everyone thinks those people used the caves for shelter. That'd be a place to start."

His words broke her reverie. "You aren't talking about the cave where Hal was found, are you?" she asked.

"I sure am." He gave her a toothy grin.

Joyful wedding thoughts fizzled completely. "No way! There's nothing there and it's spooky."

Lionel, however, didn't turn back.

The atmosphere around the caves felt even creepier than the first time she was there. "I'm not so sure about this," she said as she got out of the truck on the flatland and looked up the incline to the narrow cave entrance.

"Prospectors gotta have a sense of adventure," Lionel said, beginning the steep walk. "Let's see what we can find." Before long, he plunged inside.

She took a deep breath before entering the cave, then stopped near the entrance. It took a moment for her eyes to grow accustomed to the dark. Then, without moving, she scanned the area. The ground was rock hard. Nothing could have escaped anyone's observation in here.

"Hey!" Lionel was on his hands and knees, deep in the cave. "I see something." He was brushing aside some dirt on the ground, near a cave wall.

"You do?" She could scarcely believe it. "What is it?" she asked, stepping nearer.

"I don't know. It's shiny. Like money—or gold coins!" he cried.

"Gold coins?" She was agape. How lucky was this? Forget the cookbook—maybe they found the treasure!

He picked up the object and sat back on his heels as she squatted beside him. "I was wrong. Sorry about that." He held out a brass strip curved into a half circle.

"What in the world is that?" she asked.

He stood, and they both walked outside into the sunlight. "It's just a heel rand. I wonder how in the world it got back there? Maybe this place really is haunted!"

"What's a heel rand?" she asked, taking it from Lionel before he tossed it away.

"Cowboys sometimes put them on the back of their boots, where the leather meets the heel. It protects the leather. More common is when we put metal caps over the toes of our boots. It's all the same thing."

"Oh, my God! I think I know who it belongs to." She'd seen one of those—only one, in fact, on Joey Edwards' boots. It was the same brass color, the same curved design.

"You do?" He looked at her skeptically. "I'd keep a lid on it, if that's the case. It just might belong to Hal's murderer."

Her eyes widened. "It looks like something that might belong to Joey Edwards. If so, he probably came here to look at the site where his father was found. I can't imagine that Joey would kill his own father."

"Don't be so sure." Lionel's mouth twisted into an ugly

grimace. "For one thing, they hated each other. For another, all Joey's money is tied up in the Halmart stores, and word has it they're going down. When Hal showed up with all those birds, Joey might have seen the ruin of this guest ranch and everything else Hal built suddenly staring him in the face. Maybe he got tired of waiting; tired of watching his inheritance going down the drain. That's just my speculation, mind you," Lionel added.

"Are you saying Hal and Joey met when Hal returned in winter?"

"They sure did."

Why had Joey lied? Angie wondered. "Despite that, Hal was his father."

"Yeah, but that only made matters worse. Hell, Hal was twice the man Joey is, especially in the ladies department."

Angie's thoughts went to Hal and Teresa, and she couldn't help but wonder how much Lionel knew.

"All that aside," she continued, "if this heel thingy was here since the time of the murder, don't you think the sheriff would have found it?"

He looked at the brass object a moment. "Ordinarily, I'd be inclined to agree with you. But you've met Monster Bum and Ball-less Buster. Hell, Deputy B wouldn't want to dirty his slacks looking under dirt like I did!"

"You may be right," she whispered as elation slowly built. Suddenly, she grabbed him in a bear hug. "We've done it, Lionel! I can hardly believe it, but we solved the case!"

"If you're right," Lionel said, seeming to enjoy the hug more than she ever expected, "then you'd better get that evidence to your man, pronto."

26

A n hour later Angie entered the sheriff's station. Deputy Buster greeted her with a scowl at her jeans and T-shirt, and directed her to Merry Belle's office.

"All this damn stuff is getting in the way of me doing my regular chores like writing out traffic tickets and such." Merry Belle was complaining to Paavo, her words muffled by a mouthful of chocolate-glazed doughnut.

"Not to worry," Angie announced as she waltzed inside. "Help is on the way." With a big smile, she placed the heel rand on the desk in front of Merry Belle.

"What the hell's that?" the sheriff asked. "Something for cowboy boots?"

Merry Belle's eyes narrowed as Angie explained told how Lionel had found the heel protector in the caves and that she believed it matched the one Joey Edwards was missing. She also said that Joey had lied, according to Lionel, and that he had met and spoken with his father.

As the sheriff listened, her face blazed a deep crimson. Paavo shook his head. The FBI agents looked disgusted.

"What's wrong?" Angie asked.

Paavo explained. "By removing the metal from the crime scene, there's no chain of evidence. We can't use it to connect Joey—or anyone else—to the location with Hal's body."

"Oh," was Angie's chastened reaction. "But Lionel was with me. We both witnessed where we found it ... before bringing it here."

Merry Belle put down her half-eaten doughnut, stood up, glared at them, then stomped over to the window. Her back was to them and they could see her shoulders start to quiver. *"Arrrrgh!"* A visceral, jungle cry erupted from her.

The window glass in front of her seemed to shake and bow. The room quaked as if from a sonic boom. Angie could swear that somewhere in the far distance, a dog howled. She, Paavo, and the FBI agents sat in utter silence, gaping at the sheriff.

"I can't stand it!" Merry Belle sounded angry and on the verge of tears at the same time. "I just want to go back to taking care of my sweet little town, but everyone's against me!"

There was the sound of running footsteps, then a fearful-faced Buster stood in the entry. "Is something wrong, Aunt Merry Belle?"

His words hung suspended in the air as Merry Belle slowly faced him. *"GET-THE-HELL-OUT!"*

Buster beat a hasty retreat.

Merry Belle's attention turned to her stunned audience. She was breathing in great gulps of air, then she stiffened, shut her eyes, and inhaled slowly. Opening her eyes, she marched back to the desk, and seated herself as she stared at the four gawking onlookers.

"What else is wrong?" she whispered with a mixture of hope and despair.

No one said a word.

"Then the rest of you can *get out!*" Merry Belle roared.

"But maybe there's something else I can help with," Angie meekly offered.

It took the three men all they had to keep the sheriff from flying across her desk at Angie.

———

Teresa ended the phone call. She used the excuse that the connection was becoming weaker as she drove. The truth was, she didn't want to hear anything more from Joey.

He was upset that the sheriff had come by to inspect his father's home. There was a stain on the floor that Merry Belle wanted to run tests on. And then she took his boots. She made it clear she wanted to tie him to the caves, to his father's and Ned's murders, and acted as if he should simply confess and get it over with. He swore he had nothing to confess.

He called to insist he hadn't killed anyone. Not Hal, not Ned.

Teresa knew that. No one took the trouble to understand him; they expected him to be like his father, and when he didn't live up, they dismissed him as weak and inconsequential. She felt he could be more than that, and for that reason, they'd become friends. Joey was no killer.

Once, the thought had crossed her mind that a jealous Ned might have done Hal harm. But that wasn't true either. Ned's only mistake was that he loved her and tried to find out who wanted to hurt her. She still couldn't believe he was gone, that she'd never again see him again.

Tears shimmered. She had loved him, but not deeply—and she knew it wasn't the kind of love Ned deserved.

It was the same with Hal. He'd offered her hope. Hope to be free of life in Jackpot, of the boring sameness of it. He'd lamented that her only interest in an old man like him was his money. She'd denied it, but if she were being honest with herself, he was right. She'd been selfish. She'd loved him in her way, but in her heart she knew she had never truly and completely loved anyone. Not the kind of love she saw in

Angie's eyes whenever she talked about, or simply looked at, her fiancé.

She turned onto Doc's driveway. Her mother was remaining at the hospital, and didn't want Teresa home alone. Her thoughts turned to Doc and her mother, and how happy they were simply being in each other's company.

Teresa wondered if she'd ever find that with anyone. That's what was wrong—the curse of her life, the thing she'd have to learn to change if she was ever going to be happy. Her problem wasn't Jackpot, not its people, not even the loneliness of life in the desert. Her problem was her inability ... no, her *fear*... of trusting enough to open her heart to another human being.

How, she wondered, does a person get over being afraid to fall in love?

27

———————

Early the next morning, Paavo went to Doc with news of the latest discoveries. Teresa had already left Doc's house to relieve her mother at the hospital.

Doc was stunned. "A part of me suspected something was going on between Hal and Teresa, but I dismissed it due to the age difference. I decided he was a father figure, nothing more. God knows, with Junior as a father, she didn't have one at home. But I never imagined she'd marry him. I can't imagine how Lupe reacted when Teresa told her." He shook his head at the thought. "Still, I don't believe Hal would have lied to the girl about it. He did some shifty things in his life, but never anything that low. If the marriage records are missing, it's because someone took them."

"Did you know Ned had met with Hal?" Paavo asked.

"No." Doc said and clamped his lips together as if he refused to speak more on that subject.

"Fine." Paavo didn't want to pursue it either. "At least now we know that if there have been attempts on Teresa's life, we have an idea of why. If there once were marriage records, then we know someone besides the Flores women knows about the marriage."

"I see what you're saying," Doc said. "Someone who doesn't want Teresa to inherit."

"Someone—and I'm afraid that someone has to be our sheriff—will have to go to Yuma and find out what really happened to those records."

"Do we really want to let her in on all this?" Doc asked. "If you're talking about official documents, this could be an inside job."

"We have no choice." Paavo's words were firm. "For some reason, I trust her."

"For some reason, I do too." Doc's jaw tightened.

"I know that Teresa and her whole family are strong Catholics," Paavo said, his words cautious and wary. "You realize, don't you, it meant that even if Ned could convince Teresa to leave Hal, and if she couldn't get an annulment, there was only one way he could ever marry her."

"Don't go there, Paavo," Doc said, threateningly. "Ned would never kill anyone."

Paavo wanted to agree, but after all he'd seen on his job, nothing surprised him anymore.

Angie headed for the cookhouse. The day before, as she went to the sheriff's office with the heel rand, Lionel had gone off in search of supplies. She had no idea how far he'd gone, but after breakfast that morning, a grumpy Lionel told her he'd gotten everything she wanted except liver pâté. Of course the fact that he pronounced it "pate" might have had been the reason for his lack of success. Or not. She'd do without the appetizer.

The next day was the big cookout. So, on this day, she planned to do as much of the preparation as possible.

Dolores was making pie crusts. "If you're looking for Señora Edwards," she said, "she just left to go horseback riding. I'm sure if you hurry, you can join her."

The thought of getting back on a horse gave Angie jitters. Between horses wanting to run off with her, ostriches pecking at her, and wild boars—so to speak—chasing her, not to mention encounters with tarantulas and rattlers, she wasn't having a great time, zoologically speaking. "No rides for me," she said. "I'm going to cook the lentils for the *dal* today; peel, seed and boil the butternut squash; and make a sauce for the salmon."

"I don't know exactly what your *dal* is, but generally, the longer food marries, the better it tastes."

"I show you what it is as I make it," Angie said.

"Good. Mr. Edwards used to like my Mexican cooking, but sometimes I'd surprise him with special dishes. He always appreciated them. He said I was the best cook he'd ever known." Dolores smiled fondly at the memory.

Angie was impressed. "That's high praise for a man who had the money to go to many of the top restaurants in the country, I'm sure."

"I thought the same thing," Dolores said emphatically.

As they worked, Angie remembered that Dolores had lived here some forty years. There had to have been a lot that she'd seen. "You knew Mr. Edwards well," Angie began. "After he came back last winter, did you think he'd leave so soon?"

"I don't know," Dolores said.

"Were you surprised to learn he hadn't left, but that he'd died?"

"Oh, yes." Dolores nodded. "I was very surprised. Very sad."

Angie would have really liked to know what Dolores thought. She tried again. "The sheriff said his death was from natural causes, but now people think he was murdered. What do you think?"

Dolores pursed her lips a moment. "He was a good man, a good boss. I don't think anyone would kill him."

Well, this was going nowhere fast, Angie thought. She proceeded to work on her dishes, and the two chatted amiably about food and cooking techniques.

The time passed quickly, and Angie was surprised when Clarissa enter the kitchen. "There you are," she said to Angie. "LaVerne brought over something special for you to try."

Again? Angie thought. The woman should have been named Lucretia Borgia. "I'm working on the meal for the cookout."

"Doesn't matter. You've got to taste it while it's warm."

"I'm not falling for that again," Angie said.

"What does that mean?" Clarissa asked, but before waiting for an answer, added, "Come on, you don't want to disappoint LaVerne. She especially asked for you. You're a gourmet cook."

"Like she is?" Angie asked.

"Exactly."

"Try it yourself." Angie went back to her *dal.*

"I plan to." Clarissa marched off.

Angie and Dolores looked at each other in astonishment. This, they couldn't miss. They hurried after Clarissa.

Lionel and Joey were already in the dining room. Near the back door, Junior was watching from safety. He obviously remembered LaVerne's goat cheesecake.

Junior must have felt Angie's scrutiny, because he seemed to grow uncomfortable and left to go do whatever he did on the ranch.

LaVerne stood proudly over a bowl. "Here it is."

Angie looked down at some kind of meat in a red sauce. After her experience with the cactus, she wasn't about to take any chances. "What is it?"

"It's another secret family recipe. Arizona stew."

Angie was aware of the others watching her. She knew why

these were secret recipes—no one else wanted them. "What kind of stew?"

"Rabbit," LaVerne said. "Right from this area."

"Rabbit?" Clarissa said, shocked. "I don't eat rabbit!"

"But it's gourmet rabbit," LaVerne explained. "For the cookout."

"Oh, all right." Clarissa took the spoon, scooped up a piece with meat and tasted. "It has an aftertaste." Her mouth wrinkled. "Something very ... different."

The others all leaned closer.

"That's what makes it special." LaVerne stood tall. "An Arizona treat. Horned toad. Dried, salted, then shredded. Just half a toad gives a lot of flavor. Want me to serve it to your guests?"

Angie gasped.

Dolores chuckled.

Clarissa looked horror stricken. Trying to keep some semblance of dignity, she hurried from the room.

LaVerne's jaw dropped, her brow furrowed, and she looked quizzically at the astounded people still around her. "Do you think that's a 'no'?"

28

"Those ostriches are a good metaphor," Teresa said when Angie opened her cottage door to a gentle knock later that afternoon. "Have I been hiding my head in the sand, too, not seeing what's around me?"

Angie invited Teresa in, but looked over the birds as she shut the door. All were females, and none had found a mate to share a life with. Of course, smelling like rotten eggs and being champion kick-boxers would tend to scare off males ... but here, there simply weren't any males for them.

Teresa's metaphor might be more accurate than she first thought.

"My mother didn't want me to come here," Teresa said. She wore jeans and a black t-shirt, no makeup, and her long hair was pulled back in a low ponytail. Her face looked tired and haggard, as if she hadn't slept well for days. "She's still nervous about Joey and Clarissa. I think she's wrong."

Angie was nervous about them as well. "If your mother is right, this isn't a safe place for you to be."

"Yes, if she's right. But I've known Joey for years. I don't believe he's a killer. Hal never forgave him for siding with his mother when they divorced, or for leaving the ranch to live with her. Hal was right—Joey was weak, but despite what Hal thought, Joey actually loved and admired his father. He simply never admitted it, especially not around his mother who's never been anything but bitter."

"I have to agree on the last part," Angie admitted. "I can't help but think everything will change for the better if a will turns up."

Teresa drew in her breath before continuing. "That's why I'm here. I remember a hiding spot Hal had. It was usually empty, but I want to check it out."

"A hiding spot?" Angie's eyes widened.

Teresa couldn't help but smile. "Don't get your hopes up. It's probably as empty as ever, but at this point, I've got to see it for myself."

They were hurrying across the plaza to the hacienda when Lionel popped up. "Well, look who's back," he said, eying Teresa.

"Hello, Lionel." Teresa's expression looked like she'd rather step on him than have a conversation.

"You hoping to find someone to give you work?" he asked with a smirk. "Guess I'm the one who hires and fires around here these days. Leastways, until Saturday, when the estate is divvied up."

"I don't want work." She glanced at Angie, and then said, "I'm looking for Joey. Have you seen him?"

"He took off an hour or so ago. Clarissa was riding him real good. He's probably at the Stagecoach Saloon."

"Poor guy," Teresa said.

"Poor?" Lionel snorted. "Not likely. Want me to tell him you were looking for him? I'm sure he'll be real happy to hear it."

"That's fine."

"We'll be in the common room," Angie added, linking her

arm with Teresa's and moving away from Lionel. "If Joey returns soon, I'm sure he'll join us."

"He won't be back before happy hour ends, that's for sure," Lionel said with a smirk.

They walked on, feeling Lionel's eyes watching them.

From the common room, Angie and Teresa waited until Lionel disappeared in his trailer, then they hurried to the hacienda.

The front door was visible from the plaza, so they went in the back. The doorjamb had been repaired, and the door locked, but Teresa's old key worked. Angie quickly realized this wasn't the sort of area where people thought to change their locks.

As Teresa wandered through the house, Angie couldn't imagine what it must have been like for her knowing she'd once been married to the owner of all this, and that if their marriage had been done openly, it all might have gone to her.

Teresa visibly paled at the blood-stained kitchen floor. When she saw the torn up floorboards, she murmured that her mother might be correct—there could well be danger here.

She headed up to the bedroom and blanched at the sight of drawers opened and clothes on the floor. She lifted one of her dresses from the floor, then threw it back down. "Clarissa saw this?"

"I'm sure she did," Angie said, looking at the strange heap and shaking her head.

"She had to have realized it was mine. I wonder if Joey noticed it."

"I don't know," Angie said, wondering why Teresa cared.

Teresa went into the room Hal had used as an office and went straight to his desk. She opened a drawer, removed the papers from it, and then lifted out a secret bottom. Angie gawked in surprise.

There was nothing in the drawer except some Mexican pesos in high denominations, and a small carved black stone.

"Oh, no," Teresa murmured as she picked up the small object.

"What is it?" Angie asked.

Teresa shook her head. "It's an amulet. Mexican. Foolish old man!"

Angie realized it was the same as the one Paavo had found at Ned's. "Is that the symbol of the coyotes? The people who transport illegals across the border?"

"Those people are called coyotes, but that isn't what this is." Teresa put the amulet in her pocket and restored the drawer the way it had been. "It answers a question for me."

"What question?" Angie asked.

Teresa turned away. Angie thought she wasn't going to answer, but then she said, "It's a symbol of a drug cartel. They could have given it to Hal because he was helping them ... or as a warning because he wasn't. As to which it meant, who knows? But whichever, it could have had a lot to do with why he left the first time, or maybe why he was killed when he came back."

"Has it been there long, do you think?" Angie asked.

"I'm not sure. When I was with Hal ... as his wife, I looked here a couple of times to see if Hal was hiding anything that would give me a clue as to what was troubling him. But it was always empty. After he disappeared, I never thought to look here again."

"Paavo found a similar coyote charm at Ned's house."

All the color left Teresa's face. "Ned's? No, impossible. He wouldn't get mixed up with cartels." She shook her head.

"Do you have a key to Ned's place, or know where he kept a spare one hidden?" Angie asked suddenly.

"I know where he kept one hidden, yes, but—"

"Then, let's go. I want you to see the amulet he has, to make sure it's not one of these." Angie thought they should pick up Paavo on the way, as well. Teresa might know more than she thought, and Paavo needed to hear about it. "I think it's a clue as to who killed him and Hal—a big clue."

Teresa looked nervous. "Maybe."

"We'll go then?" Angie asked.

"Yes."

"Let's pick up Paavo as we go through town," Angie added.

"No," Teresa said. Her next words made Angie suddenly uneasy. "There's a back way to the lake that's a lot faster."

The road was rutted and unpaved. It followed Ghost Hollow Creek to the Colorado River, bypassing the town. Also, from that road, a person could veer north into the foothills and high desert plains. The land was all but untouched by humans, except for a few fire roads and old Indian trails.

Teresa was driving her big Ford pickup. As they rode through the silence, Teresa told Angie stories of her life after Hal disappeared, and how Ned started coming around more and more. She soon realized that his feelings for her were much more than friendship, and it troubled her.

She tried hard to ignore him but—

A sound, much like a backfire, caused the women to jump and turn in their seats.

"What—" Angie began, as Teresa sped up.

"Someone just shot at us," Teresa yelled.

"Shot at us?" Angie cried. She clutched the dashboard. "Maybe it's a mistake. Maybe you had a blow-out."

Another shot sounded as the ping of a bullet hit the roof. Teresa drove off the road toward the creek. "That's no blow-out," Teresa said.

"Hurry! Can't this truck go any faster?" Angie cried. A rear tire exploded, making the truck jostle and jerk.

Teresa floored the gas pedal, but the truck was straining badly.

"Who's doing this?" Angie cried. "How do we stop them?"

"I wish I knew."

Reaching the brush along the bank of the creek, the truck continued forward only a few feet before the land dropped precipitously. The truck died in a tangle of shrubbery and vines. "Run," Teresa shouted.

"Run?" Angie could barely get the word out. "You're kidding me, right?"

But Teresa had already opened the driver's side door, leaped to the ground, and headed toward the creek.

Angie was petrified, frozen, when she realized that was the worst spot for her. She forced herself from the passenger side, clutching her purse against her chest as if it might protect her from a bullet, then dropped low and left the truck. She scurried, stumbled, and slid down the bank, then half-crawled after Teresa. "Wait!"

"Hurry!" Teresa ran along the bank.

With her heartbeat so loud it was drumming in her ears, Angie eventually found her footing and followed Teresa.

Breathless, they both soon stopped, crouching together behind some scrub. "We've got to find a place to hide," Teresa said, panting.

Angie was also taking deep breaths. "Can we make it back to the hacienda?"

"It's about six, seven miles," Teresa answered, breathless.

"What about the lake?"

"About the same."

"You're right," Angie said. "Let's find a place to hide."

They crept further through the thicket.

Teresa paused and looked around. "I recognize this area."

"You do?"

"Remember, I lived and worked at the hacienda for years. I know the land." Teresa headed east. "This way."

At a bend in the creek, she found a grooved area, not exactly a cave, more like a hollow just a couple of feet deep. They crawled behind the brush and huddled inside, facing outward to search for any sign of danger. They waited, hoping against hope that their pursuer wouldn't find them.

As they waited, Angie realized what sixth sense had made her take her purse. Her cell phone was in it.

29

———————

Paavo hung up the phone.

He was in Merry Belle's office and had just finished speaking with the handwriting expert he'd often gone to for help in San Francisco. For a preliminary reaction, he had faxed the man a copy of the note that had been put in his pocket. It had been written on newsprint—some white space on the weekly *Jackpot Press Democrat.*

The fact that the writing was done in a childish block print could mean the writer was young or poorly educated, but it more likely meant that he or she had watched a TV show or movie which stated that block printing was the easiest way to disguise one's handwriting. The expert didn't think reviewing the original rather than a fax would do much good, and went on to lament the popularity of shows that gave away such valuable information and made police work ever more difficult.

Paavo thanked the expert and turned back to Merry Belle. He hated that he'd reached another dead end.

That had been the same result the day before. Agent Cragin managed to break into Hal's computer, only to discover that nothing important was on it. The only thing of interest, in fact, was that Hal had used "4clarissa" as his password. It gave Paavo pause that even after so many years, it was Clarissa's name that Hal had chosen. All in all, it seemed rather sad.

He and the FBI agents searched the computer's documents for a will. They found a generic form, but none of the blanks had been filled in.

They also read through old e-mails, trying to find any indication of why Hal might have taken off, or why he might have been killed. What they found was typical of older people—he had scarcely used his new, high-powered technology.

Paavo didn't know if it was because this case was cleaner than most or because he was in this unknown territory with none of the usual forensic and crime lab information, but all he was doing was growing increasingly frustrated at the lack of evidence and detail he had to work with. It seemed it wasn't a case that would be solved by forensics, but by understanding the emotions of the people involved. There were two layers— one, what everyone was saying and doing, and the other, what they were feeling. He had gathered about as much as he could of the first. He would have welcomed some straight talk about the second.

His cell phone rang. It was Lupe Flores. She was with Doc. The two were worried about Teresa, who had gone to see Angie earlier in the day. Lupe tried Teresa and Angie's cell phones, but neither worked, and no one answered the guest ranch number.

"I left Angie at the cabin," Paavo said. "I'll go see what's going on."

For a long while, Angie all but held her breath to be sure she made absolutely no noise. When her nose began to tickle from the nearby sage, she almost panicked. Fortunately, the tickle went away.

After an hour of silence, though, boredom began to set in. She took her cell phone from her handbag and tried to make a call. There was no service. So much for being clever.

"Why is it," Angie whispered, "that there's phone service at the cave where Hal's body was, and none out here?"

"There's service at the caves?" Teresa asked.

"Yes. I don't get it."

"Me neither—unless someone put equipment out there—boosters or receptors or whatever. Why would anyone do that?"

"Makes no sense to me," Angie said, but then offered. "If drug dealers are involved..."

Teresa looked thoughtful, but didn't respond.

Minutes slowly ticked by, an hour seeming like an eternity, until Angie couldn't take it any longer. "What do you think about making a run for it?" she whispered.

"Run where?" Teresa glanced at her. "We don't know where the shooter is, if he's given up, or is sitting out there waiting for us to move. He can be anywhere between here and the hacienda, just waiting for us to return."

Angie recognized the logic of that, much as she didn't like it. "Okay, let's think about this. Whoever is after us has got to be someone from the guest ranch. They're the only ones who saw us leave, right? All we know is it's not Clarissa. She's no shooter."

"But she is," Teresa countered. "She used to enjoy skeet shooting. Hal told me she was good at it. I can see her thinking of me as nothing more than a clay pigeon! Also, she could easily have paid someone—a stranger, or someone in town who wanted money, which could be just about everyone in this area. Maybe she hired someone who wants to leave here so badly that he'd do anything at all to get enough money to go."

Angie had the eerie feeling that Teresa was, in a sense, describing herself.

"Do you want to take the chance of leaving this hiding place while it's daylight?" Teresa asked.

"No," Angie admitted, cautiously eyeing her companion. "It's not worth the risk. If whoever wants us dead is still out there waiting, with this wide-open desert, we wouldn't have a chance. Night can't come soon enough."

Paavo rushed into the bungalow to see if Angie had left him a note. The door was unlocked, which wasn't like her. Growing up in a city, she never left anything unlocked if she could help it.

There was no note in the bungalow, but it felt different—violated—as if someone else had been there. When he looked around, however, he saw nothing amiss.

The cookhouse was empty, as was the common room.

On his way to the office he spotted Junior leaving the stables. He was wiping grit from his face, as if he'd just gotten back from a ride. Paavo called to him.

A rebellious sneer flickered across the man's features. He skulked closer. "You want me for something?"

"I heard Teresa came here to meet Angie. Have you seen either one this afternoon?"

"Hell, no," Junior said. "I been out on the range with those stupid, ugly, smelly, filthier than dirt birds."

Paavo eyed him sharply. "Come with me."

He rapped on the trailer door. Lionel stuck his head out. "Oh..." he gulped at Paavo's fierce expression, then came out. "Something wrong?"

"I'm looking for Teresa Flores and Angie," Paavo said.

"Uh... Teresa?" Lionel acted as if he never heard of her.

"She was here."

"Oh?"

"Listen, Lionel," Junior spoke up, "I know you sure as hell

don't miss a god-damned thing that happens on this ranch, so what the hell did you see?"

Lionel glanced at Junior, then said, "Oh, *that* Teresa. Didn't you see her, Junior?"

"I was feeding the ostriches," Junior mumbled.

"So you did see her," Paavo said to Lionel. "Did you talk to her?"

"She was looking for Joey," he said.

"Joey!" Junior roared.

"That's all I know. Then, Buster showed up."

"What was Buster doing here?" Paavo asked.

"Said he was looking for Miss Angie. I told him she might be in the common room with Teresa, but apparently he couldn't find her there. In fact, there goes Buster now. I wonder where he's been all this time."

Paavo turned to see Deputy Buster's old Jeep pulling out from behind the workhouses. At the same time, Joey darted out from the common room and hurried across the plaza toward his bungalow.

Lionel waved. "Joey! Come on over!"

"Me? Why?" Joey asked.

"Have you seen Angie or Teresa?" Paavo asked. At Joey's confused expression, he added, "They were together, here, early this afternoon. No one's seen them for hours, apparently. Did you?"

"No. I was taking a walk, trying to clear my head," Joey said. "Teresa's missing?"

"Were you just talking to Buster?" Paavo asked.

"Buster?" He looked around nervously. "No. I'd rather not have anything to do with him. Is he here?"

Lionel suddenly found his tongue. "Come to think of it, I saw a truck that may have been Teresa's leave the ranch earlier."

"Back to town?" Paavo asked.

"No. It went the other way," Lionel said, scratching his chin stubble. "Out the back road toward the lake."

"If they broke down on that back road, no wonder no one has heard from them," Joey exclaimed. "I'll get a truck and look for them. It's four-wheel-drive territory."

"I'll call the sheriff," Lionel said.

"Tell her to search the main road. Joey and I will take the back road to the lake," Paavo said, then to Joey, "We'll use both our vehicles. We can cover more territory that way."

"I'm sure they're all right," Joey offered. "Teresa knows the desert."

"I hope so," Paavo said, although with a killer around here, it wasn't the desert that worried him.

This had to have been one of the longest days of Angie's life. Not even the occasional rustle of a leaf broke the absolute stillness. In fact, there were no leaves, just prickly desert scrub and cactus. There was no wind. Not even a stray animal or bird.

Angie thought she'd lived a hundred years before night fell.

Most desert creatures had the sense to stay sheltered during the day. They came out at night.

The night was dark now. Beyond dark. Pitch black.

Owls hooted. Coyotes howled, and sounded very, very near. Angie couldn't help but wonder what else was out there.

Quietly, the two women talked.

Angie told Teresa about her family and growing up in San Francisco as the fifth daughter of a wealthy shoe store owner turned real estate investor. Teresa told her about growing up in Jackpot, the only daughter of a woman who worked hundred hour weeks in her restaurant.

Teresa had vowed her life would be better. Maybe that was part of Hal's attraction—a large part, Angie imagined. Around the time Hal left, Maritza's health began to deteriorate, and Lupe needed Teresa to help her with both the restaurant and her grandmother. She felt stuck.

Angie understood how, given that, she couldn't just up and leave. As they talked, they found a lot in common—love of family, respect for their parents' toils, and wondering if they could ever do anything with their own lives to make a difference.

Now, hungry and thirsty, they decided to make a move.

Stiff and sore, crouching low, they made their way back to the truck, listening for footsteps or any indication that whoever had been stalking them was still around. They heard nothing.

The truck held food and water. Teresa took three water bottles from the truck. They shared one, saving the others for their long walk back to the guest ranch—or wherever cell service would work again.

Angie's real hope, though, was with Paavo. Once he returned to the bungalow and discovered she wasn't there, he would come looking for her.

He'd find her. Wouldn't he?

"What food do you have?" she asked.

Teresa pulled out one can of chili beans, another of Vienna sausages, and a can opener.

"That's it?" Angie said, trying to keep the disappointment out of her voice. She wasn't a fan of Vienna sausages—the meat in them was always a little too soft to suit her, and what was that gelatinous stuff they sat in?

"It's pre-cooked and nourishing," Teresa said, waving a can as temptation. "We don't dare build a fire."

"You're right," Angie conceded.

Teresa opened both cans and set them on flat rocks. She lifted out a sausage, as did Angie.

Dejection settled like a shroud as Angie stared at her makeshift dinner. She hadn't eaten since breakfast. The front of her stomach was touching the back, and all she could think about was how much she wished she were with Paavo instead of stuck out here with a strange woman and a crazy killer with a rifle.

She dipped her sausage into the can of chili beans and then gave a deep sigh as she morosely took a bite, then another. At least it was more edible than LaVerne's food.

In seconds they'd devoured the food.

"Let's hope Paavo gets here soon," Angie said.

"Stiff upper lip," Teresa said encouragingly. "We can do it."

They skulked closer to the road, both anxious to be on their way back, despite their intent to wait.

Light flashed in the distance. Angie gripped Teresa's arm and pointed.

It was a set of headlights, and a second set followed not far behind. It was the first set, though, that intrigued Angie. High and wide like on a truck or SUV, it wasn't a "normal" headlight set, but Xenon hyper-whites. The only car she'd seen in Jackpot with those headlights was the Mercedes she had convinced Paavo to rent.

She grabbed the knapsack, rummaging madly through it until she found the flashlight, and ran toward the road.

"What are you doing?" Teresa tried to grab and stop her, but missed.

"It's Paavo," Angie called, still running.

"Wait! You've got to be sure."

"I am sure." She frantically waved the flashlight toward the vehicles.

Suddenly, the lead car slowed, then made a U-turn and stopped. The second car did the same.

Doors slammed.

Angie stood as if glued to the spot, praying she'd been right.

Fear that she'd made a deadly mistake kept her quiet until Paavo called her name.

"I'm here!" she shouted, relief and joy propelling her forward.

He met her half way. "Are you all right?" he asked, holding her tight.

"Yes." She nestled against him. He felt so good, so warm and secure, that she nearly cried. "We were shot at—and Teresa's truck tire blew out and we ended up in some brush, nearly off the bank and into the creek."

Joey hurried toward Teresa. "Someone shot at you?" Joey asked. He hugged her, and for a moment she let him, but then pulled away and folded her arms as if she were cold.

"Did you see anything? Any sign to tell who it was?" Paavo asked.

"We couldn't see anyone," Teresa replied, moving toward them. Joey stood back and watched her go.

"We were trying to go to Ned's," Angie said. "We should still do it so Teresa can see the amulet he had. She found one hidden in Hal's office."

"In his office?" Paavo asked, then peered into the darkness. "Let's get out of here. We need to talk."

30

———

Paavo, Angie and Teresa piled into the Mercedes SUV, while Joey went off on his own to call for a tow truck to take care of Teresa's vehicle.

Teresa listened with growing sadness as Paavo explained to her that the obsidian carving was no longer at Ned's home, and that the FBI agents had confirmed Hal's involvement with a group of drug smugglers in the past—before he left for Mexico.

"Everything makes more sense now," Teresa said bitterly.

"What do you mean?" Paavo asked.

"When Hal brought the ostriches to his ranch, I asked him how he was going to handle them." Teresa folded her hands. "If he was going to breed, raise, and sell or slaughter them, he'd need help. It wasn't the sort of thing people in town would be interested in, I was sure. He said help wasn't needed. I didn't understand at the time, but now I think I do. The ostriches were a cover, a means for people not to question that Hal still had money coming in—drug money. Caves are often used as places to move drugs—caves like on Hal's land. The fact that cell phone service was available out there makes sense now, doesn't it? He must have put some kind of system out there. The whole thing was a plan to make money. He had money, but he was obsessed with becoming as rich as he'd been when he had Halmart stores."

"If that's what the cave would be used for, why was Hal's body put in it after he was murdered?" Angie asked. "That doesn't make sense to me."

"Maybe it was a message—telling the cartel drug smugglers that the land, the cave, was no longer a safe haven," Teresa said. "Or what would happen to anyone who tried to double-cross them."

"Who would want to give a warning like that?" Angie asked. "Ned? He also had an amulet."

"I don't know," Teresa insisted. "But I do know Ned couldn't have been involved in Hal's murder."

"If he found the amulet somewhere," Paavo said, "it might have told him what Hal was involved in."

"Ned was trying to find out who wanted to hurt me," Teresa said, blinking back tears. "But his searches, instead, led him to Hal's killer."

After Paavo and Angie brought Teresa back to Doc's house, they headed for Merritt's Café.

Paavo called Merry Belle from the car. He needed to give her the latest information. She was in a particularly bad mood when Paavo called, not only because she'd been asleep, but because she couldn't find Deputy Buster. He wasn't at the station, and hadn't been since early afternoon.

LaVerne, on the other hand, was delighted to see Angie and Paavo enter the diner. She practically sang the words, "I'll bring you something extra special."

"No!" Angie shouted. "I want something off your regular menu. Something basic, like chicken potpie. Wait, on second thought, I don't want to eat bird." Visions of ostriches came to her. Would she ever be able to eat fowl again? "Let's make that pot roast."

"Pot roast?" LaVerne looked stricken. "But you're a gourmet cook. Gourmets don't eat pot roast! I've got something extra special in the freezer. It'll heat up real fast. It's a thick turtle soup—made from Arizona turtles. Or tortoises. I never can remember which is which. But anyway, you'll love it. Not as much as my prairie dog soufflé, but those stupid Feds followed when I left the diner with my shotgun, so I couldn't get any this morning."

"So you always knew the fishermen were Feds?" Angie asked.

"Of course!" LaVerne said with a huff. "They first came around when Hal showed up with his ostriches. Then, they came back when his body was found. What else could they be? Maybe looking for drug smugglers that used to frequent this area."

"You knew about the drugs as well?" Paavo asked.

"I've got eyes, ears, and a brain, don't I?" LaVerne said, indignantly. "I've been reading about it in a few 'special' internet sites I go to, plus my shortwave radio. Forget talk radio and podcasts—shortwave is where you get the real story!"

"Why didn't you say anything earlier?" Angie asked.

"I did! To you." LaVerne looked affronted.

"But you said there were terrorists involved," Angie pointed out.

"Well?"

Angie stared at LaVerne. It all sounded remarkably far-fetched. She was surprised that Paavo offered no objections. Maybe the world was far-fetched these days.

LaVerne frowned in dismay at them both. "I'll bring you my turtle soup." With that, she turned and walked away.

"No, you won't!" Angie shrieked, and then stood. LaVerne

gawked at her. "I don't want your turtle soup. I don't want any of your so-called gourmet foods! You're as much a gourmet as Roseanne Barr is anorexic! I'm hungry, I'm tired, I'm sick of the way everybody gives us only half-truths but all of you know exactly what's going on. You're wasting my vacation!" As LaVerne backed toward the kitchen, Angie marched after her. "All I've eaten since breakfast is beanie-weenies. I want real food! No turtles, no prairie dogs, no javelina, and definitely no toads! I want something I can eat and enjoy!"

LaVerne flatted herself against the door to the kitchen, mouth agape. Suddenly, her face crumpled. "That is the meanest thing anyone's ever said to me! Not even Clarissa was so cruel when she didn't like my rabbit-and-horned toad stew. You're just jealous of my cooking, that's all!" She took off her bifocals to wipe sudden tears. "I know others around here don't appreciate it, but I expected you would! Pardon me for being so wrong. I'll go get your boring pot roast!"

It was late when Angie and Paavo returned to the guest ranch. All was quiet, but Angie knew the next day would bring work-men, cooks, and chaos as the big cookout finally happened.

Instead of going inside, they stopped on the porch of their cottage, and turned to face the night and the plaza.

"I can't help but feel," Paavo said, his thumbs hooked to his pockets as he surveyed the surroundings, "that all our questions about these deaths will come to a close tomorrow, and that, if we're lucky, the pieces will finally fall into place."

"What do you think is behind this? Drug smuggling? The inheritance?" she asked, hooking his arm with hers and leaning close.

"If whoever killed Hal was interested in the inheritance, why hide Hal's body? They'd have made it look like an accident or suicide and collected."

"So … the drug smugglers?"

"It's possible, sure, but why? If anything, it seems Hal was planning on working with them. No, it's something else." Paavo was quiet a long moment. "Hal's paranoia grew after he married Teresa. Only one month later, he ran from the country. Maybe it was because of the cartel—maybe at first he said he wouldn't work with him, and they threatened him. But that's only speculation."

"None of it makes sense."

"We're missing something," Paavo said firmly. "But we'll find it. Hopefully, tomorrow."

"And the day after that," she murmured, "if things are settled here, we'll be going back home. I wish we'd had more time to simply enjoy this area." Angie rested her head against his shoulder.

"I'm surprised at how much I've remembered," Paavo said, wrapping an arm around her. "Good memories about Doc, Joaquin ... Ned. Even as a boy I loved the desert on nights like this. The quiet, the peace."

Stars seemed so close she felt as if she could reach up and touch them. After the dinginess and sadness of the town, the guest ranch was like a different world. The plaza sparkled nearly white in the moonlight. No wonder Hal had built this home as a sanctuary. It would, in fact, make a wonderful destination-wedding site. Not hers, though. She knew too much about the town and it held too many sad memories for that.

"Despite everything," she said. "I have to admit that this area is lovely. I can see why you enjoyed coming here as a boy."

His voice was little more than a whisper as he said, "I wish I'd realized, as a boy, how kind these people were to me, how open and friendly."

"You couldn't tell?" She glanced up at him, surprised.

His gaze seemed to turn inward. "I didn't let myself know. I was a tough little kid, and did all I could to shut people out, to not let them get close."

"You did it to protect yourself from more loss," she said, holding him closer. "I can understand it. At least, you've grown older and wiser. You can see it now."

"It isn't that I've grown wiser." Blue eyes caught hers. "It's that the barrier was broken down."

"Broken down? What do you mean?"

"You, Angie." One finger lightly brushed her cheek. "Without you, that little boy would still be outside, looking in."

She smiled at him, her big detective who could fight hardened criminals, but was just a big softie when it came to love. His admitting as much caused her heart to swell. "If that's the case," she whispered, lifting her face to his, "I couldn't be more grateful."

31

———————

Merry Belle walked into her office the next morning. It was quiet, which was good. She didn't see Buster—and that wasn't.

Last night when she joined Paavo and Angie at Merritt's, she hadn't planned to eat dinner as Paavo filled her in on the evening's events. But Angie's pot roast looked too good to pass up.

Between having eaten two dinners and the fact that some loony with a gun had bushwhacked Teresa Flores and Paavo's little girl friend, Merry Belle hadn't slept a wink all night. Not to mention the exposure of Hal Edwards' illegal activities. She'd long suspected Hal's ties to drug smuggling, given the way some known cartel members descended on the town when he returned and then—*poof!*—he disappeared and so did they.

Somehow, she had to find Hal and Ned's killer—she figured it had to be the same person; the town wasn't big enough for *two* killers—so the Frisco cop and the Feds would leave, and the town could go back to being the sleepy little haven she loved and protected.

"Where the hell is Buster?" Merry Belle demanded from the

night deputy sleepily sitting at the front desk where Buster should have been.

"Don't know. He hasn't called in."

As the sheriff poured herself a cup of coffee, she frowned. "You call his place?"

"Couple times. Either he ain't home or just don't want to answer."

"He phones in, you make sure he talks to me," Merry Belle said as she marched into her office slamming the door behind her. She sat at her desk and glanced up at the picture of the governor on the opposite wall. As a little pick-me-up, she took a Mr. Goodbar from a drawer and chomped into it.

The telephone rang.

"Buster, you mealy mouthed—oh." It wasn't him. It was the crime lab in Phoenix calling with some results.

Merry Belle gulped down the mouthful of chocolate as she listened, then shared a smile with the governor. The blood on the kitchen floor in the hacienda had been Hal Edwards' and the heel protector was definitely from Joey's boots. Now, if only she could find a way to tie those two facts together.

Joey had to be the killer. Goodbye, Joey Edwards! Patricide should be worth the death penalty, minimum.

Still ... she wished she didn't have this nagging feeling of uncertainty. Paavo clearly had his doubts and Merry Belle was more uneasy than she cared to admit. She had the evidence, though. What else did she need?

A little after seven that same morning, Angie's phone-alarm woke her. There was already activity outside in the plaza area. She got out of bed and with as little noise as possible prepared for the day, trying not to wake Paavo.

Outside the bungalow were a half-dozen men Angie had

never seen before working to pitch an enormous tent in front of the hacienda. Others rushed about with hammers and wood.

The ostriches had the sense to stay out of their way. She didn't blame them.

As she crossed the plaza to the cookhouse, Lionel spotted her. He bent over an ice chest, pulled a beer from it, and raced her way.

"This is gonna be something" he said. Angie reeled from the blast of early morning beer breath. "Gonna give Hal a real send off," Lionel went on excitedly. "And maybe it's the last time I gotta put up with Clarissa and her brat."

"Why would you think that? Won't Joey get the property?"

"Not if the sheriff arrests him for killing Hal," he said with a smirk. "I'm thinking she just wants to wait until after she's done eating her fill. When do you think she'll do it?"

"That's up to her—if she thinks she has enough evidence," Angie replied.

"Hell, what more does she need? She's got the heel protector," Lionel insisted. "Now we can really celebrate."

Angie was surprised to find that Paavo's doubts about Joey's guilt had crept into her thoughts as well. "It takes time to build a case."

"Sheriff Moon Bottom damn well better not take too long! Doc's gonna be here this evening to divvy up Hal's estate," Lionel whined. "Hal's killer shouldn't get his money. It should go to a relative who loved him. Like me!"

Yeah, right. She wanted to say everything should go to Hal's widow, Teresa. But this wasn't the time, and it wasn't her place to bring it up, especially without proof. Instead, she backed away. "I have to get to the cookhouse, Lionel, and prepare my contribution to the feast."

Lionel seemed lost in thought a moment, then jerked in reaction to her words. "Okay. Might be Joey's last good meal for a spell—if the sheriff does what's right. Maybe Clarissa's, too."

"You must really hate them." Angie was fascinated by the malice that filled Lionel's face.

"Me? I don't hate nobody," Lionel declared, then grinned. "I just can't stand them."

"I really have to start cooking." Angie walked away. Despite his denials, she was sure he hated them with the force of too many years of resentment.

"Lemme know if you need anything," he called.

Paavo was surprised at how late he had slept, and by how quiet Angie could be when she wanted to. It had taken Merry Belle's call to wake him. She had phoned to say she was on the way to Yuma to get a certified copy of the confidential marriage record or find out exactly why none existed. The ducks were lining up, he thought.

As he sat in the living room, aware of all the activity outside the bungalow, and grateful for the coffee Angie had made, he was more certain than ever that today would be the day when there would be a resolution to the mystery of Hal Edwards' death. Hal's death had led to Ned's—of that he was certain—and Paavo felt as if he was waiting for the proverbial other shoe to drop.

He looked at his watch. It was almost ten. He'd had trouble getting to sleep last night, thinking about these cases. Whenever he had insomnia in San Francisco, he would still wake early the next morning. Was it the weather out here, the quiet, or despite everything was he simply more at peace with himself than he'd been in a long, long time?

The door opened. "Hello, sleepy head," Angie said as she swept in. His heart did a little rumba, as always, just seeing her. "I brought you some breakfast. A mushroom and cheese omelet, home-fried potatoes, perfect bacon, and toast with marmalade."

"Looks great," Paavo said as Angie put the plate on the coffee table. "I think I'll keep you."

"Not if you say things like that."

"I don't want to overdo it with praise."

"Yes, you do."

Paavo agreed. Between bites, he filled Angie in on Merry Belle's errand. Although Merry Belle was eager to confront Joey Edwards, Paavo wasn't yet satisfied with this case. Ironically, he'd felt more confident in other cases he'd had with weaker evidence. Attempts to frame an innocent person had crossed his path before.

"But Joey's got to be the one behind this," Angie said. "I know I thought Joey couldn't be a killer, but now I'm convinced he did it."

"Let's wait and see. The whole town knew Joey showed up at the guest ranch last winter when his father was here, and knew about their crummy relationship. Anyone could have planted something of his in the cave."

"That's too clever by half," Angie said. "You wait and see, Inspector. I'm with Merry Belle on this one."

Outside, they heard the sounds of people arriving. It was going to be a busy, festive day.

***

Merry Belle reached Yuma in no better mood than when she left Jackpot. Deputy Buster had finally phoned in, hung over and morose about his job and his life. He sounded oddly guilty and kept apologizing as if he expected to be blamed for something. He received a sobering tongue-lashing. Merry Belle's always low reserve of patience was bone dry as far as Buster was concerned.

The ride through the desert had been tedious and hot. When she entered the Yuma records office, the lone clerk behind the counter all but froze at her "I'm-taking-no-bureaucratic-bull-shit" stare.

"May I help you?" he croaked.

"I need to see the confidential marriage records for five years back. Now."

"But they're confidential," he said in a voice so soft and nervous Merry Belle could scarcely hear him.

"No shit."

"I mean ... they're sealed," the clerk stammered.

She cast him a withering glare. "That's two things you've told me I already know. Get me the damn records."

"I ... I..."

"I'm the sheriff of Jackpot and this is part of a murder investigation."

"Jackpot?"

"That's right. What of it?"

"The sheriff was here a week or two back and demanded to see the records. I showed him."

"I'm the damned sheriff, bub. Here"—she flashed her identification—"satisfied?"

"I'm confused, uh, Sheriff Schwartz."

"Me, too, fellah. So, why don't you describe this so-called sheriff."

"Well, he wore a badge, and even flashed an I.D. And, uh, he was tall, probably in his sixties or so. And his hair was pretty long. Dirty blond and kind of scraggly."

Merry Belle's squinty eyes narrowed even more. "What color eyes?"

"Uh ... I don't know. They were mostly bloodshot."

Merry Belle drew in her breath. "Was he skinny?"

"Hmm, yes, I'd say so. His uniform was way too big for him. I figured he'd lost weight or something."

"Damn that Junior!" she murmured, then louder. "He's going to lose a lot more than weight before I finish with him!"

The clerk blanched.

How could Junior have gotten a uniform and badge? she wondered. Then, she knew. "Did you notice anything special about the uniform?"

"No ... I don't ... uh, wait—yes! It had some kind of dark purple-red material—uh, piping I think they call it—along the pocket flaps, collar, and down the front near the buttons. In fact, it even had a checkered handkerchief in a pocket. Downright elegant! It surprised me."

Merry Belle was ready to chew the counter. She was going to kill them both with her bare hands. "Okay, enough of that," she said. "I'll take care of the impersonator. Right now, I want to see those records. This is a murder case."

The clerk shook his head. "This is all too irregular."

"Irregular my ass! You're obstructing justice," Merry Belle yelled as she leaned toward the cowering clerk. One hand hovered near her mace canister.

He crumbled. "Come around," he sputtered, "and follow me."

The clerk motioned Merry Belle behind the counter and led her across the work area into a large, brightly lit room filled with ceiling high shelves.

"The confidential marriage records are all in one book in this locked cabinet," the clerk explained as he fumbled for his keys. "There are very few of them. It's something that's rarely used anymore. And now, a fake sheriff, a distraught young woman, and a real sheriff all want to see them. It makes me curious as to why."

"Tough!" she said.

In a few moments he placed a ledger-style book on a nearby table. "This is the book I gave the sheriff." At her glare, he amended it. "I mean, to the impersonator."

Merry Belle grunted and began turning pages in the book. She frowned and started flipping pages back and forth, stopping to run her finger along the inner spine. Her shoulder sagged and she sighed. "Looks to me like there's a page missing."

"That's impossible," the clerk protested.

"See for yourself."

The clerk hovered over the book examining it, a look of pained outrage on his face. Again and again, he ran his fingers over the pages as if willing the missing page to reappear. "I don't believe this."

"It's gone and I think we've both got an idea who took it," Merry Belle said glumly. "Was that guy left alone with the book?"

The now pallid clerk searched his memory, eyes closed and hands clasped as if in prayer. "Yes, I remember. I had to take a call. I had been expecting a call from my supervisor. I left you alone... I mean the other sheriff."

"He's not a sheriff!" Merry Belle was beyond rage and stood in fuming silence as the clerk explained that there were no other copies of the record either on microfilm or computer scanned. She nodded as he rambled on about when and how and by whom records were scheduled to be preserved.

Boredom competed with fury as the clerk continued. Unable to stomach any further bureaucratic minutia, she snorted and marched out of the archive toward the exit.

All she could think of was that she needed to get back to Jackpot as soon as possible and confront both Buster and Junior. Why would Junior want to take away proof of his daughter's marriage to Hal Edwards? It didn't make sense to her.

She turned toward the door, but the clerk jumped in front of her and continued explaining why none of this was his fault, and that he was an innocent employee just doing his job.

She began to huff and puff as he talked, distress giving way to all-consuming wrath. Finally, she told him if he didn't stop talking, she had no choice but to shoot.

32

All Angie's enjoyment at working in the controlled chaos of a busy kitchen fizzled when LaVerne Merritt entered. Normally, Angie liked the pace of action and the chatter with other cooks as she worked. The cookhouse bustled even more than usual with several young Mexican women Dolores had hired to help. They dashed about, following Dolores' instructions to the nth degree.

Angie and Dolores had been taking a great interest in each other's preparations. Dolores was busy cooking vast quantities of barbecue sauce for the meat, a cauldron of chili, baked beans, ham hocks, mashed and boiled potatoes, plus dips, a huge green salad, potato salad, cakes, cookies, and pies. She even made her own tortillas and bread. It all smelled quite wonderful, and Angie had the suspicion she would be eating more of Dolores' cookout fare than of her own.

"Something smells like it's burning." LaVerne's nose was high in the air as she put two large shopping bags on the counter.

Angie and Dolores made no comment. The kitchen helpers bent low over their respective work stations.

"What you cooking today?" Dolores asked LaVerne.

"Since *some* people have told me they don't like my special recipes, I've changed my plans." LaVerne pressed her lips to thin slivers. "Why knock myself out trying to catch gecko if nobody will appreciate it? Besides, Clarissa phoned and said I was to cook only simple food. I have excellent recipes for macaroni and cheese, tuna noodle casserole, and deviled eggs. That's what I'll prepare."

"Sounds yummy," Angie said with a smirk.

As LaVerne took over the largest cutting board in the room and unpacked her supplies, she looked hurt.

"Look, I'm sorry for last evening," Angie said. "It was rude of me."

"Rude? Crass is more like it!" LaVerne harrumphed, and adjusted her bifocals. "Don't worry. I know jealousy when I hear it."

"Jealousy?" Angie bit her lip. She wasn't going to argue. She continued to work.

LaVerne glanced smugly her way, then put on a pot of water for the elbow macaroni. As she began to remove the shells from two dozen hard-boiled eggs, she glanced at the pureed butternut squash Angie was scooping from the blender. "What's that? It looks like baby puke! Or worse."

"It's going to be a squash timbale—a custard."

LaVerne snorted. "Squash? That's so boring!"

"Not the way I make it!" Angie reached for some paprika.

"It won't stand up at all to my deviled eggs." She began to slice the eggs in half and scoop the yolks into a bowl. "And what's that other thing? Mashed beans? Why is all your food ground up? Do you think people in Jackpot don't have teeth?"

Angie's eyes narrowed. She pulled some cloves off a head of garlic. "It's called *dal.*"

"That's not what *I'd* call it." LaVerne smirked.

"The best thing about today," Dolores said, "is that all the bickering around the hacienda should end."

Yeah, right, Angie thought, with a glower at LaVerne.

"Of course, if Lionel gets kicked off the property," LaVerne said, as she took bottles of dry thyme and parsley from Angie's workspace and sprinkled some onto her eggs, "he might bump off Clarissa and Joey and then you wouldn't have to worry about them, either." She chuckled wickedly. "I'm hearing rumors, though, that there was something between Hal and Teresa. I can't imagine that's the case. No one could have kept such a thing a secret!"

"I could," Dolores murmured.

Both Angie and LaVerne faced her. She looked up, as if surprised that they'd heard. "Well, why not?" she asked indignantly. "It made my boss look very foolish. An old man like that —he should have been ashamed!"

"I wonder if Lionel knew about it as well," LaVerne mused. "If so, he might have worried that Hal would write her in and him out of his will."

Angie took her spices back.

"Lionel didn't know," Dolores said, her face contorted with disgust.

"Well, you found out!" LaVerne said. "Are you so much more clever than Lionel?"

"I cleaned Mr. Edwards' house—changed his sheets. There wasn't much he could hide from me." Dolores's words were quietly spoken and she turned away. Still, Dolores's irritation at LaVerne came through to Angie even as she was busy guarding her coriander and cumin.

"Don't be so sure about Lionel. He acts dumb, but he's not." LaVerne wouldn't let the conversation drop, despite the shell game she was playing with Angie's sea salt.

"Oh?" Angie asked, grabbing the salt once she finally spotted where LaVerne had hidden it. She was slicing the salmon into thin slabs. Afterward, she'd cover a slab with curled leeks, roll it up like a pinwheel, and cut it into individual portions to be sautéed.

"He's not dumb at all." LaVerne grimaced. Her macaroni was cooked, and she was mixing it with mild cheddar cheese. "Dumb is people who think they're great cooks and don't even have a job."

"I beg your pardon!" Angie put down her knife.

"Well, you never talk about a job," LaVerne said. "Most good chefs I've ever heard of do something with their ability."

"I've had lots of jobs!" Angie cried.

"And obviously lost them all."

Angie seethed. "You have your nerve criticizing my talent! With the ingredients you use in your so-called 'special' dishes, you're lucky you haven't killed anybody!"

"I take great care with my cooking!"

"If that's the case, talk about a major waste of time!" Angie glared at LaVerne. She picked up a knife and continued slicing the salmon.

LaVerne glared back so fiercely her weak eyelid no longer drooped. She pushed her sleeves up past her elbows, grabbed a huge wooden spoon, and began stirring her concoction. "I can't understand why anyone would be making fish at a barbecue!"

"Clarissa wanted it," Angie said. "And my salmon roulade is prized by many."

LaVerne rolled her eyes. "This is cattle country. It figures you and Clarissa would get it wrong. Birds of a feather."

Angie could take no more of LaVerne and turned to Dolores. "I learned recently," she said as she began to work on the stuffing, "that Hal might have been involved in drug smuggling, and working with some cartel."

The kitchen suddenly turned absolutely silent. Dolores froze. The kitchen helpers stopped chopping, mixing, and stirring the various dishes. Making no comment, Dolores quietly picked up a knife and began to chop more celery. The young women warily went back to work.

Big mistake, Angie thought, once she began to breathe again.

As Angie worked with professional alacrity, knives clattered, spices flew, and bowls clanked. LaVerne did the same, struggling to work even faster than Angie.

Angie noticed and began to stir and mix her ingredients at breakneck speed. LaVerne did all she could to keep up.

They tussled over the Kitchenaid mixer, swiped spices, sniped at smells, tastes, and the other's lack of perfection when mincing, slicing and chopping. Accusations flew.

"Too foreign."

"Too plebeian."

"Too much garlic."

"Too much butter."

"Too hot."

"Too bland."

In the end, as Angie slumped in a chair, exhausted, she was sure the Gunfight at the OK Corral had nothing on them.

Merry Belle had roared out of Yuma in a blind fury, her mind coming up with a thousand ways for Buster and Junior's slow, painful deaths. She considered feeding them feet first through a wood chipper, but rejected it as too humane. Looking down at the speedometer, she realized that she was close to setting a land speed record for a Hummer and slowed down. She wasn't about to let the two off the hook by killing herself.

Ahead, lonely and dilapidated in the desolate desert landscape, was a gas station with an attached diner. Merry Belle pulled over and strode inside. The look on her face plunged its occupants into an uneasy silence. She felt better after a couple of bacon cheeseburgers, an order of fries, and a vanilla milk shake ordered "for the road." Self-discipline restrained her from the pie. She did have to leave some room for the cookout.

To the great relief of the diner's patrons and staff, she soon trudged back to the Hummer. There, she raised Buster on the car radio.

She greeted him with, "You're dead meat!"

"I already told you I'm sorry! I know I did a bad thing." He sounded on the verge of blubbering. "But I was just curious and then I nearly got caught and ran and then got to drinking and didn't hear the alarm and--"

"Quit jabbering! I've been to Yuma. You let Junior wear your uniform!"

After a long pause, Buster said, "I didn't catch that. I got interference on the radio." He began tapping the mouthpiece hard, causing great bursts of sound to pop against Merry Belle's eardrums.

"I'm going to interfere with your life expectancy," she roared. "Cut that out! You know damned well what I said."

"Junior didn't do nothing wrong," he whined. "The wimpy clerk must've told you a bunch of lies."

"Damn it, Buster, you're dumber than dumb," Merry Belle yelled. "If Junior didn't tell you, then how'd you know the clerk's wimpy?"

There was a sullen silence.

"You there, Buster?"

"Yes, Aunt Merry Belle," he replied meekly.

"Don't call me that! You're disowned!"

"But I told you I was sorry," Buster cried.

"Listen up. I'm more than halfway home. I better see your sorry face in my office when I get back. And you better have some answers. Don't you even try to lie! You're too dumb."

More silence.

"You heard me."

"Yes, ma'am."

"You be there. And what was that you said about nearly getting caught?"

Buster croaked, "Ten-four," and hung up.

"Ten-four, my ass!" Merry Belle slammed the handset down and in a cloud of dust and gravel sped away from the diner.

Buster stared, confused, at the radiophone.

It seemed Aunt Merry Belle only cared that he'd helped Junior. She didn't seem to mind at all that he'd broken into Angie's bungalow to study how her clothes were put together.

He'd been so engrossed in the way darts had been added, seams finished and hems unevenly stitched so that they fell in a more interesting flow than if they'd been sewn straight, that he'd been startled when he looked the window and saw Paavo's SUV parked. He was so worried about being caught, his hand slipped as he was shutting a drawer and the clasp on his wristwatch snagged an Emilio Pucci scarf. Then, when he pulled it out, the expensive scarf tore. He didn't know what to do, so he grabbed it, stuffed it in his pocket, and ran like the dickens.

Maybe he should have simply confessed.

But nobody in Jackpot understood his interest in clothes design, and he knew better than to try to explain. The unfortunate thing was that he was also realistic enough to know that nothing would ever come of this enthusiasm. As much as he might want to be the next Joseph Abboud or Yves St. Laurent, deep in his heart he knew he not only lacked the money for classes and the brains for study, but—truth be told—the talent and imagination as well. So, Jackpot's deputy he'd remain.

And his secret passion would stay just that. A secret.

All that aside, it seemed Junior was the one who had most upset the sheriff. Buster hadn't seen any harm in lending a friend his uniform. He was surprised more people didn't want to borrow it. Its maroon trim made it pretty. He'd been honored when Junior had asked.

Maybe that was his calling—to design great uniforms! He knew more about law enforcement uniforms than most designers, that was for sure.

Now, though, unless he was mistaken, Junior had done something that was going to cause him trouble.

The more he thought about it, the more nervous he became, and the more certain that he didn't want to face Merry Belle alone.

Finally, shaking and desperate for help, he reached for his cell phone.

By the time Angie stepped out of the cookhouse, people from town were crowded onto the plaza.

The workmen had completely transformed it. Long serving tables were arranged inside the large tent. A smaller tent served as a makeshift bar with a table laden with liquor bottles and glassware, and beer in ice-filled washtubs. A small combo of fiddlers and guitarists played jaunty tunes. Flags, banners and balloons were attached to any available space. Propped up on the veranda was a large, sepia-toned portrait of Hal Edwards as a handsome, smiling young man, casually leaning back against a barn, one leg bent and his foot on the wood.

Looking at the poster, at the joy and promise in it, she couldn't help but feel sorrow at the way it had all turned out, both for Hal, and those whose lives he'd touched.

Was it his fault, if rumors she'd heard were correct, that Clarissa had been all but forced into marriage with him by parents who prized Hal's money more than their daughter's feelings? Or that the young woman Hal had turned to in his unhappiness simply wanted a way out of her dreary life?

The twists and turns life takes, Angie realized as she gazed at the poster, were completely unpredictable. Despite all the planning and care one might do, surprises could still turn up and bite you.

Beyond the tents and near the far corner of the hacienda, a barbecue pit had been dug. Smoke rose from the glowing embers beneath the turning spits on which huge sides of beef and pork slowly rotated. An enormous, florid and toothless man with the filthiest apron Angie had ever seen danced around with a bucket and hand mop slopping a cooking sauce onto the meat. On a large table near the pit were rows of skewered chicken parts and plump sausages.

The whole scene was a vegetarian's worst nightmare.

Angie saw that Doc had arrived and was in animated conversation with Paavo. She was glad to see Doc looking much better than when she was last with him. The man had gone through a terrible ordeal, but was holding up. She walked up and gave him a hug. "I'm so glad you decided to come here today," she said with a smile.

"I never was one to stay in bed, my head under the covers, lamenting things that can't be undone." Doc gave her a stern look. "I was just telling Paavo that something's got me on edge today. He says he's feeling the same way."

"I know." A shiver went down her back. "I hope it has nothing to do with the cookout, though. Everyone here has worked hard on it. Even LaVerne."

"Uh, oh," both Doc and Paavo said at the same time. After a momentary chuckle, Doc asked, "Is the chuck wagon ready to roll?"

"Not yet," Angie replied. "Lionel has to hitch up the horses. The meat is still cooking, so we've got plenty of time. Have you seen him or Clarissa?" She looked around the plaza.

"No," Paavo said. "I haven't seen Joey either."

"They should be here. Clarissa is, at least in name, the hostess. But if we're lucky, neither of them will show up today," Doc said. "They'd do nothing but ruin a good party."

"Are Lupe and Teresa coming?"

Doc shook his head and a worried frown passed over his face. "They're staying near the hospital."

"I see," Angie said. She was sorry that, the way things stood, nothing could develop between Doc and Lupe. They deserved happiness together. At the same time, she understood Lupe's position. Life wasn't always fair.

"Even though not much food is out here yet," she added in a forcibly jovial tone, "they've put out the beer. I'll bet you could go for some, right Doc?"

The faraway look in his eyes had Angie considering that he, too, had been thinking about Lupe. But then he gave her a sudden smile. "Music to my ears."

The black truck skidded to a stop in front of Junior's old and battered truck and RV trailer.

"Thanks for coming so fast," Junior said, climbing out of the trailer onto the dirt road.

"So, Merry Belle knows too much." The driver got out of the truck.

"Yeah, but we can handle her." Junior swaggered closer. "I think we should go see Teresa. I'll talk to her. Tell her it's all up to me—just like we planned."

"No." The voice was firm. Something about it made Junior's blood run cold.

"What do you mean?" he asked.

"Get inside your truck, behind the wheel."

Junior's eyes grew wide and round at the gun now pointed at him. He hesitated only a second, then climbed onto the driver's seat. "What's this about? You and me are together in this."

"Are we?"

Junior held his hands out, pleading. "What are you doing? I've got the proof of Teresa's marriage—the church and civil records—just like we need. I'm her father. If she wants to inherit Hal's property, she has to agree to give me half or I keep the proof and she gets nothing! You'll get your share. That's our deal. You and me—partners, right? In everything. I'll give you a bigger percentage if that's what you want. Or ... or maybe we could split it three ways with Teresa. What does she know about money? But you and me—we appreciate the fine things in life. We'll each take a third, right? Without me—and you—Teresa gets nothing. She has no proof, right?"

"Junior, shut up."

His face fell, and he stared as if he couldn't believe his own ears. "What are you saying? It's our plan. It's a good plan. We're going to be rich."

"Wrong."

Fear and uncertainty made Junior's voice crack as realization flashed across his bloodshot eyes. He gripped the steering wheel, looking for the truck's keys, but they were deep in the pocket of his Wranglers. "What do you want?"

Silence.

"You used me, didn't you?"

More silence.

"You set people up! You killed Hal and Ned! And ... my God! I understand now. Everything. I understand everything." Junior's face paled, his voice turned quiet, as if figuring it all out was slightly miraculous to him.

"Congratulations."

A gunshot sounded, and Junior would never figure out anything again.

33

———

With a woeful Deputy Buster beside her, Merry Belle drove along the narrow road where Junior Whitney had parked his trailer. She could hardly wait to get her hands on him.

The sheriff came close to achieving warp speed as she held her foot steady on the accelerator. Despite the high speed, she felt like she had driven for hours before spotting her objective. Merry Belle slammed on the brakes, kicking up dust and fishtailing to a stop. She jumped from the Hummer shouting for Junior to come out and face her like a man.

As the swirling dust cloud settled, she saw an outline slumped over the steering wheel of the truck.

She raced over and pushed Junior back against the seat. His chest was covered with blood, his eyes opened but sightless, his expression showed both fright and bewilderment. She touched his neck, hoping against hope to find a pulse. There was none.

Merry Belle gently closed his eyes.

Buster stumbled into the brush and threw up.

Angie watched as Lionel led a couple of horses toward the chuck wagon. For some reason, the process was making her increasingly nervous.

Paavo's cell phone rang. Angie and Doc listened in shock to Paavo's side of the conversation. He was grim when he disconnected.

"Junior's dead," he said flatly. "Shot. I'm meeting the sheriff."

"It's all coming to a head," Doc said in a barely audible voice, "just as I thought it would."

"I'm coming with you," Angie said.

"No." Paavo answered with a finality that left no room for argument.

"Let's take my car," Doc said. "I've got all my gear in it. I am the assistant coroner, after all. I... I'll do the certification, then call Lupe. You might not know, but they were married."

Paavo gave him a silent nod as they walked across the plaza to the parking lot. Doc got behind the wheel of his car.

Paavo paused by the passenger door and looked apologetically at Angie. "I'm sorry I'll miss your big entry on the chuck wagon."

"I'm sure it'll be quite boring," she said, her heart heavy that death had once again come to this town.

"Be careful," he warned.

"It's a chuck wagon—what could go wrong?" She tried to smile, but failed. "You're the one who'd better be careful. There's a killer out there, Paavo."

They kissed and Paavo got in the car.

As Doc's Cadillac pulled away, Angie felt afraid. Not only for Paavo, but for all of them.

She walked back to the plaza and the lively celebration. *I'll keep this to myself,* she thought. *Let the living have their fun.*

Lionel was waving at her like a demented maestro. "Where you been?" he called. "It's time." He ushered her to the chuck wagon.

Angie looked at the two horses hitched to it. One, Chloe, looked bored but calm. The other was Ranger. She didn't dare go near him. His teeth looked awfully big, her fingers awfully small, and she didn't like the way he stared at her as if she offended him.

"All right, Miss Angie. Time to set yourselves up front and ride the wagon over to the tents where everyone is waiting," Lionel said with a grand flourish of his battered Stetson.

"Let LaVerne and Dolores get up there first," Angie said.

Dolores laughed, nudging her forward. "LaVerne doesn't do stuff like this, and I'm just a hired hand."

"I can't do it alone!" Angie stared up at the chuck wagon's seat. It was high above the ground. Her legs didn't want to move.

"Get up there, girl," Dolores said. "You're our guest of honor. Go on, before the food gets cold!"

"But I don't know how to drive a chuck wagon!" Angie said, her voice tiny.

"You just pull back on the reins to slow them down, and say 'whoa' when you want them to stop," Lionel said.

Dolores leaned forward and whispered to her, "Don't worry —me and Lionel lead the horses, but no one's supposed to know that."

"But still—"

Propelled by Dolores, Angie found herself sitting on the bench seat with the reins in her hands. Ranger turned his head back toward her with another nasty look. What was with that darn horse? "I don't know about this," Angie murmured, trying to hide her unease.

Dolores chuckled. Angie looked for Lionel and saw him near his trailer. So much for counting on his help!

"Time to roll!" Dolores said, taking the reins and walking Ranger forward. The chuck wagon lurched and swayed. Angie almost let out a shriek as she felt the ancient wood strain and creak. Eventually, the contraption began to roll forward.

Although her imagination saw it as something akin to a chariot race, the chuck wagon moved slowly. They reached the corner of the hacienda, and to her surprise and utter relief, Dolores led the horses so that they turned smoothly onto the plaza. A cheer went up from the crowd, Ranger's ears stretched flat. He snorted and tried to surge forward. Angie pulled back on the reins, holding them so tight her fingers cramped. He settled down before Angie went into cardiac arrest.

Cheering and applauding, the crowd watched the chuck wagon approach the tents. Angie knew she had to get the look of utter terror off her face and scanned the crowd for support. Clarissa and Joey were on the veranda looking glum and bored.

She found Doc's old friend Joaquin nodding at her. Angie almost managed to smile back.

As they reached the tent where she was supposed to stop, she looked for Dolores and Lionel to help her.

Neither was nearby. Nearly spinning like a top in the wagon seat, she searched the crowd trying to find them. Where were they? What had happened to them?

Suddenly, the tent was right beside her. Ranger continued on, almost past it. She had to do something.

"Whoa," she cried, and pulled back on the reins. Nothing happened. The horses continued forward.

"Whoa, whoa," she yelled louder, half-standing as she pulled back hard on the reins. "Please! Please stop!"

To her shock, Ranger and Chloe stopped in perfect position. Amazing, Angie thought, nearly numb with relief. *Maybe I am a real cowgirl after all.* Her grin was a mixture of euphoria and stunned incredulity.

As people applauded, she stood and waved at the crowd, feeling very good about herself. Why had she been scared? How silly of her. Too bad Paavo had missed her grand entrance.

Suddenly, there was a ruckus from the far side of the hacienda. Startled, she looked over her shoulder to see a cloud of dust billowing into the sky. At the same time she heard a strange and ominous pounding.

"What--"

The word wasn't out of her mouth when her voice choked. She let out a shriek.

Of horror.

The entire flock of ostriches was running toward the plaza like a seven-foot tall tidal wave. "Oh, oh!" she cried, unable to even form words. People began screaming and running, while she tried to decide if she was better off leaping from the chuck wagon and running as well, or staying on it and hoping the ostriches went around her.

She didn't need to make the decision.

***

"I always said he should rot in hell for the way he treated Lupe and Teresa," Doc muttered as he looked at Junior's body. "Maybe now he is."

As Doc proceeded with the examination for his coroner's report, Paavo walked over to the sheriff and Buster. There was worry and upset on Buster's face, anger on the sheriff's, but also a deep weariness.

"Any ideas?" Paavo asked.

"He wasn't much," Merry Belle said in a low voice, "but I knew him my whole life. He was pretty nice sometimes when he was a boy, but it all went to hell in a bottle of Jim Beam. What a waste. The town failed him."

"People fail themselves," Paavo said.

"Perhaps."

They took one last look at the body. "Buster," Merry Belle said, "you going to tell us about it?"

"I don't know, I told you!" Buster was near tears. "Junior gave me money to borrow my uniform. That's all. If you paid more than minimum wage, I wouldn't have to do such things!"

"If you worked more than the minimum, I might think about it!" she yelled.

Paavo had them both calm down and tell him what was going on.

Spooked by the charging birds and the shaking of the earth, Ranger reared up and rocketed forward with Chloe sharing the sudden panic. The reins flew from Angie's hands as she somersaulted backwards over the bench seat to land on the wagon bed floor.

While ostriches bounced like pinballs off tents and tables they ran into and knocked over, the two horses plowed straight through the crowd, pulling the chuck wagon—and Angie—with them.

Angie held onto whatever part of the wagon she could as she crawled forward trying to reach the seat and retake the reins. She watched townspeople scatter as pots, plates, dishes and trays flew from the chuck wagon, spraying everyone and everything in its path.

Her carefully prepared scrolled disks of salmon spun from the wagon like flying, fishy Frisbees, pelting people's hair and clothes. Deviled eggs shot out over the plaza like ping-pong balls from a toy bazooka.

Everything, including Angie, went airborne as the wagon

bounced over bumps and ruts. Once again, she was knocked back onto the wagon's bed that now had a lake of punch and a tuna-noodle casserole sloshing over it. The ingredients all but glued themselves to her hair and clothes like giant leeches. The final straw was when a pot of beans, which had been secured, broke free and spewed red beans like a volcano until it tipped over, adding a gooey, slithery swamp to the tuna-noodle punch.

Even the ostriches were showered with corn, chili, and Angie's fancy *dal*. A banana cream pie hit the cowlicked bird smack in the face. She halted, momentarily stunned.

As the wagon swayed and shimmied, Angie kept trying to scramble to her feet, but slipped, slid, and didn't get anywhere.

To her amazement, she saw Joaquin on horseback, racing through zigzagging ostriches toward her. Miraculously, he soon reached the thundering Ranger and Chloe and somehow, using his skill as a horseman, got the two horses to turn back toward the plaza. Angie skittered sideways as the circling wagon tilted on two wheels. She covered her head, sure the cart was going to flip over. In an endless flash of time, cornbread bounced off her head, ham hocks pelted her, and another violent tilt of the wagon caused her to land face down in a puddle of salsa, that had also, somehow, ended up on the wagon's bed.

The wagon righted itself, and next thing Angie knew, Joaquin grabbed Ranger's bridle and shouted "Whoa."

What a blessed word! Her heart pounded with relief.

The two frightened horses came to a sudden halt in a cloud of dust. Equally abruptly, the wagon stopped. Angie and everything she was sitting in lurched and sloshed forward, then—in demonstration that for every action there is an equal and opposite reaction—momentum tossed her and the food like a whiplash toward the back of the wagon.

"Noooooo," she cried, scrambling to grab hold of something, anything, to save herself. Her goo-filled fingers could find nothing that wasn't slick. Feet first, she smacked into the chuck box. It hit the tailboard, causing the old wood to split like tissue paper.

The chuck box flew off the rear of the wagon onto the plaza.

And, riding atop a tidal wave of churned food like a kid on a water slide, Angie shot out after it.

34

Lying on the ground, eyes shut, Angie's first thought was that this absolutely hadn't happened to her.

"Is she okay?"

"Did you see her fly?"

"What a set of lungs!"

"Never heard nothin' screech like that lil' gal."

She opened her eyes to see the ostrich with the cowlick silhouetted against the harsh sun and staring down at her.

With a groan, she struggled to sit up. Joey knelt at her side. Joaquin stood beside him while others, including LaVerne, hovered near.

Clarissa looked like she'd laughed for the first time in years.

"Can you move your legs, Angie?" Joey asked. "Now your arms. Okay. How's your head? It hurt?" He looked around. "Where's Doc Griggs? He should be here."

"I'm okay." Angie blinked a couple of times and shoved away the ostrich who was trying to peck at her hair. She wiped congealed slop off her face, hands and arms, but her hair was so full of gelatinous goop it was sticking out from her head like some spiked helmet.

"Let me see her," Dr. Westlake said, working his way through the crowd. As he introduced himself to Angie, she stood up, to everyone's relief. She'd finally met Dr. Griggs' replacement.

"I'm fine," she repeated after he studied her pupils and declared her all right. "Thanks to Joaquin." She would have given him a hug if she wasn't covered, head to toe, with the food they'd planned to serve. Instead, she gave him a big smile as she said, "My hero."

He blushed.

A few people handed her paper towels, oversized napkins, and dishrags to wipe off her clothes and hair. She'd half expected to see Dolores there to help, but she guessed Dolores was busy trying to see if any food could be salvaged.

As she sopped up as much gunky food as possible, she was looking at the old chuck box at her feet. It lay on its side, the ancient wood split, with the bottom several feet away from the case. Stuck up inside the back of the case, as if it had been pushed behind a drawer, was some paper. Every instinct told her it didn't belong there.

"What's that?" she said as she reached for it. It crackled with age and dryness as she grabbed hold, pulled it from the case, and unfolded it. "It's a letter."

"A letter?" Joey asked. "What's it say?"

Angie saw that it was two pages, written in a flowery European script. She read aloud.

Dear Jim,

I regret that it became incumbent upon me to leave without saying goodbye. I thank you for all the help you gave to Miss Lane and myself.

I entrust to you the journal of recipes I developed with great care in the course of my Westward sojourn, and with it, a letter. Please send them both to my nephew, Oscar Tschirky, in care of the Waldorf Hotel, NYC, NY. A dollar is enclosed, which should cover the cost of postage.

Thank you,

Wm. V. Beerstraeden

She peered up into the chuck box. Unfortunately, both the dollar and the journal were gone. She turned to the second letter.

My Dear Oscar,

I am sending you my journal. I hope you enjoy the recipes I've created entirely with native fare. I have no need for them, and I'm sure they will benefit you in your new endeavor.

Do not worry about me, Oscar, although this is the last time you shall hear from me. God has provided extremely well for me in a most wonderful and unexpected fashion. Because of it, however, I must disappear and can never be found. Accompanying me is a most kind and virtuous woman named Miss Daisy Lane. She has consented to become my wife. I have never expected such happiness in this life.

I wish you great success in your career.

Your most loving uncle,

Wm. V. Beerstraeden

"God has provided extremely well..." Angie reread the words. Was Beerstraeden referring to the Dalton money? Maybe he and the not-so-virtuous Daisy Lane ended up finding it, "*God has provided...*"?

What else could he have been talking about?

Joey took the letters from her and read them. "The money's gone," he whispered, obviously reaching the same conclusion as Angie.

"Yes." She had to agree. When the attack was made on Hoot Dalton and his money—whether by the stagecoach drivers or outsiders—Beerstraeden and Daisy must have grabbed the money and then ran off with it. She guessed they might have joined up with a cattle drive for safety as they left the desert—

perhaps with Beerstraeden helping the cook. That could explain how his letter got stuffed into the back of a chuck box.

"There's no treasure?" LaVerne asked.

"No treasure," she replied. Around her, Angie heard the others' disappointed murmur. No one really thought they'd find the Dalton treasure, yet up to this point, the hope had been there, the dream of riches alive in every one of them. She understood what they were feeling. Up to this point she'd hoped to find the cookbook, and with it, imagined the fame it might bring her. Now, her dreams, as well as everyone else's, were gone.

Her thoughts went to Dolores again. If she had been there to take hold of the horses, they might have been under some control when the ostriches stampeded. The food in the wagon might have been saved ... and her own version of Mr. Toad's Wild Ride might never have happened.

Angie shook off the feeling, the disappointment, that Dolores—who she'd thought of as a colleague in cooking and even a friend—seemed to have so little concern about her.

Continuing to brush more of the food off her clothes, she looked at the people around her, sadly discussing the letters she'd found, and realized that was what she'd been dealing with all week—hopes and dreams for a better future.

Hopes and dreams. They were so often the key—the reason for so much good in life, and sometimes for so much that went badly.

Hal Edwards had hoped Clarissa would love him. Clarissa had hoped for happiness in wealth, since she'd given up love for money. Teresa had hoped to leave town. Doc hoped Lupe would be with him one day. Lionel hoped to find peace in a bottle. And Joey, poor Joey, hoped for self-worth. Even Dolores must have had hopes and dreams ... but of what?

Many of them, she'd discovered, had been looking for something more in life. And when such desires were shattered, the disappointment was fierce.

With that thought, she realized why the pile of clothes on the floor of Hal's bedroom had struck her as so odd. They should have been an immediate clue.

Tossing them that way wasn't the sort of thing a person did when searching for a will... that was the sort of thing done because of anger, jealousy, and loss... when there was no more hope.

And why, when Dolores had spoken to her with such pride over the way she'd taken care of Hal and his hacienda over decades, hadn't she gone into his bedroom and do some basic cleaning—to at least pick up the clothes thrown on the floor?

Obviously, Dolores knew about Hal and Teresa's affair, if not about their marriage. But to leave the mess in the bedroom, for anyone to find...

Angie looked around. She saw Lionel standing near his trailer, LaVerne picking up food and tossing it in garbage bags, Clarissa still staring at her and chuckling.

"Where is Dolores?" she asked people standing nearby as she scanned the crowd. No one knew.

She hurried toward the cookhouse. Joey followed.

"Joseph!" Clarissa called, commanding her son to her side.

Joey ignored her and continued on with Angie. "Are you all right?" he asked. "What's wrong?"

"I've got to find Dolores," Angie said. Quiet Dolores, who'd practically brought Hal back to life after his stroke, working with him for years to help him regain his strength, who had never married, and stayed in the background, loyal to him. Had she felt more than loyalty for the man?

The cookhouse was empty, the food and equipment left unattended.

They hurried to the cabin where the help stayed. Joey

showed Angie to Dolores's room. It was empty, as well. Everything was neat. Too neat. She was gone.

Joaquin Oldwater appeared in the doorway, breathing heavily as if he'd run to the room. "I heard you asking about Dolores." He gave her a strange, confused look. "Some little boys saw her leave in her truck. They said she had a rifle and some other things with her. But you can't think..."

Her brow furrowed. "I don't want to, but..."

Joaquin nodded. "You may be right. There were signs. Damn! I didn't want to believe them." He drew in his breath. "She drove out the back road."

"Toward the lake?"

"Or into the foothills," Joaquin said. "It's an area where a person could hide out forever."

"What's going on?" Joey asked, looking from one to the other.

Angie ran to her bungalow, leaving a trail of tuna, noodles, chili beans, and butternut squash in her wake. There, she thrust the Beerstraeden letters into a drawer, yanked off her wet and goopy T-shirt and jeans, pulled on clean ones, then grabbed the car keys, her phone, and ran out to the SUV.

"Lionel has to be behind this," Doc announced as Paavo and Merry Belle examined Junior's body and the surrounding area for clues. They gave Deputy Buster the job of guarding the area, and not touching a thing. "I don't see who else could have gotten Junior to do such a thing."

"And I can't see Lionel pulling it off," Paavo said as he and Merry Belle cordoned off the area with fresh tire tracks right in front of Junior's trailer. "Or shooting Junior this way. They'd seemed to be fairly close, and Lionel had been friends with Ned. It even seems he cared about his uncle."

"Who else could it have been?" Merry Belle all but moaned with desperation.

Paavo ran his fingers through his hair as he thought out loud. "Junior must have come here to meet someone. If that person is our killer, it's got to be someone Junior trusted, maybe was working with. It means Junior was duped, and that's what got him killed."

"That makes sense," Doc said. "So the question is, who could have gotten Junior to do something like this? Who could convince him?"

"Joey or Clarissa?" Merry Belle suggested, rubbing her aching back. "Both of them would want to hide the proof that Teresa was married to Hal so Joey could inherit Hal's estate."

"But Junior couldn't stand Joey or Clarissa. I can't see either of them working with the other," Paavo reminded them.

"Junior might not have been a good father," Doc said, "but in his way, he did love his daughter. If she had a chance to inherit Hal's estate, he wouldn't work against her to give it to Joey."

Buster had been listening, and called out, "Junior didn't like any of them out at the ranch, except maybe Dolores." He smirked. "They once had a thing going, in fact, for a short while after Hal first took off. Didn't last long, though. Once we got proof Hal was still alive, Dolores dropped Junior like a week old tamale that'd been sittin' in the hot sun."

"Junior and Dolores?" Doc looked appalled. "I didn't think she'd give him the time of day!"

"Didn't she live at the ranch for years taking care of Hal?" Paavo asked.

"She doted on Hal," Merry Belle said. "Thought the sun rose and set on him. Nursed him through his sickness, took care of his physical therapy. You name it, she did it."

The three looked at each other as the same thought struck.

Buster was confused. "Why are you all silent all of a sudden?"

Doc spoke first. "Hal wanted to keep his marriage to Teresa a secret. We all assumed it was because of Clarissa, but that never made a lot of sense. What if it was because of Dolores? Because he feared her jealousy? But somehow, she found out. I wonder if he felt his life was in danger because of her—or if, in his way, he did care about her and couldn't handle the guilt he felt throwing her over for the much younger and lovelier Teresa."

Paavo frowned. "I haven't heard much about Hal's character. I'll go with your thoughts on that score."

"Thinking back," Doc mused, "I suspect, in his way Hal loved Dolores—he should have. She was the only one who never abandoned him, stayed through thick and thin—very thin. At one point, he was facing bankruptcy. And that was how he repaid her devotion. I can understand him not being able to handle the guilt he felt bringing Teresa to his home, right under Dolores' nose—and to his bed. Whether Dolores knew they were married or not, she knew what was going on. Maybe she confronted Hal about it. And since he was unbalanced anyway, it was enough to push him over the edge, to run away from it all."

Disgust darkened Merry Belle's round face. "He should have understood her better."

"When he came back," Doc theorized, "I wonder if Dolores thought he'd returned for her. But when one of the first things he did was try to get Teresa back..."

Paavo finished the sentence. "Dolores couldn't take it and killed him."

"She probably knew Hal was once involved with drug smugglers as well," Paavo added. "In fact, those FBI guys said one of Hal's housekeepers had relatives who worked with a cartel. That could have been Dolores. Although she never did anything, she could have gotten them together with Hal—as a way for Hal to bring in needed cash when most of his was gone. If she killed him, she could have gotten them to help her move his body to a cave—it would warn any smugglers to stay away. We also know Ned was looking into the attacks that killed Teresa. What if he realized it was Dolores—attacking Teresa out of jealousy? She could have killed him, or had her friends do it. A coyote amulet put in Ned's house would point to Ned being involved in drug smuggling, and throw responsibility for his death there."

"I could see Junior letting her use him," Doc said. "For a few bucks and a good bottle of whiskey, she'd get him to do her dirty work, break into the church and my office, looking for a will or any evidence about Teresa's marriage. She must have somehow convinced him that it would be to Teresa's benefit— or to his."

"Hold on, you all," Merry Belle said. "You can't go blaming Dolores when I've got proof that Joey's the killer! I've got the heel rand. I don't believe Dolores would try to pin the crime on Joey."

"I don't either," Paavo said. "But Lionel would. It was an action of opportunity, that's all. He didn't know about Hal's marriage. He thought Joey stood in the way of his inheritance. And if Joey was locked up for Hal's death, Lionel was next in line."

Merry Belle grimaced. "It does make sense, I guess."

Paavo added, "Lionel probably found the heel rand on the ranch. The day he went out to the caves with Angie gave him the perfect opportunity. He brought the heel rand with him and then supposedly 'found' it. He was probably also the one who put the note in my jacket pocket, knowing I'd eventually find it."

"Lionel often said that all he ever wanted was for life to go on as it had during the five years Hal was away," Buster added. "He liked being boss."

"But wait—I still don't see why Junior helped Dolores," Merry Belle said.

Doc and Paavo looked at each other.

"That's true. We've already come up with lots of speculation," Paavo said. "It's time for answers, concrete answers, that only Dolores can tell us. Let's get back to the cookout and ask her."

35

Dolores made her way through the narrow trails that led to the foothills. Much as she would have liked to try to brazen this out, to continue to be unseen and unnoticed as she had most of her life, she was afraid that this time she couldn't pull it off. She'd been so shaken and upset by Junior's call that Merry Belle was onto him, she hadn't thought clearly. She knew Junior would fold immediately under Merry Belle's furious questioning, and had gone after him with a gun that could be traced back to her.

Also, the visitors troubled her. Paavo Smith was a real cop, not someone who didn't want to make waves like Merry Belle. And where the people in town paid no attention to Dolores, Angie Amalfi wasn't that way. Angie noticed things. Noticed *her.* That was why she'd tried to scare them into leaving. It hadn't worked.

Dolores was afraid to stay put. So she created an opportunity to get away. It had been easy to stampede the ostriches by shouting and waving a red tablecloth at them like some crazed toreador. When everyone's attention was on the chaos, she threw a few things into her truck and ran.

Now, she began to speed.

Calm down, she told herself. It would take a long time before the people at the ranch put everything together, and she'd have a good head start. The disruption she'd created at the cookout should keep people too busy to miss her for hours. No one ever thought about her until there was work to be done, anyway.

If they did put two and two together, they would figure she had headed for the Mexican border. Let them think that. She just had to get into the hills, the high desert. She could hide out there a month or more before turning south.

It wasn't the first time she'd been on the run; not the first time she'd had to live in the desert, relying on her skill at hunting and foraging for sustenance. She'd been only twelve years old when she crossed into this country with her uncle and cousins. She could do it again.

Thinking about them, about the uncle and two cousins who were dead now, about all she'd been through in this country, and about Hal Edwards, a great sorrow filled her.

Tears clouded her vision.

The evil she'd done... How could Hal have treated her as he did? After the way she'd stayed at his side when everyone else, even his own wife, left him; the way she'd nursed him back to good health after his stroke; the way she'd worked with him, making him do his physical therapy exercises, how she alone had made him strong again. She did it because she loved him. To her, he was the handsomest, kindest, most loving man the world had ever known. And when he'd turned to her, when he realized how much she loved him and gathered her to him, kissing her, loving her, she'd never been happier. She would have done anything for him.

But once he was healthy again, she wasn't good enough for him. He's always had an eye for women—for Clarissa, who was wealthy and beautiful, and then for Teresa who had youth instead of money, and also beauty.

Five years ago, Hal had tossed Dolores aside, expecting her to be happy to go back to her "place" ... in the kitchen. She'd told him she loved him, and how she felt about him treating her so badly after all they'd been to each other. And when that didn't move him, she told the cartel he had cheated them. *That* caused him to leave—to run and hide. She thought he'd gone for good, and she was all right with that. Let him wallow alone in Mexico.

But then he came back. He told her he'd eventually convinced the cartel she'd lied about him, and that he came back because he loved Teresa. He confessed he'd married her—not only in a civil wedding in Yuma, but he even had the marriage blessed in the church. Now, he would do all he could to get Teresa to forgive him for how much he'd hurt her, and to let all the world know they were married.

The last straw was when he suggested she find a husband before she was so old no man would want her.

She wiped the tears that kept falling and falling.

Now, she had to get away. She couldn't let them catch her. The state would kill her; take her life, like she took Hal's. And Ned's. And Junior's. And possibly even Maritza's, a good woman who never did harm to anyone.

"Damn you, Hal!" she cried, her foot pressing down even further on the gas pedal. "I hate you!"

The road curved sharply around the hillside. She swung the wheel hard as she tried to wipe away the tears that were blinding her. Her vision cleared just in time to see in front of her, jutting slightly onto the road, a large boulder.

The tires made an agonized shriek as Angie drove her SUV away from the parking area. Joey was with her, riding shotgun.

The ostrich with the cowlick stood by the side of the road, its eyes wide with surprise and curiosity as she zipped by.

Angie sped into the desert. She had to find Dolores. Most likely, Dolores wouldn't think she was being followed, and might not go too fast.

Somehow managing to keep control of the SUV, as she neared the area with the caves, she noticed she had enough cell service to call Paavo. The phone kept cutting out, but he understood well enough to tell her to go back to the ranch.

"I'll be careful," she said just as the cell failed completely. She doubted he heard her.

***

"There's a whole maze of old trails, some fire roads, and dry creek beds Dolores could drive through," Merry Belle said. She'd left Deputy Buster in charge of the crime scene, Doc with him, while she drove the Hummer. Paavo was at her side. "If Dolores gets far enough and starts hoofing it, she can hide out for years. She knows the desert, knows how to survive in it."

"She's desperate," Paavo said grimly, hands clenched, "which means Angie's at risk."

"You told her to not to go after Dolores," Merry Belle reminded him.

"And?" Paavo's response came through gritted teeth.

"Don't worry," Merry Belle said with sudden insight. "We'll probably find Angie stuck off the road. Anybody who doesn't know those trails won't get very far."

"I hope you're right. I don't want her catching up to a murderer."

Merry Belle got on the radio to request aerial back up from the State Police as they sped past the hacienda and onto the back road.

"Turn there," Joey yelled. "Or you'll end up on the road to the lake. I don't think that's where she's going."

"Agreed." Angie made the sharp turn, and found herself on a narrow fire road. The higher the dirt trail went into the foothills, the more twisted and winding it became, the surface rougher and more treacherous. The constant bounces and jolts made her already banged up body ache even more.

She tried to call Paavo to tell him the road she'd taken, but the signal was gone.

"I'm never leaving home again!" she muttered as she pressed forward.

"And miss all this fun?" Joey asked. "You're doing fine."

The Mercedes skidded as she careened around an unexpectedly sharp bend. Before her, Dolores' black pickup jutted onto the roadway. It had crashed into a boulder, leaving the hood crumpled. The driver's side door hung open.

Angie stomped hard on the brakes. The SUV went into a spin. As the back end skidded on the rocky road, the side of the car swiped against the pickup with a grinding whirr. Finally, the SUV bounced off the roadway and the engine died.

"I guess I spoke a little too soon," Joey grumbled, rubbing his head where it had bumped the windshield.

When Angie realized she was still in one piece, she stared with horror at the black truck, certain that Dolores was going to leap out of it with guns blazing.

She didn't.

Joey reached over and tugged at Angie's shoulder. She immediately realized the wisdom of his action and quickly bent down the same way. The two of them cowered behind the dash.

"Where do you think Dolores might be?" she whispered. "She's not in the pickup, so she must have gone off on foot. She could be far ... or she could be watching us this very moment."

"I don't know," Joey whispered back. "She must have been hurt in that crash. She might be lying across the seat, or dead. I don't like this."

"But the door's open. I think she got out."

"That's likely, too," Joey said, not exactly helpfully.

"Do you think she'd hurt us?" Angie's voice was tiny. "To me, she seemed like such a nice lady."

"Hurt us? Are you kidding? Her actions show your theory about her was right—and that means she's killed three people that we know of—including my father!" Joey cried. "Of course she'd hurt us!"

Enough said. Angie turned the ignition key. When the engine refused to turn over, she pumped the gas pedal. Still nothing. She kept trying.

"Stop," Joey whispered. "It won't help."

"Paavo and the sheriff shouldn't be far behind," she said. "If Dolores is gone, we can simply sit here and wait."

"You don't know how fast the sheriff drives," Joey said. "If her big Hummer zips around the blind curve too fast, it could flatten this car with us in it. We should try to walk down the road to meet them."

"Okay." She pushed the door open when a shot rang out. The bullet tore a wide hole in the windshield and the rest of the glass spidered. The console between the driver's and passenger's seats splintered from the bullet's impact.

Angie gave a yelp, pulled her door shut and locked it, then crawled completely under the dashboard.

Joey was already down there.

"Maybe that wasn't such a good idea," Joey said.

"At least we found out where Dolores is," Angie added, trying to stay positive even as she peeked up at the cracked windshield and the ruined console.

"Get out of that car! I need it." The voice was shrill and quaking, and came from high above and off the road.

"Don't listen to her," Joey whimpered.

"I'll give you one minute to think it over and get out. Then, I'm coming down. I don't want to kill you, Angie! But I need your car."

Angie reached up to try the ignition key again, but before doing so, whispered to Joey, "What do you think she'll do if she finds out the engine is stalled?" Angie asked.

"Probably kill us," Joey answered glumly.

Angie pulled her hand back, fast. At Joey's words, any positive thinking she might have had switched to negative. Thoughts of Paavo came to her, of the beautiful wedding they'd never have, and her eyes filled with tears. Why had she been so ridiculous about the ceremony and the locale? Who cared how extra-special it was? It was a wedding, for pity's sake, not a royal inauguration!

Then she heard the roar of a fast approaching vehicle.

"Oh, my God!" Joey covered his head. "It's Merry Belle!"

Angie screamed.

The impact could have been heard in seven counties. Or so it seemed to the two inside the sheriff's Hummer. When Paavo had gotten his breath back from the jolt of his safety belt, he saw that the Hummer hadn't crushed the SUV as he imagined. It was a fender-bender, true, but at least the SUV didn't resemble an accordion.

It had been a complete shock to round the bend, Merry Belle going at bat-out-of-hell speed, and to see both Dolores' pickup and SUV right in front of them.

Merry Belle braked, all the while roaring profanities. By some miracle, she had managed to stop "almost" in time...

She then backed up and pulled in right next to the SUV.

Angie's head popped up from inside the SUV just long

enough to catch Paavo's eye. A French-manicured fingernail pointed toward the hills. Then she ducked again.

Rifle in hand, before Paavo could say a word, Merry Belle sprung open her door. "I'll show her!"

"No, wait!" Paavo tried to grab her, but she jumped out and ran for the cover of Dolores' pickup. She wasn't fast enough. A shot fired from above. Merry Belle dropped instantly to the ground, clutching her leg.

"She shot me! I don't believe it. I've actually been wounded in the line of duty!" She was more in rage than pain, and dragged herself to the cover of the truck. "Now, I'm really mad."

More shots rained down on the window of the Hummer. The bulletproof glass dimpled but held. Paavo lying flat, called to Merry Belle, "How badly are you hit?"

"Leg wound. Lots of blood," Merry Belle gasped. "But I'll live to see Dolores pay for this."

"Stay put." Paavo repositioned himself on the front seat and pushed open the passenger door. It was no more than a foot away from the driver's door of the SUV.

Looking out, he had a clear view of the SUV's shattered windshield. "Angie, are you all right?"

A muffled voice yelled back, "Yes."

He breathed again with relief. "Don't stick you head up again," he shouted. "Just listen. I want you to open the driver's door—kick it open—if you can."

He waited. At last Angie's door swung open until it met and overlapped with his. Angie looked up, wide-eyed with fright, from under the dash. Behind her, he saw Joey's head pop up. "Maybe we'll have our wedding after all," she murmured.

"Not if we stay pinned down like this," Paavo warned. "Dolores is panicked right now. You can't trust that she'll be at all rational. Remember that."

Angie's face fell even as she nodded, and Paavo noticed the

strange bits of ... something ... plastered to her hair. "You sure you're not hurt?"

"Only my pride."

Joey cried out, "Just get us out of this!"

Dolores fired again. Shots bounced off the windshield of the Hummer and into the hood of the SUV.

"Angie, listen to me. I want you two to come into the Hummer. It's safer, and the windshield's bullet proof. The doors will provide you some cover, but you're going to have to move faster than you've ever moved before."

"It's so far!" She looked so scared he wondered if she could move at all. "You mean it?"

"I've never been more serious."

Dolores felt woozy. Every part of her body ached from the earlier crash of her truck, but especially her neck and head, which had seemed to bounce like a tennis ball between the windshield and the back of the seat. It had been all she could do to drag herself from the truck. She knew she'd be found if she stayed on the road, and so had worked her way up the hill. Going overland was the way to safety.

It had been hard. Every step jarred her, and her neck felt as if it were on fire. She was halfway up the hill, halfway to safety, when she heard a car engine.

She thought she'd caught a break when she saw Angie in the driver's seat, Joey with her.

If only they'd listened to her, gotten out of the SUV and walked away, she would have let them go.

Or was it too late for that?

Then the Hummer showed up with the sheriff and a real cop.

Her head ached; she couldn't think. She couldn't walk very

far; she needed Angie's car so she could run away. That's all she wanted; to go far, far away; to forget about all this.

Why didn't everyone simply leave her alone?

Angie moved about on her seat and took a deep breath. She sprang out feet first, hit the ground, caught her balance, took a step and dived into the Hummer. As Paavo pulled her in, shots hit the open doors, causing them to swing shut.

Paavo and Joey pushed them open again, and Joey followed Angie's lead.

Bullets slammed into the glass. Frostlike, webbed lines spread over the windshield, but it held.

Paavo faced Joey. "We can reach Merry Belle by going out the driver's door. I'll go first, then provide cover while you follow. Angie, you stay here and keep your head down."

"That's all?" she asked.

"That's enough. You ready, Joey?"

He gulped and nodded.

Using the door for some cover, Paavo fired towards the hill as he and Joey scrambled out of the Hummer and ducked behind the pickup.

"Glad to see you all," Merry Belle said. She was pale, and her trousers were heavily blood stained. Her belt was wrapped as a makeshift tourniquet on her thigh. "Don't sweat it, Paavo. I've got the bleeding under control," she said, sweat glistening on her face. "I also watch *ER* on TV."

"Can I do anything?" Angie called.

"No!" the others called back.

"Okay," she murmured.

Facing Joey and Merry Belle, Paavo said, "The way we're pinned down, we have to look up into the sun to keep track of

Dolores, and it's not going to work. I've got to get up there and get around behind her."

"How?" Merry Belle asked. "We *are* pinned down,"

"I'll draw her fire. We'll do some play-acting. Angie can help. You know the drill, MB?"

She smiled like a Cheshire cat. "Got it."

"Can't we wait for help?" Joey mumbled.

"We don't have the luxury," Paavo said. "She's desperate and will probably make a move soon. If I'm up there with her, it should at least guarantee a standoff until help arrives."

"He's right, Joey," Merry Belle said, handing him her revolver. "Follow my lead. I don't think Dolores will shoot back right away—she'll probably be ducking."

Joey paled at the gun in his hand.

"Angie," Paavo gave a loud whisper. "Merry Belle will cue you in."

"Cue me?" Angie asked, confused.

Paavo helped Merry Belle position herself, and lean against the truck. "Do your thing, San Francisco," she said.

"On the count of three," Paavo said, "start shooting."

He tucked the Beretta in his waistband and positioned himself like a sprinter.

"One... two... *three!*"

With a groan, Merry Belle raised herself up. Joey rose with her and both opened fire as Paavo ran. The noise was deafening.

Paavo dashed toward the rocks as shots suddenly rained down from Dolores' hiding place. He clutched at his chest and went down. His body rolled to the shelter of the rocks.

"Paavo!" Angie screamed, horrified. She couldn't move for a moment, then began to scramble out of the Hummer.

"Stop!" Merry Belle commanded, then dropped her voice. "Your man's acting," she hissed.

Behind shelter, Paavo gave a thumbs up. Angie gaped, feeling all but faint. His plan slowly sunk in, yet there was blood on his upper left arm. That was no act. He pointed at his arm and gave another thumbs up.

"You can act, too," Merry Belle said. "Start yelling and crying."

It took Angie a moment to catch her breath. "Paavo, Paavo!"

His smile blinded her, and as relief coursed through her blood, she got into it even more. "Oh God! I'll come to you, my darling!"

Merry Belled picked up her cue and yelled, "Stay down! He's dead, dammit! Dead!"

"Noooo!" Angie let out a scream that might have had distant wolves howling.

Dolores opened fire again, peppering the hood and roof of the Hummer. Merry Belle fired back. Joey tried to join her, but he was so pale, and shaking so hard, he dropped the revolver.

"Go away!" Dolores shrieked. "I'll kill you all if I have to!"

"Give up, Dolores," Merry Belle yelled. "You can't get away from us."

"Oh, Paavo," Angie wailed, really loud. "Oh, my love! My life! Dead! *Dead!*"

Merry Belle gaped at her with an expression that said her stomach was turning nauseous. Joey looked at her with something akin to revulsion.

Angie grimaced. No one had ever appreciated her acting.

Meanwhile, Paavo carefully worked his way up the rocks.

Dolores' most recent shots had given away her position.

"I'm sorry, Angie!" Dolores called. She wondered what they were up to, and if the cop was really dead. "I didn't want to do it, but it couldn't be helped. Please—put your guns down and back away from the Hummer. All I want is to go away. I'll never bother you again."

"You'll give us as much chance as you gave Junior," Merry Belle snarled.

"I didn't want to hurt him," Dolores complained. "But I had no choice."

"Like you had no choice about Ned... or Hal?"

"Ned figured it out. He asked questions of people I didn't think he knew. He came to me, asking about Hal. Somehow, he figured it out."

"How did you get him to go with you to the caves?"

"I didn't force him there." Dolores was crying. How she hated to think about any of that. "All I did was to tell him I had found Hal's will, that it gave everything to Teresa. I said I'd hidden it in the cave where Hal was found, and would give it to him if he'd let me go. He believed me. He didn't know..."

All was quiet for a moment, then Angie called out, "Didn't know what? What do you mean?"

Dolores didn't want to talk any more. Her head hurt, she was tired. If only she could leave...

"Tell me!" Angie demanded until Dolores couldn't stand to listen to her a moment longer.

"He didn't know *me!* No one really saw me most of the time," she cried. "Not even Hal. He used me, let me work for him, love him—and he never even saw me. Am I invisible? I prayed Hal could see me with his heart as well as his eyes. Perhaps he did, once. But then he turned away, became blinded by youth—by Teresa. She never really loved him. I know that. I should have been his wife. Me, only me."

Angie again glanced over at Merry Belle. She was sitting back against the truck, breathing hard. Loss of blood and pain had gotten to her, and for that reason, Angie had lowered the driver's side window and took over distracting Dolores with questions. "You're a liar! If you really loved Hal, you wouldn't have killed him!"

"He left me for that young nothing after I spend my life

caring for him!" she shrieked. "How could he—what's the word? —forsake me for her? Howt?"

Angie had no answer, but she knew she had to keep Dolores talking to help mask the sound of Paavo sneaking near.

But suddenly, she saw the ostrich with the cowlick walk up to the Hummer and begin to peck at the door. The foolish bird had followed her all the way up here! It was going to end up fricasseed if it didn't watch out. "Go away!" she whispered.

The ostrich stuck its head against the passenger's side window and one big black eye peered inside at Angie. "You'll get yourself killed!" Angie hissed. "Now, go home! Run!"

The bird just stared at her.

Angie called to Dolores, "You wanted to kill Teresa, too, didn't you?"

"No! I'm a good person, not a killer! But I also didn't want to see her as the owner of all Hal's things—to profit from his death when she was the cause of it! That wouldn't be fair! I got Junior to steal the proof of her marriage. That's all. But then Ned started asked questions, and Junior wanted to give the proofs to Teresa, and everything went bad. It wasn't my fault!"

"Why did you hurt Maritza?" Angie asked.

The ostrich went around to the back of the Hummer, apparently fascinated by the sun glinting off the red taillights.

"I watched her walk to the restaurant alone. I followed and asked her what she was doing. She just looked at me, and I could see it in her eyes. She knew. She got scared, then said, 'You loved him.' And I had to stop her!"

"Give up, Dolores!" Merry Belle called. "Come down here."

At that, Dolores shot at Merry Belle again. The bullet bounced off the rocks.

The ostrich ran, but soon returned and began to peck at the side-view mirror on the rented Mercedes. "Go away!" Angie said, trying to shoo it from harm.

Merry Belle returned fire, but as she felt in her pockets for rifle bullets, she found she'd used the last one.

Joey handed her back her service revolver.

She just stared at it.

"Shoot!" he cried.

Dolores shouted again. "The sun is behind me. You'll never see me coming. I need the Hummer! Give up."

"Your story is horrible!" Angie yelled, needing to make noise, hoping Paavo had time to climb up behind Dolores by now. "You make excuses, but you're just a hateful, jealous woman. No wonder Hal dumped you!"

"I thought you were my friend!" Dolores shrieked. "You're going to make it easy for me to kill you!"

"Why are you just sitting there?" Joey said to Merry Belle, nearly in tears. "Paavo needs you to shoot!"

"It only has blanks," Merry Belle wailed. "I didn't want to carry live bullets around Jackpot with me! What if someone got hurt?"

"Blanks?" he repeated.

"Blanks," she said morosely. "Until today, with this rifle, I've never shot a gun with real bullets anywhere except a shooting range."

"Oh ... my ... God!" He took the gun from her. "If I have to, I'll use it. At least it makes a lot of noise."

"She could kill you!" Merry Belle said.

As Joey and Merry Belle quivered with dismay, Angie knew that if Dolores wasn't distracted, she might notice Paavo.

Desperate to find a stray bullet or two—maybe even a little gun—Angie rummaged through the Hummer's glove compartment. It was stuffed tight with papers, junk food wrappers and heaven only knew what else. Merry Belle seemed pretty careless about everything else, why would she be any different with guns and ammo?

She pulled everything out of the glove compartment. Something had to be there to help.

In the very back, under everything else, was a black strip of some kind. She pulled it out. It was a lace garter.

What in the world? She held it up. It was big—so big it probably could have fit around both her thighs at once. So big it probably fit Merry Belle....

Merry Belle and a black lace garter? But then she turned it and saw it was a promo piece for a Las Vegas casino. That made some sense … she guessed. She pushed away the torturous image from her mind.

The ostrich continued to peck at the mirror.

Angie looked from the ostrich up to where Dolores was hiding. And as she did, a plan formed.

Glancing at the ostrich, she reached up to remove an earring.

She wasn't wearing any! She hadn't put any on that morning, mostly because she didn't want to be bothered by the birds while she worked on the cookout.

Her heart sank. So much for her great idea.

But then, another thought came to her.

A horrifying, ghastly, appalling thought...

Still, she needed to create a distraction, and that should do it.

The only bright, shiny thing the ostriches loved that Angie absolutely had refused to remove was—her heart nearly stopped at the thought and she clasped her fingers over it—her engagement ring.

How could she even think...? But Paavo was up there...

She tested the garter belt. It had a lot of stretch left in it. It should work.

Practically holding her breath at the all-but sacrilegious act, she took off her engagement ring and waggled it so that the sun caught the facets of the beautiful diamond. The diamond she loved more than any she'd ever seen anywhere, anytime...

Intrigued, the ostrich did an about face and headed toward her.

As the ostrich watched, Angie stretched the garter belt between her thumb and forefinger, then placed the ring against it and pulled back like a slingshot.

Quickly moving her hands through the Hummer's open window, she aimed upward, in the direction where Dolores hid, pulled back as hard as she could on the elastic, and let go.

The ring flew high in the air, up, up, she watched her most precious possession fly, sparkling in the sunlight, until it landed on rocks just behind Dolores. Angie cringed as it bounced and scraped against the rough ground.

The ostrich let out a raucous squawk and clambered up the hill, its little useless wings flapping, its heavy legs pumping.

"What the hell!" Dolores stood up as the bird neared, aiming her rifle at the beast.

Before she fired, Paavo stood up behind her, shouted her name and told her to drop the gun. Instead of obeying, Dolores spun around, facing him.

The ostrich didn't stop, but ran right into her. Dolores flipped head over heels in one direction, her rifle in another.

Then, as Angie watched, the worst possible thing happened.

The ostrich found her ring.

And swallowed it.

36

---

ngie sat in Jackpot's medical clinic waiting room, Joey beside her. Paavo had gone into an office with Doc, who had insisted on personally cleaning and dressing his gunshot wound.

Half the town, it seemed, was milling about. Word had spread quickly about Junior's murder, Dolores' shocking confessions, and the shoot-out. Sheriff Merry Belle Schwartz, who was also in the clinic being treated, was lauded as a hero, her reelection guaranteed for many years to come.

Angie rubbed the empty spot on her ring finger.

"We'll get it back," Joey promised, seeing her forlorn expression.

She turned to Joey. "You can give the ostrich ipecac or something to make her throw up, right?"

He looked abashed. "I'm afraid that won't work. Ostriches swallow sand and stones to help them digest food since they have no teeth. Their stomachs are tough. Your ring is staying at the guest ranch a while longer."

"Oh, no! What am I going to do?" Angie wailed.

"Don't worry," Joey had said with a wide grin. "Everything will come out all right in the end."

The worst day of her life had just gotten a whole lot worse.

"We'll clean it up real good for you," Joey continued, "sterilize it and everything. No one will ever know."

"I'll know," Angie said mournfully.

Just then, Lupe and Teresa found her and Joey. "My mother woke up this afternoon," Lupe said to them both, "right after Doc contacted me at the hospital and told me about Dolores. First, he called and told me about Junior, then later, about Dolores. I could hardly believe either call, and yet, it's almost as if some evil that had dwelt in this town has been lifted. My mother's going to be all right. Her mind, everything about her is much better than the doctors expected."

"Thank goodness," Angie said.

"We heard you helped as well, Joey," Lupe said, facing him without her usual hatred. "Thank you."

"I did nothing," Joey replied, looking abashed by Lupe's words. He also appeared surprisingly composed, even likable. Angie wondered if being away from Clarissa was what did it.

"I'm sorry I ever suspected you," Angie confessed to him.

"I'm sorry, too, that you could have thought so poorly of me," he said quietly. "I can understand it, though. Murder does terrible things, and not only to the victim. Ned was a friend, and frankly, I suspected him of killing my father."

"You did?" Teresa asked.

"I'm sorry." He scooted over to give the Flores women room on the bench. Teresa sat beside him. "Did you suspect me as well?" he asked.

"I never did, Joey."

He looked at her, swallowed hard a couple of times, then simply whispered, "Thank you."

"I should have known it was Dolores," LaVerne announced, joining them and wiping the dust from her bifocals. She was slightly breathless from dashing over to the clinic to get all the latest information and zeroed in on the little group. "That woman would never talk much at all to me. There was definitely something wrong with her."

"Was the cookout ruined?" Angie asked.

"Ruined?" LaVerne gave her a big smile. "It was bigger and better than ever! Only a small portion of what Dolores and I cooked was on the chuck wagon you practically destroyed. Later, the entire town showed up to find out all they could about the shootout. They especially liked my macaroni and cheese." LaVerne's eyebrows arched. "Too bad all *your* food was ruined."

Angie had had it with her. "Just why did you come here, LaVerne?" she snapped.

LaVerne squared her shoulders. "Actually, I came to show you something. Those old letters got me thinking. The recipe journal—maybe it wasn't written by one of my ancestors, after all. In fact, my great grandfather's name was Jim—the name of the man who received the letters. He was a cook on a cattle ranch." She handed Angie an ancient leather-bound volume. "Will you look at it? Is it worth a lot of money? Am I going to be rich?"

"Oh, my God!" Angie whispered as she looked at the book in her hands. Could it be? LaVerne had put plastic wrap on the cover to protect it. Angie's heart began to beat a little faster. The book's pages were brown with age, but it opened easily. She turned to the frontispiece.

It read "Recipes Developed on My Travels West" and was signed Willem van Beerstraeden. "This is it!" she cried. "The missing journal!"

She turned the page. The first recipe was for "Gila Monster Egg Surprise."

Her face fell, and she knew she didn't want to learn what the surprise might be. Actually, the surprise would be that anyone would think—ever—of eating Gila monster eggs.

She quickly turned more pages, her heart dropping more and more as she read. "Fried Porcupine Quill Crunchies," "Kangaroo Rat Bisque," and at least thirty ways to fry, sauté, broil, stew, boil or grill rattlesnakes and its varieties, such as sidewinders and diamondbacks.

All in all, Angie thought, the recipes LaVerne had chosen to cook weren't half bad compared to what else was in there. She gave a deep sigh. "I think I now know what Oscar Tschirky meant when he said he didn't want the recipes to fall into the wrong hands, and that he wanted to retrieve it for the family's name and honor."

LaVerne's eyes widened. "He meant we're going to be rich, didn't he?"

Angie shook her head. "I think he wanted it so no one else would see it."

"What?" LaVerne shrieked. "No!"

"These recipes are horrible! No one should eat this stuff. Half the animals are poisonous, the other half endangered. You shouldn't even be cooking from this book. No wonder van Beerstraeden gave away his recipes. If he learned anything at all from Oscar, he knew how bad a cook he was."

"These recipes are awful?" LaVerne asked glumly. "I thought gourmet food was supposed to taste that way. Damn! I surely would have liked to become rich."

Angie stared, equally doleful, at the book. "And I surely would have liked to have been the one to discover how Oscar of the Waldorf came up with his famous recipes. Maybe he really did develop them himself."

"It's too bad," LaVerne said with a heavy sigh.

"Yes, it is." Angie tried to give the book back to LaVerne, who refused to take it, and promptly left.

Angie felt Paavo's hand on her shoulder. She looked up to

see him standing behind her. He'd heard everything and now seemed to be struggling not to crack even the tiniest of smiles.

"It's not so bad, Angie," he said, patting her.

"Not bad at all, except that my engagement ring is somewhere I don't want to think about, my fiancé has been shot, I spent hours and hours chasing a recipe book by a chef who has no idea about good food, and the worst cook on the planet had more people liking her food than mine! Sometimes I feel I live under a very black cloud."

Maritza was still groggy when Paavo and Doc walked into her hospital room. Doc had asked Paavo to take her statement about what happened that day at the restaurant. Merry Belle wanted to take it, Doc said, but she was crankier and more obnoxious than ever with that leg wound.

Maritza spoke slowly and explained that something had made her go to the restaurant. Once she was there, though, she couldn't remember what it was. To her surprise, Dolores entered, and that was the last she knew.

It was good enough. Paavo and Doc were ready to leave when Maritza said, "When I sleep, though, then it come to me."

They stopped.

"I see Mr. Edwards—Hal. I know it's a dream, but it seem so real. He come and remind me of the day he see me at the restaurant. I'm in my chair. He give me an envelope and say to hold it for him. That I will keep it safe. He trust me. I put it in a drawer of the chest under the picture of Our Lady. I know she will not let anything happen to it until Mr. Edwards want it back."

"What was in the envelope?" Paavo asked.

"Mr. Edwards doesn't tell me. But I think it's important. If not, why does he come into my dream?"

Lupe easily found the sealed envelope Maritza had spoken of. She handed it to Doc.

Teresa, Angie, Paavo and Joey were also there to watch as Doc took out the papers and read through them.

"Although I suspect it'll be challenged"—Doc glanced at Joey—"this appears to be a properly executed, witnessed, sealed and notarized copy of the last will and testament of Hal Edwards, dated January of this year in Bisbee, Arizona."

"What does it say?" Angie asked eagerly.

Doc read the will aloud. In it, Hal requested that his cattle ranch be sold. Of the proceeds, to Dolores Huerta, who had been loyal to him for years and stayed with him through his stroke and rehabilitation, he gave the sum of two hundred fifty thousand dollars."

"She won't be collecting that," Angie said.

Doc continued, "Of the remaining, which should be well over a million dollars, half is to go to Jackpot's medical clinic and half to building the town a proper library."

"Wow," everyone murmured.

"To my cousin, Lionel," Doc read, "his trailer and twenty-five thousand dollars in cash. To my ex-wife, Clarissa Edwards, the knowledge that if only you'd loved me the way I loved you, I would have given you the world. To our son Joseph Edwards"— Doc cleared his throat and eyed Joey before going on—"the recognition that I failed you as a father, but Joey, you failed me as a son."

Joey's face fell, then he nodded and bowed his head.

"And finally, to my wife, Teresa Flores Edwards, I bequeath the remainder of all my worldly goods, after all legal obligations are met, including the Ghost Hollow Guest Ranch, stocks, bonds, and bank accounts. See list attached."

Doc held out the long list, then placed the will on Maritza's chair.

Everyone stared at it in silence.

37

The next afternoon, Angie and Paavo stopped at the Stagecoach Saloon on their way out of town to say goodbye to Doc and others who had gathered there to wish them well. Since their Mercedes SUV had been destroyed, Joey let them use his Lexus for the drive to the airport. He'd retrieve it sometime soon. He planned to return Los Angeles long enough pack up his things.

He was moving to Jackpot, to the Ghost Hollow Guest Ranch, and was going to be its new manager. He'd offered his services to Teresa, and she'd gladly accepted them. Lionel didn't have the energy or brains to make it the kind of resort it should be—a first-class one, and a possible destination-wedding site as well.

As Joey had explained the evening before to his appalled mother, he'd always liked both the hacienda and Teresa. Liked, not loved, he emphasized. Teresa had always been kind to him—kinder than anyone else, in fact. He didn't want to fight the will. He had no reason to. And for the first time in his life he put his foot down and told Clarissa that if she tried to fight it, he'd do all he could to oppose her.

Sheriff Merry Belle was at the saloon as well. She leaned against a crutch, Buster beside her. She recounted time and again the 'Shootout at Ghost Hollow Ridge,' as she called it—a day that would live in infamy, at least in her own mind.

Buster took Angie aside and apologized about her Emilio Pucci scarf, offering to buy her a new one. She told him to forget it, she had plenty of others. She also promised to send him a bunch of her favorite high fashion catalogues and magazines so he could study them to his heart's content. He was thrilled.

Doris Flynn's appearance saved Angie the need for a trip to the library. She handed Willem van Beerstraeden's letters and recipe journal to the librarian. Doris clutched them to her heart and promised to give the materials a prominent place in a glass case in her new library with a plaque thanking Angelina Amalfi and LaVerne Merritt for the generous historical gift. It might even bring a few more tourists to Jackpot.

Whether that happened or not, the whole town believed Angie deserved the plaque simply for convincing LaVerne to stop cooking her "old family gourmet recipes."

Angie invited Teresa to come to San Francisco for a visit. Teresa agreed. She planned to spend a year or more traveling. There was much she had to sort out in her mind, and much sorrow to forget. It was time for her to get to know who Teresa Flores Edwards was, and what she valued in her life.

To Angie's surprise—and Teresa's own—she added that after the year ended, she'd very likely be happy to come back to Jackpot. She'd kept her heart wrapped up in a protective shell all these years, and she couldn't help but suspect that to work her way out of it, the best place was home.

Angie suspected she was right.

Doc and Lupe were together, arms around each other's waists, beaming, and looking for all the world like young lovers. Angie was glad to see it.

Even Joaquin Oldwater had stopped in to give his best wishes.

Soon, the time came for her and Paavo to leave, to make the drive to Palm Springs and then a short plane ride back to San Francisco.

Angie felt strangely melancholy about saying goodbye to so many new friends. She had a special hug for Doc.

Doc told her that she and Paavo were good for each other, and she told him that the same went for him and Lupe.

Lupe took Paavo's hands. "Don't stay away so long, next time."

"I won't," he promised and gave her a warm embrace.

He then turned to Doc and held him a long moment as thoughts of the friend who wasn't there hit them hard. Both were misty eyed when they parted.

Merry Belle stood near the front door, ready to rush—or hobble—outside if need be to protect Jackpot.

Paavo said goodbye to her with a handshake, but at the last moment, leaned forward and kissed her on the cheek. Merry Belle blushed twenty shades of red, then gave him an affectionate tap on the chest that nearly sent him through the saloon window.

With smiles and grins, and more than a little sadness, Angie and Paavo left.

As they passed Merritt's Café, both stuck an arm out the window and waved at LaVerne, who was watching, her nose pressed to the glass and a coffee pot in hand.

Just past town at one point where the creek neared the highway, Angie found herself studying the horizon.

"Beautiful, isn't it?" Paavo asked.

"Yes," she replied. The more she'd come to know the desert, the more she appreciated it. She, who was a city girl through and through, was surprised at the beauty she'd found in lonesome stretches of land broken up only by a cactus or some low-lying scrub, at the horses, the cattle, and even the hard-working people in the sleepy Western town.

"I never did get to go fishing," Paavo said. "And I used to enjoy it as a kid. I enjoyed it a lot, in fact."

"We'll do it someday," she promised.

"I wonder what's going to happen to Ned's business," Paavo said quietly. "If it'll be put for sale?"

Her head swiveled toward him at warp speed. "For sale?" Her throat felt like it was closing.

"You don't think you'd be happy working on boats and gutting fish for your husband?"

She was speechless.

"Don't worry, Angie. Not now. But..." he looked out at the empty vistas and smiled wistfully, "maybe someday."

"Maybe so," she murmured as she eased herself against the passenger seat. She'd hoped that from this vacation she'd learn more about Paavo, and she certainly had. Learning so much about him as a little boy, seeing his bravery now, as a man, and throughout watching the love these people had for him, and him for them, made her appreciate and love him even more—something she hadn't thought was even possible.

Now she just had to settle on her wedding site. Her mother's idea, the church in San Francisco where everyone else in her family had married, looked better with each passing moment. Especially since it had nothing whatsoever to do with the old west, cowboys, horses ... or ostriches.

THE END

Dear Reader,

Reviews are gold to authors. If you've enjoyed this book, a review on the **Salsa and Secrets** *site where you purchased this book would be most appreciated.*

If you'd like to continue to follow the adventures of Angie and Paavo, the next serving is titled **Deadly Ever After.** A dream wedding, a city full of suspicious deaths, and a killer determined to crash the party. Gourmet cook Angie Amalfi and Inspector Paavo Smith must stop the murderer before her Big Day turns into a deadly Last Supper.

Gourmet cook Angie Amalfi has planned the wedding of her dreams, but while she's perfecting every last detail, San Francisco is suddenly plagued by suspicious deaths. Inspector Paavo Smith has his hands full juggling a fiancée in full bridal frenzy, a homicide squad stretched thinner than phyllo dough, and a string of cases that seem to circle closer and closer to Angie. The more he investigates, the more it looks like Angie herself could be a target.

Can Angie and Paavo stop a killer in time, or will their carefully planned wedding day turn into a deadly Last Supper?

To find out more about Angie's long, long awaited wedding, grab your invitation now for **Deadly Ever After.**

(But first, don't miss Angie's recipes on next page.)

FROM ANGIE'S KITCHEN…

Here are a couple of recipes Angie learned in Arizona, plus a favorite pie recipe. Enjoy!

TORTILLA CRISP

2 (or more) large flour tortilla
1 cup shredded cheddar cheese
1 can whole chili peppers cut into strips
1 tsp garlic powder, or 2-3 finely minced cloves of garlic
salt to taste
olive oil or lard

Preheat oven to 400 degrees. Grease a cookie sheet with olive oil or, for more authenticity, lard. Place the tortillas on it, then cover them with cheese, pepper, garlic and salt. The thickness of your toppings will determine how many tortillas you'll need. Bake at 400 degrees just a few minutes until the cheese is melted and slightly bubbling.

MARITZA'S PORK STEW

3 lbs. lean boneless pork country ribs
1 tsp oil
1 can black beans
1 large chopped onion
1 can (4 oz.) chopped chilis (or 2 poblano & 2 Anaheim chili peppers, seeded and chopped)
3-4 cloves garlic, chopped
juice of one lime
1 can tomato sauce (8 oz.)
1 tsp. oregano
1 minced small jalapeño pepper
salt to taste
cooked rice
sour cream
salsa

Preheat oven to 325 degrees. Heat oil in an oven proof pot and brown the country ribs in it.

Next, add the beans, onion, chili peppers, garlic, lime, tomato sauce, oregano, jalapeño, and salt. Add enough water to cover the ribs. Cover the pot and move it into a 325-degree oven and cook 1-1/2 to 2 hours until the meat is tender and breaks apart with a fork. Add more water if needed. Remove any excess pork fat that rises to the surface before serving.

Serve over white rice. Top with sour cream and your favorite salsa.

BOURBON PECAN CHOCOLATE PIE

1 cup light corn syrup
  1 cup white sugar (or ½ cup white and ½ cup brown)
  4 oz. unsalted butter, melted
  4 eggs
  ¼ cup bourbon
  1 teaspoon vanilla
  1/4 tsp. salt
  pinch ground nutmeg
  pinch ground cinnamon
  1 cup coarsely chopped pecans
  6 ounces semisweet chocolate chips
  1 9-inch unbaked pie shell

Heat oven to 325 degrees. Heat sugar, corn syrup and butter in a saucepan over medium heat until sugar is dissolved and the butter is melted. Remove from heat and let it cool slightly.

In a bowl, add eggs, bourbon, vanilla, salt, nutmeg and cinnamon. Whisk or blend until mixture smooth. Pour cooled sugar mixture into the bowl, whisking constantly as you do. Add chocolate chips and pecans, stir together.

Pour into uncooked pie crust and bake at 325 degrees until set, about 50 minutes. (A cake tester or toothpick inserted into center should come out clean.) Serve slightly warm or at room temperature.

ABOUT THE AUTHOR

Joanne Pence was born and raised in northern California and now lives in Idaho. She has been an award-winning, *USA Today* best-selling author of mysteries for many years, but she has also written historical fiction, contemporary romance, romantic suspense, a fantasy, and supernatural suspense. All of her books are now available as ebooks and in print, and most are also offered in special large print editions. Joanne hopes you'll enjoy her books, which present a variety of times, places, and reading experiences, from mysterious to thrilling, emotional to lightly humorous, as well as powerful tales of times long past.

Visit her at www.joannepence.com and be sure to sign up for Joanne's mailing list to hear about new books.

www.ingramcontent.com/pod-product-compliance
Lightning Source LLC
Chambersburg PA
CBHW061657190726
48289CB00006B/1911